REBEL CAUSE

MINUS AMERICA BOOK 3

E.E. ISHERWOOD

CONNECT WITH E.E. ISHERWOOD

Website & Newsletter:
www.eeisherwood.com

Copyright © 2019 by E.E. Isherwood

All rights reserved.

ISBN 13: 9781675162668

Cover Illustration by 'Covers by Christian'

Editing services provided by Mia at LKJ Books

This is a work of fiction. Names, characters, businesses, places, events and incidents are either the products of the author's imagination or used in a fictitious manner. Any resemblance to actual persons, living or dead, or actual events is purely coincidental.

ONE

Long Island, NY

Ted and Emily had risen with the sun, snuck a bite from the cupboard of the stranger's apartment, then immediately jogged a couple of miles to escape the sprawl of New York City. He thought being on foot would reduce their chances of being seen by searching aircraft. However, as the morning had heated up, he'd found a small four-door Nissan, and they'd been traveling in air-conditioned comfort for the last hour.

"Thanks for making me breakfast," Emily remarked.

Since they'd been in someone else's apartment, he was left to the mercy of whatever was in the pantry. His first choice was the frozen waffles he'd found in the freezer, but the idea was crushed since the power had gone out overnight. His backup plan was the family-sized box of Tot Pop's cereal. The milk was still cold inside the darkened refrigerator, so he'd poured a bowl for them both.

"If the power is going out for good, it may be some time before we have milk and cereal again," he said from behind the wheel.

"That sucks." After a short pause, she continued, "Why do you think the power went out when it did? I thought nuclear power plants would go on forever."

He tilted his head toward her, not sure if she was being serious. If his sister had said such a thing, a woman who wouldn't know the difference between a coal power plant and a nuclear one, he wouldn't think anything of it. However, Emily was probably the President of the United States. She should know the answer to simple questions like that.

Emily smiled as if she'd heard him thinking. "What I mean is, nuclear power should have lasted longer than forty-eight hours. A coal plant would shut down as soon as the coal stopped feeding in, say a matter of hours. As far as I know, New York never got its proposed Long Island wind farm up and running. That means the power going to the television last night was from a nuclear source. I want to know why it shut down overnight."

He guided the stolen car on the two-lane road, always mindful of the derelict vehicles blocking the lanes. For a few seconds, he thought of his sister again. Silly, ditzy Rebecca. He'd watched her neighborhood burn last night. Conceptually, he knew everyone in America was probably gone, but also knowing he'd never hear his sister's laugh again killed him inside.

"Well, Madame President, I'm impressed. You seem to know quite a bit about power generation on the East Coast, including the status of yet-to-be-built wind farms in these parts."

"And?" she replied.

"And the answer is, I have no idea why we lost power. Maybe a tree branch fell on a wire. Didn't that knock out power for the whole East Coast a few years ago? Or maybe the assholes leading this shitshow went out and turned things off. If I were in charge, I'd want to conserve as many resources as I could, rather than waste running televisions inside empty apartments."

Emily seemed to think on it, and it made him reflective, too.

Who were the people invading America? He'd watched the broadcast by Jayden Phillips—or David, as he called himself now—but that only gave him the face of the beast. There had to be millions of people behind him. Those arriving planes didn't appear out of thin air. They had to be waiting for the precise moment of the attack in order to get there so fast. Same with the ships. How did they get into port immediately after the attack?

For all he and Emily had discovered, the enemy still had no name. No base of operations. No place where America could point a finger and fight back. He and Emily had surmised Jayden was currently in Colorado, at NORAD, but even that was a guess. The extent of his battlefield intelligence was Newark being overrun. New York was getting there. And the only good guys around were on a ship over the horizon.

They were silent for the bulk of the ride toward the end of Long Island. The forest-lined road was flat most of the way, but they'd gone over a gentle hill before coming to a small tourist town stuffed with cars.

"Oh, we're here," Emily said with excitement. "This is Montauk."

"It looks like we've driven into Disneyworld with all this traffic." The area was quaint, with tasteful motels and tourist storefronts, but his focus was entirely on the vehicles as he drove around several pileups.

"We have to decide if we're going out by sea or air." She pointed to an upcoming roundabout. "Left is the marina. Right will take us around the lake to the airport."

Ted drove along the shoulder, then went onto the grass inside the giant traffic circle. Based on how the cars were parked, there'd been a traffic jam taking place at the moment America was attacked. Going into the middle was the best way to avoid it. The delay gave him time to think, but he still wasn't sure what to do.

Emily spoke up when he didn't say anything. "I say we get on a plane and go find your niece. I know that's what you want to do."

Ted gripped the wheel. It was, in fact, what he'd been thinking. How did she already know him so well? However, it wasn't the professional thing to do.

"No, if you have a seaworthy boat, we'll escape Long Island and head north. We should be able to hug the coast, avoid our overhead friends, and put some distance from the men looking for us. Once we get far enough north, we can hop into a plane and go west."

She grimaced. "You still want to take on NORAD all by yourself? You know I could be wrong about the broadcast coming from a replica of the Oval Office. It might not have come from NORAD at all. Maybe there's a duplicate somewhere else made just for this invasion. Ted, that's not out of the realm of possibility for someone who can destroy our whole country in only a few minutes."

The next choice he made could mean life or death for lots of people.

Chicago, IL

Tabby stood on the elevator as she came up from the Bonne Terre mine. The clanking and herky-jerky of the hundred-year-old lift was somehow comforting, despite the threat of it falling apart under her feet.

The cage doors opened, and Mom and Dad stood there with scowls on their faces.

"What?" she asked with surprise.

Mom tapped her foot in an ageless sign of maternal impatience. "Did you forget something, young lady?"

Dad craned his neck to look behind her.

She turned around, but the elevator was empty.

"Where'd they go?" Tabby asked with confusion.

"You left your people, Tabitha. What's the first rule I taught you down there?"

Her shoulders slumped. "Always come back with the same number of tourists you left with."

"And how many did you lose?" Dad spoke with more anger than concern, which was totally unlike him.

She glanced all around the large elevator, hoping someone was hiding. That took about two seconds, leading her to an answer she couldn't avoid...

"How many?" Dad repeated.

"I've lost all three!" she yelled out loud as someone jostled her shoulder.

"Tabby? Are you all right?" A young teen boy knelt next to her. He wore a blue track suit with red sneakers, as if fully prepared to start soccer practice.

"Donovan?" Her eyes darted around the observation deck of the Sears Tower, and it all rushed back. They'd come there last night after a long day on the road trying to reach Mom and Dad at the edge of the disaster. However, after almost two days of hoping and praying, she'd come to the conclusion they were dead, like everyone else.

Her heart skipped a few beats, then seemed to have trouble regaining its rhythm. Much like in her dream, she had a cosmic revelation. It wasn't the three teens who were gone forever. It was her parents.

"Dang it. I didn't want to wake up from my dream." She sat up on the small padded bench.

"I'm sorry," Donovan drawled, "but you're going to want to see this." He stood up and motioned for her to follow him to a corner. "Just peek around."

When she got there, she saw a scene that might have been from her nightmare.

Audrey and Peter were on the floor together, behind another bench, about twenty feet away. The suspicious side of her wondered if they'd slept there all night, though it didn't look very comfortable. However they got there, they couldn't move from behind it or they'd be seen by the investigative white robot floating outside the window.

"How long has it been there?" she whispered.

Donovan took a quick peek around the corner, then leaned closer. "I don't know. Pete caught my attention. He woke me up. When I came around the bend, I saw it and where it had them."

She held her bangs to keep them from giving her away, then she looked around the corner again. "It must know we're here. It isn't moving."

"Maybe it's sent for backup," he suggested.

Tabby crouched against the wall. "Hey, Audrey. Peter. Can you hear me?"

"Yes," Peter gushed. "What should we do? This thing won't go away." Quieter, he added, "It must have seen us."

She thought back to her dream about getting out of that elevator and seeing Mom and Dad. It seemed so real, and it still lingered in her memory as if it was. It might be the last connection she ever had with them. She put herself back in the dream, desperate to ask Dad what she should do. He always had the answer, no matter the question. How did he do that?

"Tabby?" Donovan sounded worried. "We've got to help them."

"I know." There wasn't much she could do about the drone outside, but she could get her people on the move. Keep the tour on schedule. She knew how to push these kids.

"Guys!" she called out to Audrey and Peter. "On three, I want you to run to me. We're getting out of here before more of those things arrive. Get your stuff ready."

She stood up again, content she was making the right call. There was no point in waiting if they'd already been spotted. Escaping the building was the priority.

"We're ready!" Audrey exclaimed.

"One, two…three!"

Tabby peered around the corner, unafraid to be seen. The hovering drone seemed to fight against the wind, but otherwise didn't leave its position. The black orb underneath was undoubtedly a camera. By the time she'd finished studying the drone, Peter and Audrey came rushing around the corner hand-in-hand.

She waved her arm. "The elevator! Go!" she ordered. The clock was ticking. The drone operator would report movement, more would be sent, and eventually people would show up to capture them. Or worse.

"We have to hurry," she said with as even a voice as she could muster. Her heart raced beyond her lung capacity, making her take short, uneven breaths. However, she did everything possible to hide her fear.

Peter pressed the button over and over but seemed agitated immediately. When he punched the button with his knuckles, she gently shoved him aside. "What's up?"

He pointed. "The light isn't coming on."

"Shit," she said quietly. "The power's out." There were no lights on in the observation area, but the bright morning sunshine made interior lights unnecessary. If the power was out in the building, the elevators would be out, too.

"The stairs!" she said in a high-pitched voice.

No one remarked on her obvious panic. They went a few paces to the right and opened the fire door to the stairwell. She noticed a knocking sound, a little like a jackhammer, followed by the crash of glass. It couldn't be coincidence that it seemed to come from around the corner where the drone had been stationed.

"Go! Hurry!"

They all went in; she slammed the door and took a deep breath. The three kids stood on the landing with her, as if afraid of starting down 103 floors and an untold number of steps.

"What are you waiting for?" She expected a drone to tap on the door at any second. Like any good science fiction movie, it probably had heat-seeking equipment to see her standing against the cold, metal slab.

Tabby took the lead and went down the first flight.

The kids soon followed. Donovan caught up to her and went ahead, two steps at a time, which she didn't mind. He was the sports guy in their group and probably wanted to show off. Peter was the heavy-set kid; he and Audrey lagged behind.

After five minutes, her calves burned. A short time later, Peter lodged the first complaint. "I have to stop," he chuffed, nearly out of breath.

The boy did have a few extra pounds but didn't look unhealthy.

"He wants to stop for his girlfriend," Donovan taunted from a flight below. He kept one hand on his pistol as it sat securely in his police utility belt.

"No, I don't," Peter replied in leave-me-alone singsong.

"I'm not stopping," Audrey interrupted, continuing down the seemingly endless steps. "I can make it."

After another ten minutes of continuous motion, Tabby wondered if she should make them stop for their own good. Her legs were aching, and her calves felt like they were actually on fire. How were the kids keeping up?

"We're almost there!" Donovan shouted.

Tabby glanced wearily at the plaque noting the floor number. They were still on the twentieth floor. It didn't feel close to the end.

She decided to let the athletic boy lead. If no one else was going to halt, neither was she.

At ten floors to go, she had to wobble from flight to flight. Her legs were jelly.

At two floors to go, she leaned heavily on the railing to compensate for her pain. Peter and Audrey lagged a few floors above her, though she saw their hands coming down the railing when she looked up the narrow gap to the floors above.

"We're there!" Donovan shouted.

She barely heard him over her own footfalls. Each plodding step brought her closer to the end, and she could finally taste it through the pain. At the same time, she couldn't portray too much weakness, though the struggle made it seem as if she was dying a little inside. Faking positivity was high on her mind as she rounded the last landing and saw Donovan holding the door at the bottom.

"See? We made it," he said, breathing heavily.

"Yeah, we—" she started to say.

Bursts of red exploded from his chest, followed by the echo of muffled gunshots.

She caught herself on the bannister to stop, though her sweaty palms made her trip down an extra step or two. Leaning forward, she was not more than twenty feet away from her young friend.

Donovan looked right at her with eyes that said, "Tabby, help me."

He then crumpled against the door, dead.

The shadow of a walking horse-drone appeared in the doorway.

TWO

USS John F. Kennedy, **south of New York City**

Meechum led Kyla deep into the belly of the aircraft carrier, one ladder at a time. The trip through the claustrophobic interior reminded her a lot of the day before, minus the shooting. Most of the empty uniforms were gone, too; Van Nuys had asked the remaining crew to spend every free moment gathering them into piles, out of respect for the deceased. They'd all worked on that until near midnight.

"Where are we going?" Kyla asked for the third time. Meechum had practically pulled her out of the rack, where she'd spent an uncomfortable night of sleep. The hasty wake-up didn't seem normal, even for the dialed-to-eleven young female Marine, so Kyla remained vigilant for trouble.

She'd kept Carthager's M9 semi-automatic Beretta pistol in her waistband. It made her feel a little like one of those gangster rappers, but it fit snug and stayed in place, aided by the few extra pounds she could never lose around her midsection.

"We're here," the short-haired woman replied while pointing to an open doorway. The Marine went in without further comment, and Kyla followed like she wasn't quite sure this wasn't a setup.

A man spoke up. "Over here."

"Sergeant Carthager?" she replied in a low voice, though no one else was around.

"Take a seat," he ordered.

She did as requested, mostly because it seemed like she was in a spy movie. She'd been brought all the way down here to talk to a guy who had passed her in the hallways multiple times over the last couple of days. Why he needed her to sneak around to meet him was unknown.

He got right to it. "Listen, we heard what you told the captain yesterday. That it was your uncle down there, and the VP was with him. Are you absolutely sure it was the both of them?"

"I'd bet my life on it. I even texted my uncle on the flight out to confirm."

"But was it her? You have to be one hundred percent sure."

Yesterday, she'd had her doubts, but lying in bed gave her plenty of time to reflect on it. The pinned-up hairstyle matched the vice president's. Same color hair, too. She was about the right height and figure, from Kyla's recollection from television. Back when her ticket was voted into office, you couldn't look at a screen without seeing the first female vice president. Uncle Ted's mission was to fly her plane, so it stood to reason he'd die trying to keep her alive. "I'm one hundred percent, sir."

Carthager nodded seriously. "Good. I like to see confidence like that." He passed a look to Meechum, and she took a few steps back before he continued. "Meech and I have talked about this at length, and I don't see any other way. We have to bring you in on part of our mission.

Someone has to get a message to the vice president."

Kyla chuckled. "Is that why you brought me down here with all this cloak and dagger stuff? I can give you my phone. My uncle and I communicated just yesterday."

"No, that won't work. We're going to use this." He pointed to a radio sitting on a nearby shelf.

"Why? What's going on?"

Carthager put one boot on an empty metal chair and peered down at her. "Ma'am, we came on this ship because someone up the chain of command got wind a big event was about to go down. Obviously, that something kicked off before we could report back, but our FAST platoon has been doing its homework over the past twenty-four hours. We now know two things. One, we can't trust a damned person on this ship. Two, we have to get a message to the vice president, or more people are going to die."

"Why? Why are they going to die?" she asked.

"I'm afraid I can't tell you that." He continued before she could protest. "But it isn't because I don't trust you. If you're captured, they could pry it from you. You've got to trust me on this. The enemy is on the ship, and it could be anyone."

"Even the captain?" she asked lamely.

"Anyone," he said dryly.

She sat there for a few moments, then peered at the radio. "What do you want me to say to him?"

Carthager rubbed his chin, then motioned for Meechum to go to the radio. Kyla was surprised how much non-verbal communication passed between the two Marines. "We need to know where he is, but you can't use place names. There will almost certainly be unfriendly ears listening."

Since she had no realistic idea where he was, it was hard to envision a place she could tell him to go. The last place she'd seen him was in Central Park over twelve hours ago. They could be in Canada by now.

The leader went on. "Once we get him online, I'll explain how we're going to do this."

Meechum invited her to sit at the radio.

She watched as the woman adjusted the frequencies and asked her to call out for her uncle. The first lesson was to use a name only he would recognize, so she had to think it over for a minute or two.

I hope he remembers this.

"This is Reba calling for Hailey-boo, do you have your ears on?" Reba was shorthand for Rebecca, which was Mom's name, but the nickname also happened to be one of her mother's favorite singers. It was one of Mom's many contrasts—the hippy-dippy mother wearing tie-dye dresses singing country songs. Hailey-boo was the name of one of Uncle Ted's girlfriends; the 'boo' was because the woman was terrified beyond logic by ghosts.

Meechum smiled approvingly at her use of the handles. After repeating the call-out a few times, they went to a new frequency. For the next fifteen minutes, they went through the routine until a reply came.

"This is Hailey-boo. Go ahead, Reba."

Carthager leaned close. "It's a marine frequency. He might be on a boat or using a boat's radio. Tell him you're having a birthday party and need to give him a present."

Kyla did as instructed. Uncle Ted seemed to understand she was talking in code.

Her uncle's voice crackled in the radio. "I've got a few things going on, but I think a birthday party sounds nice."

Carthager whispered, "See if you can dial in where he is. Pick a place only he would know, then ask him how many miles he is from it."

She tried to think, but there was only one spot on her mind. "Hailey-boo, do you remember where we've always had birthday parties in the past? How many miles are you from there?"

They waited a few seconds before the reply came back. "We're about a hundred miles from those birthday parties. We're also about sixty miles from the place where Hailey-boo's mother and I took you on your tenth birthday."

Kyla grinned and spoke quietly to the Marines. "That's Martha's Vineyard. It was a big deal because Uncle Ted knew someone in the government who got us a tour."

Carthager tapped his temple. "It's an island, right? We can draw a circle around it and see where it meets the circle around the other place. Where was the first location?"

"New York City. Pelham Bay, to be exact. My mom's house. We always invited Uncle Ted to my parties..." She got a little sad at the memory, though the tough-guy Marine kept talking.

"Right, so he's a hundred from New York, but only sixty from Martha's. Any idea where that might be?"

"No," she replied, "but you said he was on a marine band and might be on a boat. That gives me an idea."

"Hailey-boo, the birthday party you mentioned. You aren't by chance using the same type of transportation as we used that day, are you?"

To the Marines in the room, she added, "We took a ferry from New York out to Martha's Vineyard. It took all day and was the most boring part of the trip, by far."

"We are, Reba. In fact, we're a little more than halfway on the same route, if we were going to your tenth birthday party again. I don't think you'd like how boring it is out here."

"Yep," she deadpanned to those around her, "he's on a boat."

Carthager let out a sigh of relief. "He's still alive and on the move. That's excellent. High marks for your uncle. Now, are there any other places you've had birthday parties where we might be able to get to him?"

She had a place in mind right away. "It wasn't a birthday party, but I did take a field trip he would know about. It was to a lighthouse."

Off the coast of Long Island, NY

"This is wonderful," Emily said excitedly. "Your niece is alive, and, it would seem, quite the fighter."

Emily's family yacht rocked with the waves. They'd stopped and shut off the motors so no one on the radio would figure out they were on the water. Now, he didn't want Emily to start it back up until he'd had some time to think it over.

"Yeah, she's the rebel of the family. Her mom was a pushover. She'd spend an hour to get a fly to exit through the door rather than swat it dead. Up until the past few days, I'd have thought Kyla was cut from the same material. Now I've seen her on a helicopter leaving a warzone, and she's using coded messages on the radio. I'm impressed, but also worried what she's gotten herself into."

"Don't you trust what she said? This rendezvous at the lighthouse?"

Using coded words only the two of them would understand, they'd agreed to meet at the Montauk lighthouse, which was at the easternmost point of Long Island. She'd gone there on a field trip in middle school, and he remembered it because Rebecca called him the night before asking if it was safe to let her go.

Now there was no question it wasn't safe.

He looked south, toward shore. The skies were overcast, but the thin slice of Long Island was still visible. He couldn't make out the lighthouse, but it was there.

"I trust her, but she was being coached. I'm wondering who was there with her."

"How could you tell?"

Ted had spent enough years in the Air Force to know tones of voice while on the radio. Kyla was nervous and cautious and spoke in monotone, as if reading from a script or repeating what was told to her.

"I've known her since she was a baby. As much as I'm impressed with her coding, she couldn't have come up with it on her own. She couldn't have found us on this maritime frequency. Not unless she's been taking a lot of classes down at the learning annex I don't know about." He smirked to Emily to offload some of his tension.

"So, we can't really trust her, but we have to go anyway. Right?"

There was no way he could skip on a chance to collect her. If she was with him, he could get Emily and his niece to safety in Canada. That would be a job well done by anyone's measure.

He knew what he wanted to do, but she was the president. "You're driving. What are your orders?"

It was her family's boat, and she'd driven it before with her husband, so he was content to let her pilot the fifty-foot giant. He stood next to her as she thought about the answer. However, he'd gotten to know her very well over the past two days. Much as he'd done with his friend Frank, he would eat his hat if Emily suggested they leave his niece behind.

She didn't disappoint.

"Let's go see that lighthouse."

San Francisco, CA

Dwight woke up with the feeling of a shoe in his side. Living on the streets for so many years, he'd become accustomed to the unpleasant wake-up call.

"I'm not in a doorway. Leave me be." It was his standard response.

"Hey, guy, you are supposed to be on the road. What are you doing?" The man sounded anxious, like Dwight was breaking an important rule. When he opened his eyes, he remembered it wasn't a standard day.

"Oh. I'm sorry, Jacob, I, uh—"

"It's fine. I need you up. I'm running late, too. We've got to get to the rendezvous, or they'll put us on an even worse duty, you know?" The man was dressed in the same black jumpsuit Dwight had been forced to wear; they could have been on the same pit crew for a racing team. He was average height and build, probably in his forties, with a natural, smiling face and a thin mustache. His salt-and-pepper hair was cut short, like most men in the black suits.

Dwight picked himself off the small patch of grass he'd found among the downtown buildings. "How did you find me?"

"All the bikes have trackers. One of the team leaders told me to come here and find out why this bike wasn't moving. I'm not about to go back and explain you were sleeping, so if anyone asks, you had a flat tire and we worked together to get you mobile."

Poppy swooped down from above, making him involuntarily swat her away. He dearly wanted to ask what the hell she was doing, but he knew better than to talk to the bird when people were around.

"I'm not Jacob, by the way. It's Bernard. What's your name?"

"Dwight," he replied. He'd been lured into the warehouse by a man named Jacob. If this was a new person, there was a chance he hadn't been discovered as an imposter.

"Well, Dwight. Hop on your bike and let's go. We have a lot of ground to cover today. Then we'll have a ton of work on our hands." He patted the flamethrower machinery attached to the backside of his motorbike.

It took him a couple of minutes, but Dwight managed to get himself upright and on his bike. His only thought was how bad he wanted a drink, but it didn't seem likely he could find a liquor store with his new friend lording over him. That bummed him out.

"Stick on my back tire, Dwight. Remember, they're always watching us. We have to go where we're told, or they send out the work police." He chuckled in a fashion that sounded anything but funny.

They both cranked over their motors.

Dwight looked up at Poppy, still aloft. "Hey!" he called out to get her attention. "You didn't warn me he was coming!"

The multi-colored bird seemed to cackle in laughter.

"What?" Bernard asked while cupping his ear.

Dwight shook his head, waving him off. The guy wouldn't understand his relationship with the bird, nor did he want to explain it. Normal people had a blind spot to the creature, and he didn't want to answer the questions that invariably came when he revealed his friend.

For now, he would ride his motorcycle and wait for the opportunity to flee.

He hoped Poppy, for all her practical jokes, would help him when the time came.

THREE

Off the coast of Long Island, NY

"When were you going to tell me you could fly a plane as well as pilot this big yacht?" Ted stood next to his companion, admiring her transformation to boat captain. She'd unhooked her hair clip, which let long brown hair whip around behind her as they sped across Long Island Sound.

She giggled girlishly and brushed her wild hair aside, as if boating was a way of life. "It didn't come up organically in our conversation. This is more of a forty-foot boat, anyway, not a yacht. Besides, this is nothing, I also read a manual on how to operate a diesel train engine."

"No shit?" he said with surprise.

The vice president turned, mischief gleaming in her eyes. "I'm kidding! But wouldn't you just die if I could drive a train?"

"No. I'd believe it. You're the real deal. Hell, if we were voting for president again, I'd vote against my party so you'd remain the VP." He meant it. Her past political affiliation was the only blemish on what he viewed as a pretty solid woman, not that any of it mattered now.

"This was my uncle's fishing boat. As I said, forty-footer, with an open floorplan so you can hold rods over the side. For all their Washington, D.C. insider bull crap, my extended family never strayed far from the water."

"Except for your parents," he replied. She'd told him about her mom and dad operating a flying school somewhere in Montana.

"They fly in retirement. Back in the day, they were here on the East Coast, too. They opened more than a few doors for me."

He didn't want to imagine the political maneuverings necessary to get a son or daughter into the right schools, the right internships, and so forth, on the way to elected office. Navigating politics was frustrating enough in the Air Force. It included long stints of boring duty stations on the way to the next level up. His first four years involved lots of foosball playing and goofing around, but little upward movement. Once he left the poor leadership he'd found in Tallahassee, he'd begun to weave his way through the officer ranks.

Emily piloted the boat over a large wave, causing it to crash back down with a satisfying smack. "Wahoo!" she howled with infectious glee.

Ted spent the next couple of minutes outside of his war mentality. For that brief time, he enjoyed the spray of the water shooting up on both sides as the yacht cut through the water. He glanced back at the churn created by the roaring engines. But most of all, he liked being next to the commanding woman behind the wheel.

He wondered if the boat under his feet would be enough to get them up the East Coast, over to Greenland, then to Iceland and Great Britain. It was a route he'd flown many times, and the distance between landmasses didn't seem too far.

If they could collect Kyla, that was their way back to friendlies.

"Ted, I'm getting something on the radar." She tapped one of her long fingernails on a video monitor inset into the dashboard. The readout was similar to his in-flight collision-avoidance system, but not as sophisticated or detailed. Instead of having blips for each plane in the air, there was only enough information to see the land and islands in their line of sight.

"What's the range on this thing?"

"Not sure. About fifty miles, I think."

The point on the screen moved slowly from north to south, as if it was a boat shadowing theirs. However, the color was all wrong.

"The radar tracks birds," she said matter-of-factly, "because birds lead to schools of fish. However, flocks of birds don't move that fast."

That explained the color. It was moving and in the air.

"We've got to get to shore right now." They were already headed back to Long Island, but they were supposed to go to the easternmost end to meet Kyla at the lighthouse. Instead, he directed her to go toward the beach at the nearest point. "We'll keep the boat near the shoreline and throw out an anchor. It will hide us from the snooping aircraft until we're ready to escape for good."

She changed course. They weren't more than a mile from the pristine sand of the beach. The tall lighthouse peeked above the trees to their left a couple of miles away.

"Do you think it sees us?" Ted asked with uncertainty, not sure what to make of the unfamiliar radar system.

As she drove them in, the dot on the screen stayed true to its flight path. Emily backed off the engines as they got within a hundred yards from shore. She'd found a tiny inlet, barely big enough for the boat to fit. Beyond it, there was a surprisingly large lake; it was perhaps two hundred yards from one shore to the other and surrounded by forest on all sides except the beach access point.

"Nice and easy," she said, obviously talking to the boat.

After the yacht cruised through the inlet, Emily let out a breath she'd been holding. "My uncle would kill me if he saw me doing this. He once paid eight thousand bucks to repair a propeller after striking a rock in the shallows. This cruiser is meant for deep water, not little lakes like this."

"Well, I'm not complaining." He motioned toward a nearby stand of trees at the lakeshore. As they got away from the beach along the ocean, it became rocky and less uniform on the banks of the lake. Some of the trees hung over the water, giving them the cover they'd been seeking.

"It's still coming," she warned.

The dot traveled across the screen, and Ted thought of his Air Force training. Even a weak radar system like this one was broadcasting a signal into the air. That signal could be intercepted and triangulated. "Shit, turn it off. Power everything off!"

Without waiting for an explanation, Emily flicked off the monitor, then hit more switches to shut down the bilge pumps and other accessories.

"Can I drop anchor?" she wondered.

"Do we need it?" he asked quietly.

"If we don't secure ourselves, we might float into the middle of the lake, or against those rocks."

He guessed the blip was still a mile or two out, based on where it was when she turned off the radar. It was a risk to operate machinery, but a necessary one.

"Do it," he said, not so sure of himself.

She powered some of the equipment, flicked another toggle, and they listened as the anchor slid out from a port near the front. It didn't take long for it to hit bottom, given they were in a shallow lake.

Emily powered off without being told.

When it became silent, they heard the whine of an airplane prop.

He didn't need a radar to tell him it was getting closer.

Emily's expression was as panicked as his insides.

"Should we jump?" she asked.

Ted imagined Hellfire missiles with their names on them. There was no point staying in the boat if they were found, and the continued approach of the drone made it seem almost a certainty. He silently grabbed his rifle and the backpack, prompting her to grab an AR, too.

"After you," he said with all the calm he had left.

They both leapt over the sides.

On the way down, he noticed the name of the boat written on the back: *Happy Hooker*.

Everything really is a joke with her.

Chicago, IL

Tabby's heart stopped cold for at least ten seconds, or it seemed like it as she stood on the steps looking down at her fallen friend. Audrey and Peter had come down the last flight just as Donovan was shot. They stood behind, leaning on her, as if they were also shocked beyond their capacity to think.

"We...have to go back up," she finally choked out.

The kids didn't move.

"Go!" Tabby spun around and pushed, but she almost couldn't get up the next step. Her leg muscles were burned to ash from the endless descent, so going the other direction was torture.

Audrey cried out in pain, obviously suffering the same effects. Peter reacted by pulling on the bannister with one arm, while keeping a hold on his girlfriend with the other. Together, they went up the stairs at the speed of a death march.

The robot didn't get a direct look at Tabby, but its computer brain would almost certainly figure out where she was. She fumbled with her shotgun as she followed the kids, sure it was going to be put to hard use in mere moments. "When you get to the next level, go through the door. We've got to find another stairwell."

The death of Donovan scared her to the bones, but it also gave her clarity for what had to be done to keep the others from meeting the same fate. They might climb back up to the top of the tower and delay their doom, but it was an ending already written. To stay alive, they needed to get out of the building in any way possible before more of those robots showed up.

Tabby fell through the fire door a few seconds after the kids. The three of them hunched over while they walked, desperate to catch their breath and rest their spent muscles. However, none of them stopped completely.

Audrey was openly weeping. Peter was probably crying too, but she couldn't catch up to him. He practically dragged the girl, always ahead of Tabby.

They jogged down a long hallway with a lone window at the far end. Each side was lined with glass doors to office space in the high-rise building. Those offices often had light coming through, too. They had the bare minimum to see where they needed to go.

"There! The exit sign. Go through, then down!" Tabby pointed, though the kids were ahead of her and wouldn't see it.

Was the robot behind them? Was she about to be shot in the back? If so, she wanted to at least make sure the kids got out.

"Run!" she yelled.

Peter slammed into the doorway and held it open as Audrey stumbled through and started down the stairs. He shot a worried glance at Tabby, then seemed to think about running down the stairwell too, but he stayed and held the door. "Come on!"

Tabby tasted the salt of tears. They were a combination of grief and pain, caused by the loss of Donovan and the intense efforts of the morning. She scurried through the door, grunting like a cave girl. Every footfall caused raging pain.

She gave the appearance of having a plan. "Go down, then out. Fast!"

Peter ran ahead and quickly caught Audrey. They only had to go down two flights to reach the main level, so it only took moments. Peter put his face on the glass window of the fire door to see what was out in the lobby. Tabby came up next to him, using the wall to hold herself up.

"What do you see?" she gasped.

"More of those things. It's like a patrol. They're walking all over the lobby. I see three. No, four. Probably more."

Up wasn't an option, so she looked at the stairwell heading down. If there were parking levels under the building, it might be another way out.

"We're not going through the lobby," she droned. "We'd never make it." If her legs were fresh, she might have been able to run into the lobby and escape, but she couldn't chance it in the condition she was in. She stifled her own groans and went down some more steps. "Follow me."

The next two levels were repeats of the lobby. Each time they came to a door, they checked to see if the way was clear. It was almost total blackness in the garage levels, but the robots were there. They each had illuminated strips along their flanks, giving them away.

They went down another level, but it was the bottom.

"It says mechanical room," Peter got out despite his panting.

"Go through," she advised. The door didn't have a window, so there was no way to see what was in there, but she figured it didn't matter.

They'd either be caught now or caught later. If they could skip the death climb up the 103 floors, so much the better.

Peter and Audrey went through, leaving her to wonder for a second if she should have gone first. Did she put the kids in danger?

She laughed. *Yeah, only now did I expose them to risk.*

The mechanical room turned out to be more like the entire floor. Numerous pipes, vents, and water tanks filled the space. The emergency lights gave them enough to see where they were going, but it was creepy, like being in the bottom of a ghost cruise liner.

"How do we get out of here?" Audrey complained.

"I don't know," Tabby replied, aware again of how it fell on her to get them to safety. "I'm working on it." Despite the power being shut off, the level wasn't silent. Pipes creaked and knocked, and sounds came from inside the ductwork as if the robot horses were walking inside them. "Skyscraper movies always have a connection between office buildings and the city sewer system. We just have to find it."

Peter didn't seem impressed. "That's your plan? How many skyscraper movies have you seen?"

"Shut up!" Audrey snapped at him. "She's doing her best."

Peter was already holding Audrey's hand, but he pulled her closer. "I was kidding. I'm scared of dying like Donny. I'm going to crap my pants if I don't laugh at how crazy this is."

Audrey sobbed once but managed to speak. "First of all, eww. That's gross. Second of all, I'm trying to hold it together, too."

"We all are," Tabby added. Her tummy bounced around inside her like it was on springs. "Let's find a sewer lid. I'm sure there's one here." For the next several minutes, they picked through the pipes and tubes from near the door, along the wall, and to the next corner. The sounds continued to suggest activity in the water pipes and the air ducts, but Tabby kept up the search.

"This is it!" A large metal grate had been built into the concrete floor. It wasn't the sewer lid she'd been expecting, but the smell inside indicated what was down there. She was able to lift it with Peter's help.

"After you," he insisted.

This time, she had to lead. Tabby climbed down a narrow ladder, using the dim emergency lights as her guide. Her legs were still on fire, though the new range of motion seemed to make the pain lighten up. She made it down about twenty feet but froze when she put her foot in water. At first, she thought it was disgusting sewage, like a scene out of Peter's overflowing toilet of imagination, but it seemed to be mostly clear. "It's rainwater, I think."

She descended a few more feet until she hit bottom. "It's only up to my waist."

The kids took their time coming down, which gave her a few moments to herself. The erratic clanging of the mechanical room was gone. It was almost perfectly silent, save for the occasional lapping of water against her legs.

Tabby still had the little aquatic flashlight strapped to her arm—a relic of her escape from the mine. She tapped it on to give herself a little light, but the small beam was swallowed by the oppressive darkness in both directions.

Must I always end up in dank caverns?

FOUR

USS John F. Kennedy, **south of New York City**

Kyla hung around Meechum enough to start feeling like she was at least an honorary Marine. The other woman never sat still; she was always checking weapons, cleaning equipment, or talking with her peers about the serious and the inane. They loved to joke with each other during the downtime, and sometimes even during battle. However, as she and Meechum ran across the deck of the carrier to the waiting helicopter, no one was screwing around.

"Why are we running?" she asked Meechum on the sly.

Most of Carthager's squad was with them. Eight or nine Marines appeared loaded to the gills on their way to their flight. She was proud to be a part of the team going to bring back her uncle, but it didn't feel right. It seemed rushed.

The rotors above the dull gray machine were already spinning, speaking to the efficiency of the Marines. Meechum ran close to her. "It's like I said, we can't trust anyone on the ship. We're going to borrow the Seahawk, you know?"

She fell a step behind the other woman, recalling something that had happened to her mom not long before the end. A man called on the phone saying he was with the cable company and wanted to talk about her bill. After some back and forth, the man explained that Mom's checks over the last six months had all bounced, and she would need to send a new one, for the full amount, to a PO Box. She was prepared to write a check, but she'd mentioned it to Uncle Ted before she got it to the mailbox. He immediately saw it for the scam it was.

Was she missing the obvious here on the ship?

What if the Marines were the bad guys? They could whisk her away and then use her as a bargaining chip to get to Uncle Ted and the VP.

She replayed her time with Meechum, trying to explain how she could have gone through New York City if she was the enemy. None of it added up...

Still, Kyla was wary when they reached the helicopter. She almost skidded to a halt when a familiar man appeared in the cargo door. Captain Van Nuys waved pleasantly.

"Oh, shit," she said with surprise, though under her breath.

"Good morning, Marines. I'm glad you could make it. We're going ashore." The captain waved to four men already strapped into the compartment. "I could use your help, but there's only room for two. I'll take you and you." He pointed to Meechum and Kyla.

Carthager got up to the edge. "Sir! Respectfully, I'm the commanding—"

"Thank you, son. I know. That's why I need you here watching over my boat."

Meechum shared a look with Carthager. Her squad leader offered an almost imperceptible nod before stepping back.

The door gunner was a new addition since the day before. The man hugged a giant machine gun at the edge of the cargo bay, presenting a threatening image. Kyla considered turning around and running from the sudden change in plans, but there was nowhere to go. The captain could order her onto the helicopter, even if she didn't want to go. Therefore, it seemed logical to play along.

As she got inside, Van Nuys pointed to her rifle. "You won't need that in here. I'll take it for you. Keep it safe." His lips formed a smile, but his eyes only conveyed a dead-serious order.

She handed it over without complaint. She'd only had it for about ten minutes—another assist from Meechum. The captain could do whatever he wanted with his team, including making them surrender weapons. However, Kyla carefully observed how he didn't take the rifle from Meechum.

"You'll get this back when we land," he shouted above the growing rotor wash.

She wondered if that would be true.

Is everyone a bad guy in hiding?

Long Island, NY

Ted and Emily treaded water as the buzz of a propeller got closer. The thick tree line made it hard to see until it was almost directly overhead. For a few tense seconds, he expected bombs to fall through the trees, but when the Predator was in the clear, he caught sight of both Hellfire missiles still secure under the wings.

"It's going for the lighthouse," Emily said, using her finger to indicate the route.

A few seconds after she'd said it, the drone drifted into a turn toward the lighthouse to the east of them. It went right, over the trees and out of view.

"Shit," Ted breathed out, "maybe it was a programmed turn. This is the end of the land mass. Maybe that one is searching between here and New York City. The lighthouse would be a convenient waypoint for a turn."

They slogged to shore, staying under the trees. The black yacht looked expensive and out of place parked on the glassy surface of the inland pond.

"I didn't even need a bath," Emily said with surprisingly good spirits. She'd managed to keep her head above water, sparing her hair. Ted knew from experience how women hated to get their hair wet for no reason.

"Me either," he agreed, remembering the nice hot shower from last night.

As they walked up the bank, he was pleased he'd managed to keep his prized AR-15 dry. Emily didn't have the same upper body strength, so hers got a little wet. She looked at him sheepishly.

"It'll dry out," he said, sensing the question on her face.

"Phew. I'd hate to ruin one of your babies."

He laughed as he walked into the woods, tugging at the sopping wet straps of his pack.

"Are we still going? Aren't you worried about that plane?" she asked in quick order.

He shrugged. "It didn't circle around up there, so it probably didn't see us, or the boat. If they see it now, no one can possibly know where we're headed. Not based on the radio broadcast."

"Unless someone knows where Kyla went on her field trip." She tore off her long-sleeve shirt and tossed it on the edge of the boat to dry out. It left her wearing the black tank top, which was as casual as he'd ever seen her. She also pulled out a stretchy headband to keep the hair out of her eyes.

Ted shook his head. "Don't worry about that. I barely remembered where it was. Our secret is safe. Let's hit it."

They walked in the woods for fifteen minutes. They still had an hour to reach the lighthouse and look over where they'd be meeting. It couldn't hurt to check it out, on the off chance it was being used for some unknown reason by the enemy. It seemed unlikely, but his military training wouldn't allow him to take anything for granted. His "uncle card" also needed punching. If he failed to look out for Kyla before and during their secret meeting, he'd never live it down.

Ted used his rifle butt to punch through a thick bundle of vines. "This is like being in the jungle."

She huffed while clearing some small branches with her arm. "I wouldn't know. The closest I've been to the tropics is Florida."

"Well, that's close. I spent some time there myself. The jungle is a lot like Florida, only hotter, wetter, and deadlier."

"Sounds wonderful," she said sarcastically.

He almost fell through some brush onto a two-lane blacktop road. Once he straightened up, he saw their destination. "We're here."

The lighthouse didn't seem as tall as he expected. It was made of brick, about fifty feet high, and all white except a thick line around its middle, which was painted maroon. The black walkway and windows sat at the top, though the light wasn't switched on in daytime.

"We've got about an hour to get in there and search for trouble." There were a few cars in the parking lot, but they were most likely from before the attack. All the spots at the front were empty, suggesting no one was inside. If the assholes in charge had come, he expected they would park in the handicapped and first row spots.

"I'll follow you, Major," Emily replied. "Don't forget where we came from. If we need to escape, we've got to get back to the *Happy Hooker*."

He stopped. "Yeah, I've been meaning to ask you about the name..."

It made her smile. "It means happy fisherman, not what you're thinking."

Ted smiled with her. "Oh, no, I had no other ideas in my head."

The moment of mirth felt good, but with the sight of the lighthouse ahead, he was already plotting his course back to the boat. Kyla's life could depend on his ability to get her there.

Nothing was funny about the danger they might face...

Amarillo, TX

Brent had never spent such a sleepless night. Even during his missions in the rice fields of Vietnam he'd managed to catch a little shuteye. Now, with a new purpose in his life, he'd spent the night going over the prison's defenses, planning for where attacks might come from and drawing up lists about where he needed to go the next day. In the light of a new morning, he yawned his jaw sore.

He'd drawn up a duty roster and called everyone together to let them know how the day would go. After sharing it, he waited for the inevitable complaints from the ex-convicts. Surprisingly, none came. They all got in their vehicles and followed him out of the prison.

They were exes because he'd preemptively commuted all their sentences. They were smalltime criminals, at best, so he was confident he could talk to a judge in the far future and make it legal. His immediate concern was that they continued to stick with him, and not run for the hills. After rescuing Trish, he thought they'd go their own way, but they didn't. A little extra incentive couldn't hurt.

Trish rode with him. The other five men spread out in three different pickup trucks, giving his convoy a total of four vehicles. As they drove toward the city, she seemed anxious to not let the conversation lapse. After talking for several minutes about the incident in her trailer the day before, she looked ahead.

"You know where you're going?" she asked. The young woman now carried a shotgun and a regulation Glock 22, like the other men. She told him she wasn't going to get caught flatfooted and unarmed ever again.

"I always know where I'm going," he bragged. "Thataway!" He pointed out the front window, making her laugh.

He couldn't spare anyone to stay back at the prison to guard it. If someone came to take it, one or two men wouldn't matter. Brent needed those extra guns out on the road. He planned on taking a tour of Amarillo to see if any of the invaders from the radio broadcast were already there. If not, maybe they could set up some booby-traps, like his days overseas. Even if there were only seven of them, he wasn't going to give up Amarillo without a fight.

"Last night, you said we were starting a rebellion," she stated. "Do you think we have a chance of defending this land with what few people we have?"

They were inside the city limits of Amarillo, away from the corn fields and prairie around the prison complex. It gave him a new perspective on how empty the world had become. "Only a small percentage of colonists took arms against the British government. It doesn't take much to win a war if one side wants it a lot more than the other. We learned that in Vietnam back in my day, and in Afghanistan more recently."

"Yeah, well, I—"

Brent caught sight of motion out the front window. "There!" he interrupted. "A plane."

It was a big military transport. Essentially the same beast that carried him around while he did his time in the service fifty years ago. He'd recognize the configuration anywhere.

"It's coming down," Trish added, seeing it herself.

Brent waved for the other vehicles to follow, and he led them on a winding route eastward across the city. Most roads were wide and flat, leaving plenty of room for the abandoned cars to roll and stop, which kept the routes clear in the aftermath. He used that luck to get them close enough to the airport to see more planes landing. They parked out of sight and had to walk a short way along a tree-lined road before he found the perfect vantage point.

Trish kept close to him. "Those aren't our boys, are they?"

"No, I don't think so." He wished he'd gone to Walmart as he'd suggested the day before. He desperately needed a set of binoculars for reconnaissance. "That guy on the radio said they were taking over; I think we're seeing the first wave."

"There has to be at least a thousand soldiers over there," she whispered.

"More than that," he deadpanned. Even with his bad eyes, he observed lots of movement from groups of soldiers in dark uniforms. Each of those transports could carry about three hundred soldiers, and there had to be more than twenty planes on the ground with a few in the air. Assuming they were bringing men, rather than equipment, the number of invaders could be in the thousands. And they might have made multiple trips.

"Are you positive they ain't ours?" another man asked.

If those were friendly forces, led by American service members, they'd have patrols roaming the city, helicopters on overwatch, and a protective cordon set up around the airfield itself. The force arriving as he watched showed absolutely no fear about being attacked from outside the airport. Why should they? Everyone in Amarillo was supposed to be dead, and they were the ones who caused it.

"Boss, what do you want us to do?" one of the men called out from some trees a hundred feet down the roadway.

Brent scanned the area, sure there had to be a way to fight back against them. Those four-engine jets weren't cheap. Taking out even one might severely wreck their timetable. However, his decision didn't come easy. He was about to get them into a war at much worse odds than those colonials ever faced. Whatever the number of colonists who went off to fight, it was more than seven people.

On the flipside, those early Americans had nothing comparable to the weapons of modern day. As long as there were no fighter jets, one tank could wipe out that entire airfield without getting a scratch on it. Not that he knew where to get a tank.

However, there were other ways to fight.

"Retreat, for now. We're going to come back with the right tools."

FIVE

Montauk Lighthouse, NY

Ted and Emily watched out the windows of the lighthouse visitor's center at the base of the tall spire, but he kept looking over his shoulder due to the creepy vibe inside. The place was filled with the fallen clothing of twenty or thirty tourists who happened to be in there when America was attacked. It made him think back to a similar situation on day one: Andrews Air Force Base had been filled with the same bundles of clothing. He shuddered before looking out at the beach again.

"You think she'll bring a helicopter back for us? After getting dirty in the ocean water, it sure would be nice to get a shower on an aircraft carrier." Emily stood at a nearby window, checking out a different stretch of beach. Because the lighthouse stood at the end of a peninsula, they had a great view of the shoreline in three directions.

"Yeah, that's my guess. If she's coming, it will be the helo." He patted his AR-15 out of habit.

"Do you think she'll show?" she asked.

As Kyla's uncle, and the brother responsible for promising her safety, he thought about whether it was right to bring Kyla to shore, even using code words. She was safe where she was, or at least safer than being on the mainland. However, he had to balance her safety with the need to get Emily in the opposite direction. If he got her to the aircraft carrier, it might free him up to concentrate on protecting his niece going forward. Assuming, of course, Emily didn't tap him for a bigger job now that the nation was at war.

While he'd been chewing on an answer, a small dot appeared on the horizon to the south. "I think I see something." He stared, afraid to lose track of it. After half a minute, he was positive what it was. "It's a transport helicopter, and it's heading this way."

Emily spoke with grave seriousness. "So, do you think she'll show?"

He cracked up right away, letting out a deep gulp of tension he'd been saving. "Yeah, that's probably her. However, I'm not sure I want it to be. The more I think about it, the more I believe it is dangerous to be around us. I should have had them send an empty helicopter to pick us up." He cocked his head toward her and spoke with dry wit. "Why did you let me agree to this meeting, Madame President?"

She rolled her eyes. "Stop second-guessing everything. Your instincts are good. Yeah, it's risky for Kyla, but based on what I saw of her hanging onto that helicopter as it hauled ass out of New York, your niece can take care of herself."

He still could hardly believe that was his sister's daughter. "Yeah, I guess you're right. It looks like the helo is going to touch down about a mile away on the beach."

Emily came to his window to get the most direct view. "Yep, they must be worried about an ambush, same as us. Still, it looks like we'll be getting out of here pretty soon."

The dull gray helicopter hovered over a flat expanse of beach, and then descended into a swirling tornado of sand kicked up by the rotor wash. He observed figures climbing from the aircraft and then running into the woods at the edge of the beach. He counted at least six people, maybe up to ten. "Damn, it's like they planned it that way. I couldn't see the crew unload, so I don't know how many we're dealing with."

"What's that?" she asked as she tapped his shoulder and pointed into the air.

"Shit, a drone!" he snapped.

There wasn't anything he could do but watch out the window. The pilot of the helicopter never stopped spinning the blades, so he was quick to dust off as soon as his people were out. Ted assumed the pilot knew he'd been spotted when he banked hard to the right and flew a few yards above the water. The Predator drone veered off its predetermined course to pursue.

"Go!" Ted shouted.

The pilot went out to sea for a short time before he banked and headed for shore. As Ted watched the two aircraft close distance with each other, he lost sight of the helicopter behind some trees. The drone swooped in and descended below the tree line after it. For the next few seconds, he watched with the expectation there'd be an explosion.

After half a minute of not seeing anything, he realized Emily's hand was still on his shoulder. Her fingernails dug into his skin as they watched. However, he didn't want to ask her to remove it; the human contact reassured him he wasn't alone against the entire world.

Eventually, she seemed to notice what she'd done. "Oh, I'm sorry. I don't know my own strength." She slapped him on the shoulder, laughing gently.

"It's okay. I didn't see if there was an explosion. Did you see anything?" She was standing a foot away, so he didn't expect her to see anything different.

"They both went out of sight, but I didn't see any smoke or fire. You think he made it out?"

"Dunno. However, we've lost sight of the incoming men. I think we should abandon this location and get somewhere we can rc-establish visual contact. I want to see how many there are, where they're going, and if Kyla is with them. If we stay here, they can walk right through those woods without us knowing a thing about them when they get here."

"I won't argue tactics with my general," she joked.

"Major, ma'am," he said in a formal tone. "My rank is major."

"You bumped me up to president," she said sarcastically, "So I'm bumping you up to general."

He hastened toward the door but halted as if to think it over. "General MacInnis. I like it, but that's one hell of a battlefield frocking. I don't even think regulations will let me skip lieutenant colonel and full-bird colonel."

She strode past him and opened the door. "I can't have an army without a general. As long as you keep calling me president, I'm going to call you general. We can argue pay grades and deal with HR when we're on that carrier."

All he wanted was to get Kyla safe. Battlefield ranks meant squat when there were no men to lead. Even the pay bonus didn't mean a thing when the entire economy of the United States was gone. Still, playing her game was a worthy distraction to balance out the hopelessness of being the only two people in the US military chain of command in America.

"I do as you order, Madame president," he said as he followed her outside.

Chicago, IL

Tabby was filled with fear as she walked the dark tunnels looking for a way out. A great deal of it had to do with seeing Donovan get shot. The replay ran over and over in her memory and wouldn't turn off. Could she have anticipated it? Should she have insisted on staying in front of the kids? Was she to blame for the result?

The water up to her knees didn't help.

Peter spoke to Audrey, who was shivering again. "Hey, babe, I would never complain about how you dress, but you somehow seem to always end up cold, despite it being summer outside. If we get out of here, maybe we should find you some long pants?"

The teen girl forced herself to laugh. "I'll be fine." It sounded hollow to Tabby, though her guilt-ridden brain immediately attributed it to how much the girl probably blamed her for allowing Donovan to die. It also could have been because the girl wore super-short jean shorts and a spaghetti-strap top, leaving her long legs exposed to the cold water. Audrey finally added, "Tabby will get us out of here, just like she did down in those mines."

Tabby perked up, glad to hear some words of encouragement. She stopped and turned around, keeping the light pointed down. "I'm so sorry about Donovan. I can't even imagine how you two must feel."

Peter and Audrey held hands, as they did almost all the time. They shared a look before Peter replied. "Don't worry about it. There's no way you could have done anything back there. Right now, all that matters is getting out of these tunnels."

Audrey jumped in. "And when we get out of here, we'll honor Donny like he deserves. He wouldn't want us to endanger ourselves with a memorial until we're all safe."

Tabby wanted to break down in tears on the spot, but she bit her tongue to stop the waterworks. It was tough enough leading the kids away from danger, but it would be impossible if she let herself turn into an emotional dumpster fire. She bowed her head for a second, then spun in the water to walk some more. "This way."

A few minutes later, she saw some light beaming from a grate above them. When they walked underneath, she found a ladder going up. "I'm going to check it out. You two stay here."

She climbed up the gritty metal bars about ten feet to reach the crisscrossed metal lid. Tabby watched through the slats for a few seconds, but all she saw were clouds and smoke from the fires. After taking a deep breath, she slid her fingers through the slats, intending to lift the lid and peek out. However, as she got it about an inch off its ledge, a shape up top slammed it back down.

"Crackers!" she blurted, channeling her conversation with Audrey the day before about a never-to-be-uttered C-word.

A metal foot pressed on the grate, then stepped off.

Tabby froze as the mechanical horse trotted by; her only movement was to pull her fingers back down. However, she heard its gears whir as it turned around.

It found us, she thought, instantly thinking how she could escape.

There was nowhere to go. If she climbed down, she wouldn't have time to make it. If she tried to get out, she would probably be chopped in half by a gun. The only thing she could do was freeze. As the machine arrived, she turned her face down, so at least it wouldn't identify her.

The mechanical leg hit the grate, then tapped it a few times. She sensed it was inches from her face—a fact she could have seen for herself if she'd looked up.

Go away.

The horse-robot must have stood there for a full minute. Tabby's arms burned from holding herself still on the ladder, but she was willing to die rather than relieve the pressure. The motors revved on the robot and it backed away from the grating. She sensed the light level increase as it cleared out.

"It's gone," Peter whispered from below. "Get out of there."

She opened her eyes, checked above to ensure it was really gone, then scurried down the ladder. As soon as she touched the water, she got away from the access point, so if it came back again, it would have nothing to see down in the sewer. "Follow me."

She walked for at least an hour. It was hard to say what direction they were going, but she did her best to go one way, rather than wandering in loops. She went straight at every intersection, hoping she was going anywhere but east. That would cause her to hit Lake Michigan.

When Tabby was satisfied they'd gone far enough, she found another grate and climbed to open it. She was almost positive there wouldn't be anyone up above unless they guarded every entrance to the sewer system for miles around, which seemed impossible. When she lifted this grate, no one stepped on it.

"It's a park," she said quietly. "And I see bicycles. We're taking them."

Tabby climbed out next to a basketball court in a municipal park. A few aging apartment buildings flanked the woodland property, as well as some large trees, but there were no drones. "Come on up, guys. We're getting out of the city."

Audrey had climbed up after her, but as she reached to help her out, Peter screamed in pain below them.

"Not again!" she shouted.

SIX

Montauk Lighthouse, NY

Kyla's stomach played the part of a spinning roulette ball as the helicopter swooped down and reached the beach. "I'm going to be sick," she said to herself.

For a short time, the lighthouse was visible about a mile away, but then a curtain of sand surrounded the aircraft as it touched down. Her tummy finally found its proper pocket when she jumped onto firm ground.

"I'm starting to hate helicopters," she yelled to Meechum, who ran next to her as they both headed for the trees beyond the sand. The other woman didn't acknowledge her, likely because it was far too loud to hear anything.

The helicopter powered up and lifted off while she was still on the run. More sand blew at her backside, but it quickly went away as the rotors gained altitude. Once she was in a safe spot, she looked back to watch the big military machine fly away. However, men began to yell at her to get down, which she did instantly.

The helicopter flew low to the water, but another aircraft was circling it a couple hundred feet above.

"It's a Predator!" one of the Navy guys shouted.

Van Nuys stood closest to the beach, unafraid to be seen. It appeared as if he wanted to see what was going to happen to his pilot. "The bastard has two Hellfires with the Seahawk's name on it."

A couple of seconds later, the drone launched one of its missiles. It came down at a steep angle due to the relative altitudes, but the pilot of the helicopter countered by swooping up and sideways. The missile flew in the ocean but didn't send up a giant plume of water like she expected.

The helicopter sped off to the west around the curvature of the land, and the drone dropped in behind, but it was impossible to see what happened after that.

"Dammit all," Van Nuys snapped. "If I had just one spare pilot, I could have a Super Hornet chewing up these Predators like a wolf through the sheep herd."

"Why don't you, sir?" Kyla asked with a voice far too timid for her liking. He was in charge of a super carrier, plus the other Marine ship, and he'd already sent planes into New York City, so why weren't they overhead at that moment?

The captain turned to her with sad eyes. "The enemy has more than those drones. They're landing all kinds of tech back in Newark. The few planes we have operational have to guard both the Iwo and the JFK." He walked past her toward the forest. "Come on, let's find your uncle."

She peered out over the water, hoping the pilot made it to safety. She'd never been on a helicopter before yesterday, and already she'd taken three rides. She couldn't imagine being a pilot, like Uncle Ted, and having to deal with the stress of flight every time they went up, much less avoiding missiles and whatever else was coming for them.

"You all right, dudette?" Meechum asked dryly from close by. Kyla glanced back, noticing how the captain had given her gun to the female Marine. She had it slung over her shoulder, while she kept the other one at the ready.

Kyla nodded, expecting her friend to hand over the weapon, but she only gestured for her to get moving. It was a behavioral oddity matched only by the surprise arrival of the captain to the shore party. Both were acting strange, it seemed, but it was probably because they were conducting the rescue of the President of the United States.

Kyla was the outsider.

Maybe it's just me.

Montauk Lighthouse, NY

Ted chose to watch his target from a bushy clump of trees next to the parking lot. He and Emily crouched in the weeds under the leafy canopy, and the chiggers were murdering his ankles, but at least it was a shady place to watch the wide walkway back to the lighthouse. Shirts, pants, and little dresses were the only signs of people on the concrete path. Unless Kyla's group climbed up the steep rocks next to the beach, there would be no way to get to the lighthouse without being seen.

"Well, this isn't how I planned today," Emily remarked as she slapped at a bug on her leg.

"Me either. When I finally co-piloted for the president, I assumed we'd have an actual plane." He spoke with thick sarcasm to poke fun at her.

"I was often told it would all be glamor and champagne. Photo spreads. Fancy-pants dinners. How did we get our wires crossed so badly?" She'd responded in a thoughtful voice but ended with a chuckle. "But seriously, I've thought about this day—I mean being upgraded to the presidency, not sitting in the weeds—every night for the past three years. Is tomorrow the day I have to step into Tanager's shoes? Can I do it? Am I ready?"

"Are you?" he asked in a more sympathetic voice.

She brushed hair out of her eyes, swatting a fly at the same time. "I'm not the first VP to face this crisis, you know. A number of veeps had to step in and take over the most important job in the world. Sometimes it was because of illness, or assassinations, or improprieties. During all of those crises, the rest of the world went on like normal. Looking back, it was almost silly how easy it was for those men. Here, today, facing the worst disaster of human history, I... Honestly, sometimes I feel like blending into the woods never to come out again." She batted at another bug. "Not these woods, mind you. I'm talking about a forest with no bugs, lots of food, and maybe a comfortable bed."

He couldn't help but laugh. No such place existed, though spending time with her in the woods, frontier style, didn't sound half-bad, all things considered. He'd taken courses in wilderness survival and would do all right on his own. At the same time, the humor was because they both knew retreat wasn't their style.

"Emily, I know a little about how you feel. The joke earlier about me being a general makes me appreciate the challenges of taking over a rank I have no business taking. I think your nervousness comes because there are no rules to follow anymore. There isn't an aide telling you how it goes, how to step into the dignity of the role. However, if my sister were around, she'd say we all just have to roll with it. Whatever life deals out, don't hide under your covers and worry. Hit it head-on with your best shot." He laughed a bit more. "Funny, because she was a hippy-dippy pacifist."

"Oh, I'm not a quitter. I shouldn't have said anything, but, what the hell, you're the only friend I've got." She smiled brightly at him, then slapped her wrist for another bug.

He glanced up to the lighthouse, then froze in place.

"Someone's coming."

Sacramento, California

Dwight found the motorcycle ride exhilarating. Being close to sober helped some of his normal memories percolate back to the surface. Riding his father's hog back in high school was one of the few memories he didn't mind having. The rest—from his time in the service in the wastes of the Middle East to his downward spiral kicked off when he got back—could be tossed onto the shoulder of the highway like so much trash.

Poppy soared high above. Her blue and green wings plied the skies like she was a soaring condor. He was happy to give her some room to fly, and he found himself seriously impressed by her ability to keep up with him. He drove the bike at over eighty miles-per-hour.

He followed Bernard not so much because he wanted to, but because the guy told him the bikes had trackers on them. As best he figured it, he had a good thing going with these strange people. Yeah, they had played a role the disappearances, but they seemed all right otherwise. They provided him food, water, and a motorbike to get around. It was more than anyone had ever given him on the streets.

After an hour of riding, Bernard waved him to an offramp at one of the many exits in the Central Valley of California. They played follow the leader as they went into a giant Valero gas station with a dozen lanes for pumps. Only one of them was operational, however, and a man in black overalls waved them in.

"Ahoy! Right this way." The guy indicated Bernard needed to pull forward so Dwight could use the pump behind.

After kicking the stands to keep the bikes upright, they both hopped off. Bernard acted like he knew the guy and went right up to him and shook his hand. "We're with the Folsom group. Fell a bit behind. How far back are we?"

The man eagerly shook hands in return. "Not far. They were through an hour or two ago. Hard to tell because it's pretty boring guarding this place. I wish I was going out with you and doing the real work." He glanced at Dwight, who smiled knowingly, though in his head he had no idea what the guy meant.

"Well," the man continued as he walked to one of the pumps, "of course you don't have to pay for anything. We've got you covered. Once you fill up, you're free to go."

Poppy landed on the roof of the nearby convenience shop, giving him an idea. "You got a restroom in there?"

The attendant nodded. "You bet. Nice and clean, like the boss requires."

"Cleanliness in all things," Bernard replied, along with the man. Things got silent for a moment, so Dwight looked over to the two men. They both stared at him like he'd crushed all their hopes and dreams.

"What?"

"Cleanliness in all things," they repeated, like robots.

Poppy squawked, suggesting he repeat the message.

"Cleanliness in all things." He shrugged. "Sorry, guys, it's been a long couple of days."

Bernard came to life as he spoke to the other man. "This guy had a flat tire earlier, and I think he got heatstroke while we fixed it, so he's not in the right frame of mind."

"And I've had the mad squirts since I ate at the buffet yesterday." Before they said anything else,

Dwight excused himself and beelined toward the restrooms. A tiny bell rang as he walked in the door, and for a few seconds, he returned to the normal life. The smells of the convenience store were a mix of fountain sodas, donuts, and cigarette smoke. He took a long drag, like the whole place was a cigarette.

He trotted to the back, like he really had to go to the bathroom, but he ducked down and shot over a couple of aisles to the liquor section. There, as if presented only for his enjoyment, was a full row of untouched beer, wine, as well as the good stuff.

"Oh-ho! Santa has come early this year!" He quietly mimicked the jolly elf's laugh and grabbed for a particularly large bottle of rum on the bottom shelf. When he stood back up, Bernard was at the end of the aisle.

"Hey, man, I thought you were heading for the bathroom." Bernard got quieter. "If they catch you with booze, you'll be shot."

Dwight was frozen in place, unable to process the simple words spoken by the other man. He'd shoplifted a time or two, and the worst that ever happened to him was he had to put it back. No one ever called the police on a rundown-looking man like him. But to be told he'd be shot for indulging in his one true hobby...

"I, uh, thought this would be good for cleaning the grease off my bike. I, uh, noticed it was dirty after they did some maintenance yesterday." It was a miracle he could come up with an answer that fit the situation, but he had used alcohol to clean engine parts before. Sometimes, his team got desperate over in the sandbox.

Dwight slowly put the bottle back, like it would blow up.

"Cleanliness in everything, Dwight. Remember that. We're starting America from scratch. None of the alcohol, drugs, or chemicals they pumped into their foods. It's all pure, from here on out."

Where's the fun in that?

His eyes closed to blink, but they wouldn't open back up for about five seconds. The words hit him in the feels in a way he did not expect. It wasn't from a respect for clean living or this new way promoted by his strange, new friend. It wasn't because he'd been told he might be shot if he did it again. It was because he couldn't imagine a world anything like what the man had suggested.

Suddenly, the cool uniform seemed too tight.

SEVEN

Montauk Lighthouse, NY

Ted pulled down the branches of a small bush to get a clearer view of the figure standing by the lighthouse. He had the small pair of binos he'd been carrying in his pack, which was the perfect amount of magnification for the job. The woman was dressed in Marine fatigues but didn't carry a weapon, which was unnatural Marine behavior. The only logical explanation was that it was Kyla, still dressed as she was the day before. "It's my niece. She made it."

"We saw more of them," Emily remarked as she too looked through the leaves. "So, where are they?"

Kyla walked onto the walkway close to the lighthouse, but based on her direction, she'd come up through the woods about fifty yards to their right. He suddenly imagined a whole Army battalion could come charging at him from the greenery, and he wanted to move. However, no matter who was in there waiting for him to meet Kyla, he wasn't going to leave her.

His heart raced as he thought through all the combinations of responses he could take, but it all came down to what he could do on his own. Under no circumstances could he endanger the vice president. "I've got to step away for a minute. Don't go anywhere."

"Now, Ted, you brought me here. Where the heck am I going to go?" She chuckled quietly. "I'm kidding. I'll stay put."

He crouched low as he backed away from the front edge of the trees, but he stopped for a second to observe his friend. She absently flicked a bug from her knee, then seemed to notice his pause. "What?"

It seemed like good-bye for some reason, but he didn't want to dwell on the point. "If you get into trouble, fire the rifle up in the air."

"Or put two in the chest, one in the head," she replied dryly.

His look was probably one of bafflement.

"I watch a lot of cop shows," she explained.

"Right. Do that." He smiled, then trotted into the thick underbrush of the summer foliage. Luckily, he wore long pants to keep the poison ivy at bay, though the mosquitos and chiggers had already chewed through his socks.

The lighthouse walkway came in a straight line down to the parking area, but the lot was mostly in the woods, which gave him plenty of concealment as he skirted around it. His intention was to scout the woods on Kyla's side of the walkway to see if it was indeed full of soldiers. However, he'd only gone about a quarter of the way when he realized exhaustion had gotten the better of him.

They'll post lookouts.

If he went over there, he'd be spotted. As he thought about it, he figured there might already be someone watching him. The lot was about a hundred yards long, and nearly as wide, with empty lanes that provided long lines of sight.

He had to change tactics. His first assumption was the people with Kyla were friends, or, at a minimum, weren't going to shoot him on sight. He then thought perhaps he was being overly dramatic about the whole thing. Kyla had given him the coordinates and wanted to meet him. She'd been on a US Navy aircraft carrier. They wouldn't send her out alone. Her escorts were there for her benefit, which should have made him happy. His final estimation was they would assume he'd come in on foot.

Ted searched the parking area for what he wanted. Of the approximately thirty cars in the lot, only one had what he needed. It was a white minivan with its sliding side door all the way open. Clothes were spread out around it, suggesting the owners had been in the process of loading or unloading at the time America disappeared.

It was in the middle of the lot, but he was able to use other cars to hide his approach to it. The minutes kept ticking away, leading him to worry if Emily was going to come looking for him. He'd told her to stay put, but that didn't mean she'd do it forever.

He scrambled on the pavement until he crouched next to the van. A pair of man's jeans were nearby, so he searched the pockets for some keys. When he didn't find any, he lifted the blouse of a woman who'd stood immediately outside the van door. The key fob was with her. Ted also noticed the onesie of a baby a bit under the van, as well as an empty car seat in the rear. He tried not to put too much thought into what the young family had been doing in those final moments.

Once he had the keys, he climbed in through the back and hit the button to auto-slide the door to close it. He let out the big breath he'd been holding while he studied the far edge of the lot. There had to be other men out there, but he didn't see them in his brief search.

Ted moved at sloth-speed into the driver's seat. He figured if he moved faster, he'd be obvious out to a lookout. If he moved slow and didn't draw attention, he might be able to start the van unhindered.

As soon as he was in the seat, he held his finger over the start button.

"Well, this might be stupid, but it will definitely get me noticed," he whispered.

Of all the options he could have chosen, he assumed stealing a car was the least risky to him. If Kyla's backup wanted to shoot him, he wasn't going to make it easy by walking up the path. If he did get shot at, Emily and Kyla would know to run. They could get away, he hoped.

After about thirty seconds of what-if scenarios running through his mind, he realized he was delaying the inevitable. If he was going to draw fire, he had to start the van.

He pushed the start button, then, strangely, looked at the horn.

Chicago, IL

"What's wrong?" Tabby fretted. She looked past Audrey to Peter down in the hole. He'd yelled, and she assumed the threat was bad, like a robot, or maybe a snake.

Peter gazed up at her with the look of a boy who'd done something stupid. He straddled one of the ladder bars and his face was scrunched in pain. "My foot slid off the ladder and I, uh, shattered my marbles."

It looked like a painful situation, and she tried to be supportive and encouraging as he untangled himself and climbed the ladder. His wet shoes seemed to want to go anywhere but the rungs, and he almost slid off a couple more times. She helped him out of the drainpipe and watched him slither into the grass before she chuckled. "Are you going to be all right?"

"I need a minute to collect my thoughts," he croaked.

"We can't stay," she replied quickly. "The people sending those drones around probably know we were in the sewers. We have to at least get away from this park in case they check this lid." She looked at Peter, then Audrey, then at the lid. "Audrey, will you help me slide this back over?"

The two of them were able to move it back with no problems. If the drones did come, they would see a closed lid. That might throw them off the scent, if the robots had the ability to track by smell. She wondered about the possibility as she and Audrey helped Peter to his feet. The teen girl wore a pleasant perfume, but she'd loaded up on it back at her house. After all their sweating and walking through water, it was only now getting to be tolerable.

"Do either of you know anything about computers? Is there a way to get an advantage over those robots? Can we block their signal or something?" She figured Peter was a know-it-all guy who might be plugged into technology.

They'd gone about twenty feet before Peter shook them off. "I can make it. And, to answer your question, I know about computers and tablets and stuff, but I have no idea what makes those things tick. I've never seen anything close. Like if they are remote control or working on their own. That would be important to know."

"Which one is more dangerous?" Tabby asked as she picked up one of the bikes she intended to borrow.

"I don't know for sure. A robot on its own might see things no human would notice. However, I might be more afraid of the human eyes behind the robot because a person's brain is a lot smarter than any software code. But if you're going to ask me which one these are, I have no idea how to tell."

There were more than a dozen bikes on the ground, as if children had been playing in the park when the robot people zapped America. It made her sad to steal the bicycles from the fallen clothing, but it had to be done. She was sure the kids would understand.

Before they got started, a dog came out of the small block building that served as the restrooms for the park. It was a big, burly brown dog, and it didn't appear anywhere as nice as Sister Rose's. It had a big, ugly black collar with oversized lugs sticking from it, as if the owner wanted everyone to know how mean the dog could be.

"Good pup," she cooed. Then, to her friends, she added, "Let's get out of here."

She didn't look back as she pedaled away. Tabby led the teens down the bike path, along the edge of the park, and then into what would have been a busy urban street. Cars were everywhere on one side, so she went to the other where it was mostly clear. Only a few of the out-of-control cars had veered into the wrong lanes, probably because traffic had been stopped in that part of Chicago.

Peter stood while he pedaled—a position Tabby only figured out after remembering his painful climb up the ladder. "Where are we going to go?" he asked.

Besides leaving Chicago, she had no idea where they should go next. The cordon around the disaster had turned out to be a false hope, so there was nowhere else worth going, as best she could tell. However, as the leader of her small troupe, she didn't want to give the impression she had no ideas at all. "I was thinking of going back to my home in Bonne Terre. It's the one place on earth where I think I can survive if we have to wait out these bastards."

They rode in silence for a few minutes before Audrey spoke up. "Can we come with?"

Tabby stopped her bike, as did the others. "Of course you can. We're in this together, you know? I'm not going to ditch you or anything like that. It's important to me you know that, because Donovan would never forgive me if I ruined his memory by ditching his two friends."

"What, did you think she was going to leave us?" Peter asked Audrey in a tone of voice Tabby thought sounded like he wasn't sure, either.

Audrey huffed. "I don't know. I'm scared shitless, I know that much. If Tabby left us, I don't know what I'd do. Probably shoot myself."

"No!" Tabby blurted. "Never say such a horrible thing. No matter how bad it gets, you have to keep fighting. Keep running. Keep doing whatever it takes to stay alive. Donovan and all these people you see along the streets and in the cars, they'd do anything to be in your place. We honor them by staying alive."

Audrey gently tapped a little bicycle bell on her handlebars. "So, we're going back toward home. I can handle that." All three of them were from the same region, so it was going to be close to home no matter which house they ended up in. Perhaps they could rotate, to keep the memory of family fresh for all three of them.

"Back to Missouri," Tabby said with conviction.

"To Missouri," Audrey and Peter echoed.

EIGHT

Montauk Lighthouse, NY

Kyla had been standing in front of the lighthouse long enough that she began to doubt Uncle Ted would ever show up. Though she'd discussed it all in code, maybe they'd misinterpreted each other. If so, he could be waiting for her somewhere else at that moment. It would be one more mistake in a couple of days stuffed full of them.

She looked back the way she'd come. Meechum and the captain were in the trees about twenty yards behind her, but the growth was so dense, she didn't see either one. Were they going to come out and tell her to forget about the meetup?

Kyla used her idle time to remember the last place she'd seen her uncle, besides seeing him from the helicopter. It hadn't been too long ago—maybe a month. He had some time off from his flight duties and had come up to New York City to hang out with Mom for a while. They took a Saturday to drive up to Boston and visited the *USS Constitution*, an old sailing ship. She immediately saw the irony—in the span of a month, she'd been on the US Navy's oldest commissioned ship and its newest. There was also a darker comparison to be made. A month ago, she was bored to tears on the tour, a little anxious for the trip to be over and looking forward to when Uncle Ted hit the road. Today, she couldn't wait to see him.

Uncle Ted won't let me down.

Mom always loved having her brother around and made a point of inviting him any chance she could. Kyla always attributed those visits to her being lonely, since Dad was long gone, but as she stood there waiting to see him, she found a new emotional state tied to her uncle. He always seemed to know what he was doing. He was put together and competent. For

Kyla, that represented having a solid mentor and family member in a world gone mad, but for Mom, maybe he represented a calm center to her otherwise messed-up life.

Uncle Ted was the military man with pressed uniforms who always made his bed. Mom was the woman who didn't even own an iron, much less keep an orderly house. He was—

An engine starting caught her attention. Was it Uncle Ted? One of the captain's men? They'd gone into the woods to who knows where. Another survivor? The enemy?

Kyla looked back to the captain, expecting him to pop his head out of the woods and give her some advice, but when that didn't happen, she took a step off the walkway away from Meechum and Van Nuys. If there was any chance it was a bad guy, she didn't want to give them away. Ever since Meechum had put it in her head to think more like a Marine, she tried to do justice to the suggestion.

The motor didn't sound like anything special. It wasn't a motorcycle or a big truck. It sounded exactly like a normal car on a normal street. Her guess was confirmed when a white minivan came into view at the end of the walkway down by the lot. It paid no heed to the pedestrian-only signs but sped over the blowing clothes of dead tourists.

She took a few more steps away from the pavement, but also stayed close to the lighthouse building. If the person meant to ram her, she didn't want to be out in the clearing, and she wasn't sure she could run to the woods before the van arrived.

"Please be Uncle Ted," she said quietly. If she'd been given the rifle, she would have it out and ready for action. Silently, she cursed Van Nuys. However, he'd failed to collect her pistol. She would yank it out if things got bad...

The van accelerated up the walkway, but at the halfway point, the driver honked twice and waved a hand through the open side window. Like clockwork, Uncle Ted always did the same two-honk signal when he left Mom's. It had to be him.

The operator slammed on the brakes, causing the tires to grab onto the concrete, save for one front tire, which dragged a pair of jeans under it. She stutter-stepped back a few more paces and thought about reaching for her pistol, but the van turned sideways and stopped at the last second.

"Get in!" Uncle Ted yelled through the open passenger-side window.

She experienced a wave of confusion once she had confirmation it was him. She wanted to get in, desperately, but she didn't want to leave Meechum. It was like both choices were wrong, and for a few seconds, she stood there processing a solution. Uncle Ted was right there, but the Marine was close by.

"I have to get my friend, Meechum," she lamented as she walked up to the door.

"Just get in! I'll explain when you're inside." He spoke forcefully, but also a bit on the quiet side, like someone might be listening.

She did as instructed. Whatever he had in mind, she trusted his judgement. "Okay."

As soon as she shut the door, Uncle Ted put it in gear, spun the tires, and got the van pointed back down the walkway. He mashed the gas pedal, pushing her back into the seat, but then he slammed on the brakes a couple of seconds later. He also hung out the window on his side.

"Becca, get in!" he shouted in a loud voice.

Kyla's heart leapt into her throat from anticipation.

Mom's alive?

For a brief instant, Kyla expected her mom to come out of the trees; it would be a reunion for the ages. However, a small brunette woman popped her head up over some weeds and tall grass, looking like she wasn't sure if she should come out. Uncle Ted waved her in. When she stood up, Kyla knew it wasn't her mom, though it was a recognizable woman.

"So, it was the vice president," she said dryly.

Montauk Lighthouse, NY

"Why did you use Mom's name?" Kyla asked in a depressed voice as Emily ran for the van's sliding door.

"Sorry, Kyla, it was the first name that came to mind. I didn't want to use Emily's name, in case those people you're with are after her." It didn't take long for the VP to climb in the back, and Ted had them rolling before the door slid shut. He checked the rearview mirror and thought he saw movement back by the lighthouse, but he had to turn the wheel to get around parked cars. His attention was focused forward.

"I guess it makes sense," she replied. "Those aren't bad guys. In fact, I have a good friend who helped me survive in the city. She was on the helicopter when you saw me yesterday."

"That was awesome," Emily interjected from the back seat. "Your uncle was so happy to see you get out of there and we worried about you all night, with all those planes fighting in the skies."

He guided the van around the parking lot, chirping the tires with abandon, and finally sped onto the two-lane road. There were plenty of trees to give them cover, so he let out a bit of the tension in his spine, but he didn't relax yet.

Kyla turned in her seat to face Emily. "It's nice to meet you, Madame Vice President. Me and my mom are big fans..." She let her voice trail off, and Ted assumed she was still upset about how he'd used Rebecca's name.

"It's great to meet you, too. I've heard a lot of great things about you. This guy has been trying to get to you since all this started." Emily reached from the back seat to shake hands with his niece.

"What happened to your face?" he asked Kyla. It looked like she'd been in a fight; one of her cheeks was swollen and purple.

The girl laughed. "You know that friend I mentioned? Her name is Lance Corporal Meechum. She kicked me in the face. By accident."

"Uh huh," he replied distractedly, clicking his tongue in thought.

He didn't have time for further small talk, as much as he wanted to catch up. In the short time he'd been in the van, he'd formulated a plan to shake off the soldiers who were with Kyla. When she was somewhere safe, and they could take more than sixty seconds to talk, he could establish more about who they were, whether they could be trusted, and how they were going to get Emily to real safety. "Guys, it's not going to take them long to find us. This is the only road down on this end of Long Island. We can't escape on it. So, what I'm going to do is let you out."

Ted jammed on the brakes, sending Kyla toward the dashboard and Emily toward the back of his seat. "You guys should wear seatbelts," he chuckled.

"Thanks for the warning," Emily snarked.

"Yeah, where'd you learn to drive?" Kyla added.

"I can see having two side-seat drivers is going to be Hell." He smiled at them both as they straightened out. "But listen, go into the woods and get to the boat. Emily knows how to pilot it."

"Wait!" Kyla exclaimed. "We can't leave. My friends are with the FAST Marines. They say they really need to catch up to her." She pointed to Emily. "They said they have to get a message to her, or more people are going to die."

"FAST Marines?" Emily asked. "It sounds familiar, but I don't remember the acronym."

Kyla's shoulders slumped. "I don't remember, either."

"Fleet Antiterrorism Security Teams," Ted replied in a businesslike tone. "We dealt with them a couple of times when we traveled to overseas ports where our Navy had basing rights."

"Yes," Kyla agreed. "They knew something about this terrorist attack. They were on the JFK because they tried to get ahead of it, but they were as surprised as everyone else when all the sailors disappeared."

He pushed the button to open the sliding door on the passenger side, then he turned to face both women. "Listen, we don't know who we can trust outside this van. Get to the boat, then go to Martha's Vineyard. I'll go down to the airfield we passed and get myself over there as soon as I can."

"Why can't we all go in the boat?" Kyla asked.

"He's going to play the hero," Emily said in a I'm-not-impressed voice. "So we can get away."

Put like that, he did feel a little dramatic about the whole thing, but he wasn't going to underestimate the enemy, even for a second. As long as no one saw the women get out of the van, they'd think they were with him. He'd drive around for a little bit—long enough to let Emily get the boat over to the next island. If the men who'd brought Kyla were the good guys, then there'd be no harm, no foul. If they were the bad guys...

It was a good plan...as long as they got out at that moment.

"Please, get out. Let me do my thing, and you two do yours. This is going to work."

Neither woman seemed to believe him, but Emily slid out the side door. "Come on. You and I will probably end up saving him, anyway." The VP smiled sideways at Ted, inserting a pang of regret in his side, probably as she'd intended.

Kyla opened the door, but she hesitated. "I barely got a chance to say hello after finding you again. If you die, I won't have anyone left."

He opened his mouth, thinking he was going to have to comfort her, but she went on. "So, don't die, Unk."

She hopped out, slammed the door shut, and ran into the woods behind Emily.

They grow up so fast.

Amarillo, TX

Brent launched into a little pep talk as he stood at the threshold of the building. "Gentlemen, I know I'm supposed to represent the law, or whatever, out here, but everything changed when they attacked this great nation. When we walk through these doors, I'm giving us all permission to take whatever we need to fight back. It isn't theft; it's commandeering. Do you understand?"

The ex-convicts all nodded and mumbled agreement.

"Then let's get this over with. You all know what we need." He led the way through the sliding glass doors of the Walmart. The power was off, so they had to pull them manually, but it didn't take long. Once inside, there were a few dim emergency lights in the ceiling, which cast a twilight ambiance over all the aisles, including the fallen clothes of the vanished shoppers.

"Let's add flashlights to our list," he said matter-of-factly. "They'll be in sporting goods. I'll grab the batteries."

"I need one of these," Andre said in a business-like tone as he grabbed a huge flat panel TV set up near the front door. He was normally a quiet man, mid-forties, who'd been sent up the river because he set up a fake charity and collected online funds from it.

He and Carter were cellmates, so Carter was closest to him after he'd said it. "The hell you do. It wouldn't even fit in our cell."

"So, we'll get a bigger cell," Andre joked. "Better yet, I'll kick you out and put it on your bed."

"Be my guest, you no good—"

"No extras," Brent chided, knowing they were kidding.

Carter looked back as he walked away. "If that TV is in our truck when we get outside, I'm chucking it back out."

Everyone laughed as they split up, each going to their assigned goals. Brent thought he'd done a good job of explaining what they were doing, and the men held together remarkably well for a random bunch of survivors from a state prison. However, no matter how many supplies they took from the store, or how many guns they collected, it would be dangerous business trying to fight the invaders. His acid reflux was at the high-water mark in his stomach, suggesting he make a pit stop in the pharmacy section to stock up on antacids.

One old coot leading young guns against the most destructive terrorist group in history. What could go wrong?

It all came together a half-hour later. Some of the men had lingered, leading him to wonder if they'd stocked up on illicit gear like smokes and booze, or, god forbid, fifty-inch televisions, but he didn't make a big deal out of it. They were all volunteers, and he didn't think they'd respond well to true military discipline.

"All right. Good job. We've got backpacks, flashlights, FRS radios, and all the shotgun ammo we can carry. Is there anything we're missing?" He glanced around at them, sure he saw a few extra gold necklaces and watches. Did Walmart even have jewelry worth stealing?

"Can we have a crack at the front registers?" one of the guys asked. Others laughed.

He sighed. "Frankly, I don't care. Grab all the money, if you want, but I don't think it will do you any good. No one's around to take it if you wanted to buy something. The government itself isn't around, either. It's basically worthless paper."

That seemed to settle them.

"However, I see some of you now have watches on. I want you all to go to the watch section and get your own watch. We'll want to synchronize them so we're all on the same time, down to the second."

"Why is that, boss?" one of the guys asked.

"Because when we attack those bastards, we have to do it at the same time, or some of us could die."

That really shut them up.

NINE

Montauk Airfield, NY

Ted suffered guilt for letting both women out of his sight, as it went against his keep-them-close protective wiring, but he was convinced the decoy gambit was their only viable option. After swooping in and stealing Kyla without a shot, he didn't want to depend on surprise again. If anyone was going to fire guns, it would be at him, not her. It was the very least he could do for Rebecca to take care of her only daughter.

After dropping them off, he continued on the narrow forest road for another few miles until he found the airfield. The tiny airport was a far cry from the one in Harrisburg. It had no terminals, towers, or National Guard station. Instead, it only had one small shack serving as the radio and control center, with a dozen parked single-engine craft nearby. At least it was paved. He'd been on smaller fields that were literally strips of grass.

Finding an operational aircraft was a lot more difficult, however. It didn't look like any of the planes had been caught taxiing during the attack, so there weren't any conveniently-placed Cessnas ready for him to borrow.

On a hunch, he went into the radio shack. Small fields like the one at Montauk were often manned by volunteers, and those volunteers almost always had a love of flight that drew them to the lifestyle, including ownership of planes. He went right for the bundle of clothing piled on a chair by the radio; the keys were inside one of his pockets.

From there, it only took a little effort to find the right plane out on the tarmac. It took him about six tries, but he found the right one as helicopter rotors echoed in the distance. At first, he listened to see if maybe the aircraft was heading for open water, and his friends, but it surprised him when it swooped in over the trees about midway down the airstrip.

"Oh, shit!" he cried out.

Ted didn't go anywhere without his rifle, but the Seahawk helicopter banked around about twenty feet above the trees, which gave the door gunner plenty of time to zero in on him. Fighting back against an M240 machine gun was suicide. There was no way to get in the plane and take off. He couldn't run for cover either. He was out in the open in the middle of the plane parking lot. It wasn't bad strategy on his part, but it was bad luck.

Nice going, general mayhem. You really impressed the VP with this op.

He put his hands up as the helo closed the distance and then hovered at the close end of the runway. It put him in the terrible position of praying they were good guys. As a man in a Navy uniform got out, he let his guard down a tiny bit. A Marine woman followed, and a heavily-armed seaman in fatigues came last. They hunched over until clear of the rotors, then they jogged his way as the Seahawk lifted off again. Its starboard door gunner never let him out of the crosshairs.

The Navy man was a ship's captain, based on his all-white uniform. He held his white service cap until the rotor wash faded. "Are you Major Ted MacInnis, US Air Force?" He held out his hand as if to shake. Ted wasn't about to mention he'd been promised a promotion by Emily. There were proper channels, even in the Apocalypse.

Ted took the courtesy, though he didn't like the rifles pointed at him. "We're on the same team, right, sir?"

"It depends. I'm Captain Van Nuys of the *USS John F. Kennedy*. When this business kicked off, someone put a bag over my head and tossed me in a lower hold. This Marine found me." He pointed to the woman, who wore the name Meechum; a name Kyla said was her friend. Then he motioned to the seaman. "This man with me is on my personal security team. Other than them, I trust absolutely no one."

"Probably smart," Ted allowed. After being betrayed by John Jefferies and that asshole Ramirez, he knew where the captain was coming from.

"Probably? No, it's smart, Major. I need you to get smart too and tell me where the vice president has gone." He paused for a moment. "I need to know right now."

Van Nuys undoubtedly always got what he wanted—it was one of the perks of skippering the most expensive weapon in the US Navy—but Ted wasn't in the Navy. He lowered his AR but kept it under his arm. "Sir, I'm doing what I think is right to protect the women traveling with me. You've already met my niece, Kyla Justice, but you haven't met the other woman I was with. She's my sister, Rebecca. She bears a passing resemblance to the vice president, so I could see why you would say that, but it isn't her. Sir."

The captain studied his eyes, searching for any trace of the lie he'd tossed out there. However, he seemed to make a decision and waved to his two backups. "Guys, lower your weapons."

The seaman and the Marine both dipped their barrels, which seemed to take everyone down a notch on the stress scale. Van Nuys leaned against the fuselage of the red and white airplane he'd been testing. "Major, I appreciate what you're doing out here. You're one of the first people I've met on the outside. Hell, other than those bastards at Newark, you might be the only person alive within a thousand miles."

"Sir, these forces aren't just in Newark. I saw them in DC, Harrisburg, and lots of them were inside New York City." He didn't mind giving away that detail. If the three people in front of him were with the enemy, they'd already know where they were deployed. If, however, they were on his side, they'd need to know where to avoid the enemy.

"Good to know. When we get things up and running at full strength on the carrier, we'll pound these guys so far into the ground, they'll only be able to feel the furnaces of Hell." He took a deep breath. "However, until then, I should tell you we're searching for the vice president because she's the only one who can lead our rump forces left here on the fringes of America. I've got the JFK and *Iwo Jima* with me, but we've lost contact with the rest of the fleet. We think it's that David guy. He turned the whole world against us."

Ted and Emily had watched the speech on TV the night before.

Van Nuys went on, "If we don't get some real leadership, the enemy is going to pick us apart one by one. When your niece told us she saw you and the vice president, I was sure we'd finally gotten our act together. We were finally going to fight back."

"I saw what you did in New York, sir. You delivered some good payback." He felt marginally better about the man; why would a bad guy shoot up his own team?

"I was playing defense, Major. I had to protect my extraction helo. I risked my men to save your niece, which turned out to be a good thing, especially since she claimed to have seen the vice president."

"No," he insisted, "it was a case of mistaken identity. Kyla is with her mom right now. I told you—"

Van Nuys held up a hand. "Yes, I know. It wasn't her. Why don't we get on the chopper and go back to the JFK where we can further debrief you? Then, when you're comfortable with our operation, maybe you'll tell us where to find your niece and her *mother*. We'll bring them in however you want. Remember, we're all on the same team."

"No, we're not, sir. He's lying." The short-haired Marine pointed her rifle square at Ted's chest.

Chicago, IL

Tabby and the kids rode the stolen bikes through endless blocks of the Chicago cityscape. At first, they passed taller skyscrapers and apartment complexes, but the height of the buildings decreased as they got further from downtown. Later, they made it to a monotonous section of strip mall storefronts for sandwich shops, payday loans, and autobody shops. The seemingly endless repetition, along with the utter silence of what should have been a bustling city street, threatened to drive her mad.

"Will someone say something," she requested. "Tell me what you were learning in school, or if you learned anything when you came to the Bonne Terre mine. Anything. I want to hear it."

Peter laughed a little. "You mean before the place caught on fire? I learned some people have really shitty jobs in this world. I mean, who would want to work in an underground mine, with dynamite, while always worrying if the whole place was on the verge of collapsing on your head? Not me, thanks."

Tabby knew what he meant, since she'd been there on the tour, but she could only think what the mine was doing in the present time. It was as silent down there as it was on the street in front of her. For a few pedal strokes, all she wanted to do was turn around and somehow blow up those drones. Incur a small financial penalty upon the terrorists as payback for the larger toll they'd dealt to the country. Her anger only lasted another block. The silence was broken by panting animals.

Three dogs walked in the middle of a cross street almost next to them. She didn't know the breeds, but they were medium build, mostly dark-colored, and didn't look like they had leashes or collars. Once they saw her, the creatures dropped their happy indifference and instead came at them like barking sharks.

"Go!" she screamed, immediately standing and pumping the pedals like a madwoman. Audrey and Peter followed her lead, standing and pedaling, but the dogs were at least twice as fast in their initial burst of speed.

The leader went directly for her. She allowed Peter and Audrey's bikes to stay out front. What kind of protector would she be if she left the younger kids in the dust?

Knowing there was no avoiding it, Tabby swung her foot in a clumsy kick toward the dog's snout. "Take this!" She missed its head but clipped the side of its neck. The dog veered right at the last possible second, as if realizing it was dangerous to bite at the metal contraption and the person attached to it. However, it reoriented while sprinting and appeared to search for a way to nip at her again.

Her effort to protect the teens was only partly successful. The other two dogs passed Tabby and zeroed in on Audrey. "Get them off me!" the girl screeched.

Tabby looked down to her own attacker. The little beast snapped at her shoe each time it circled the crank. She tried to kick it again, but the move cost her speed. The next time her foot came around, she kept pedaling. That should have been the end of it, but the mutt wouldn't back down. As it continued to lunge at her, she got more pissed off than scared, and she wanted to fight back.

Don't mess with us.

Tabby summoned all her pent-up anger about Donovan's murder and drew it into her lungs. She let the bike coast while bending over toward the canine's face, then let it all out with a primal scream. "Bad dog!"

The mutt spun aside and lowered its tail, as if surprised into submission.

Seeing the opportunity open, she pedaled as fast as her lungs and legs would allow and quickly caught up to the other two dogs, creating a wedge between them and Audrey. They seemed surprised to see her and drifted aside, then they dropped back. Maybe they were lost without their leader.

"Out of my way," she snapped at them.

After a few seconds of believing she'd made it, the first dog was back on her heel. It rubbed its teeth against the sole of her right foot. It was wrong to think it, since she was a dog lover at heart, but her patience snapped like a dry twig.

"Sonofa!"

She pulled the brakes on the handlebars and skidded to a stop. The change of pace seemed to catch the dog by surprise, and it slid past her. The other two mutts halted when the leader did, and the trio regrouped—shaken and confused, but not beaten. The barking started up as they closed in on her. However, the delay allowed her to pull the pistol from her waistband.

I could kill you all.

For a few seconds, she reveled in the thought of taking control of the situation. It was completely within her ability to end this threat for good. The dogs, for their part, didn't seem to understand that their fate was tied to the object in her hand. They barked relentlessly, as if psyching each other up to go in for the kill.

Yet she couldn't hurt them. Instead of blowing them away, she aimed the pistol in the air and pulled the trigger. The explosion seemed louder than any other gun she'd ever heard, including the drone machine gun back at the TV station. It scared her almost as much as it frightened the dogs; their claws seemed to dig into the asphalt for how fast they accelerated away from her.

Peter and Audrey circled around. By the time they arrived, she had the gun back where it belonged. "That was awesome," Peter announced, tapping the pistol in his police belt. "Can I shoot the next ones?"

"I didn't shoot them," she croaked. Her emotions had lost their compass. Her sadness at losing Donovan was as deep as her anger at being forced into a situation where she had to threaten dogs, of all things. She desperately wanted someone to appear who was in charge and could make sense of all that she'd seen the past few days.

Peter replied, "Well, I don't mind shooting bad dogs. Unless you thought they were good ones?"

She didn't know. They could have been the worst dogs in the world, or saints. She'd come into their territory. The unfamiliar city of Chicago. "We have to get out of here, like, right now. Let's check these cars next to the street. I'm sure one of them has keys."

Audrey straddled her bicycle as she stood by Peter, but she stepped a bit closer to Tabby. "Can I give him my shotgun?"

Tabby was surprised but accepting. "Sure, you can do whatever you want. Is everything all right?"

The girl smiled weakly. "I'm a mess, Tabby. I don't think I could have shot those dogs, even if I needed to. If Peter can, I'd rather he have this." She unslung the weapon.

"All right, Peter, it looks like Audrey is giving you a present. Don't let anyone steal it, like the last one." He'd let Gus the sewer worker take his, but if Audrey wasn't up to using her weapon, the smart play was to give Peter another chance.

Peter wheeled up with a look like he'd been given an important gift. "Awesome! Thank you. I'll call this *Audrey Three*!"

"Call it whatever you want," Audrey sighed.

Peter got serious. "I swear I'll protect you, babe."

She smiled. "I know you will. Thanks."

The two kids exchanged the gun while Tabby looked around. When they were done, the young girl rolled back over to her and acted like she was letting her in on a big secret. "Tabby, I don't want to scare you, but my meds are in the cooler back in your car…"

"Oh, no," Tabby replied immediately. Her car was still at the door of the Sears Tower, probably surrounded by enemy soldiers.

"Shush," the girl complained. "We can't go back. You know that. I'm just telling you, so you understand my issue."

"There has to be somewhere we can go to get more insulin, right? A pharmacy or whatever." Tabby scanned the street, already on the hunt for one.

"I'm fine for now. Let's get back home, like you said, then we can deal with it."

She gave her a once-over. "Are you sure? We can do this now."

Audrey nodded. "Out of here. Then we worry about me. Do you really think we're far enough from downtown to get in a car?"

She had to make an educated guess. "I think we've put enough miles between us and them. There aren't any robots flying around out here, and we should be far enough from where we last saw them in the city. I don't know about you guys, but I need to make some real time. I want to go south, toward home, and I don't want to meet any more animals."

Audrey and Peter shared a look, and some form of silent communication passed between them. Audrey seemed to speak for them both. "We're ready to go."

"Start checking the cars," she replied.

I want to be home before sunset.

TEN

Montauk, NY

"I thought our reunion would have been a little bit longer," Kyla said as the engine sounds from Uncle Ted's stolen van faded in the distance.

The forest was thicker here than by the lighthouse, so she had a little trouble keeping up with the older woman. However, once she remembered Emily had been through there before, she followed in her footsteps and managed to keep pace.

"I've only really known your uncle for a few days, but he seems to know what he's doing. I trust he's got a plan for today, too." She held a young sapling branch so it wouldn't shoot back in Kyla's face when she walked by.

"Thanks," she said as she grabbed the branch and guided it safely to her side. "Yeah, Uncle Ted is pretty intense. I think my mom secretly hated him because he always seemed to have his life together."

Emily laughed. "Yeah, I can see that about him, but Ted isn't perfect. Trust me. I've seen him make plenty of mistakes. I just hope this isn't one of them."

She noted the informal use of her uncle's name. Was it appropriate for a vice president? Her dress code didn't seem presidential either. The blue jeans and black tank top made her appear like a soccer mom at the match rather than the second-most important person in the American government. Her rich, brown hair was frizzy at the moment, though held together by a black headband.

"What's it like to be the vice president?"

"Boring," she replied without a pause. "Lots of glad-handing and chairing of big commissions, but it all amounts to nothing. As vice, I had no real power of my own. I think people treated me like royalty because I was the first woman in the office, not because they particularly liked me. Hell, your uncle didn't even vote for me."

Kyla chuckled as she walked around a thick tree trunk before rejoining Emily. "I have no doubt of that. Mom and him were on opposite sides of politics, as you probably could guess."

Emily brushed a stray leaf out of her hair. "Well, all that's gone. None of it matters. However, I'll tell you a secret only me and your uncle know." The pair walked close together as Emily spoke quietly. "The president is gone. Your uncle is the one who confirmed it. I'm the new prez. Fun, huh?"

Kyla whistled softly. "Some general overseas said everyone was gone in the line of, what's it called, secession?"

"Succession," Emily corrected.

"Right, the line of succession. Out there, they don't know you're still alive. That explains why they been acting all weird, like they're lost without anyone up top leading them. Even the captain on the carrier seemed keen to have you around once I told him I saw you in Central Park.

Naturally, they'd want to rescue the woman who would be our president."

"Did they tell you that?" Emily asked.

She shrugged. "Nobody told me nothing," she said, "besides the fact I needed to find the vice president because people's lives are in danger." Kyla briefly wondered what Meechum would think of Kyla abandoning her. She was certain the Marine wasn't tied up with any of the bad guys, but maybe other Marines were. That would put her friend in danger. A few steps later, she came to the realization Meechum probably wouldn't care one way or the other. The tough-as-nuts woman would go on being a Marine, kicking ass, doing what it took to fight the good fight.

Kyla wanted to fight the good fight, too.

"Hey, they took my rifle away back there, though they didn't take this." She cradled the M9 pistol on her hip after lifting the hem of the Marine top, which she'd left untucked. Van Nuys wouldn't have found it unless he patted her down, and she didn't suggest he try. Kyla gestured to the rifle slung over Emily's shoulder.

"You got another one of those? I'd feel a lot better having a big one."

Emily laughed out loud. "I don't have any extras, but did you know your uncle's coffee table was a gun-storage locker?"

"No way," she gushed in reply. "I've sat at that thing a million times. Are you serious?"

"I'm serious as a—" Emily stopped and held out an arm to halt her, too.

"Ladies," a man's voice called out. "I'll kindly ask you to put the rifle on the ground." They'd reached a clearing next to the boat, but a sailor stood on the deck. He pointed a military-grade rifle at her and Emily. Did he hear them talking all the way in?

For a split-second, she thought Emily was going to go into superhero mode, rip the rifle off her shoulder, and start firing. However, she carefully pulled it over her shoulder, holding it by the strap, and set it down in some weeds. Emily said, "We don't want any trouble."

Kyla had no way of knowing if the man heard their full discussion, but much like she didn't volunteer the pistol for Van Nuys, she didn't mention it to the new guy.

The sailor breathed hard, like he'd run the long way through the woods in order to beat them to the boat. He tipped his camouflaged canvas hat toward them. "Do as you're asked and you won't get in any trouble, I promise you that."

Kyla recognized the man from the helicopter ride. He'd come over with her and the captain. "Hey, I flew over here with you," Kyla said. "She's with me. We're cool."

He sounded angry. "That's not how it works. You should have done what we asked you and brought her and your uncle into the lighthouse. Now, you're a suspect, too."

"Suspect?" she replied with her own anger. "I'm the one who brought you where you needed to go. How the hell does it make me a suspect?"

Emily spoke with a level voice. "Kyla, take it easy, okay?"

"Screw that!" she replied.

The man held up his hand. "Quiet. I'm going to call this in." He keyed his radio and it beeped a couple of times, like it was making a call.

She stood next to Emily, trying to stay calm like the other woman. Kyla figured someone like her would be used to high-pressure situations of life and death.

Life or death?

Kyla did have a rifle pointed at her. Her heart got up to a gallop and she immediately imagined they were about to be in big trouble. Maybe even accused of a serious crime. The man's tone sure sounded like it.

She glanced around, desperate for a way out. They'd emerged from the thickest part of the forest, though they weren't far from it. If they could take a few steps back, maybe they could escape.

The radio warbled. A man's voice replied from the speaker, loud enough for her to hear it. "This is Nighthawk, go ahead."

"Hey, boss, yeah, I found them at the boat, like you said. What do you want me to do with them?"

"You have the vice president, and the young woman?"

"I do."

The radio was silent for ten seconds, and Kyla felt a black hole spring to life in her stomach. She listened intently as the radio squawked again.

"Kill them."

Montauk airport, NY

"Drop your weapon, sir." Meechum took a few steps back but kept her rifle pointed at Ted's chest, which made him very receptive to laying down his AR and defusing the situation. "And the Sigs." She motioned to the pistols on his hips.

"There's been some kind of mistake," he said as he put the three weapons into a pile. "I'm not lying."

The Marine wasn't done. "Sailor, check him for knives and other goodies."

After getting patted down, Ted was relieved of his backpack as well as the Ruger LCP pistol he always kept in his front pocket. She'd gotten the drop on him so completely that he'd lost all of his weapons in one swoop.

"I saw the other woman," the Marine replied, not at all worked up. "I know the vice president when I see her. Your niece confirmed my suspicion. My orders are to bring her in to our base at NORAD."

"NORAD?" Ted asked her with surprise, knowing for a fact the Cheyenne Mountain facility had gone offline with the attack. "Is that your headquarters? You're with the invasion?" He looked to Van Nuys, sure he was going to give the order to the caught-in-the-middle sailor to secure her weapon, and for a second, it looked like he was going to turn around and do it, but his radio came to life. He gently grabbed the radio from his belt and raised it slowly, as if to show the Marine he wasn't holding a weapon.

"This is Nighthawk, go ahead."

A crackling voice came from the speaker. "Hey, boss, yeah, I found them at the boat, like you said. What do you want me to do with them?"

"You have the vice president, and the young woman?" Van Nuys made a point to look into Ted's eyes, like he was a little pissed but also disappointed he'd been lied to. Ted's intuition was off kilter after seeing the Marine announce she was playing for the other team, but he wanted to believe the captain was going to stand up to her. If he did, Ted was ready to attack her, too.

"I do," the man's voice came back.

Ted toyed with the idea of rushing the Marine alone, but she was at least ten feet behind the captain, as if she knew someone was going to try. Van Nuys took a long time to reply, but Ted realized he'd been working a pistol out of a holster toward the front of his hip. It was out of sight of the Marine. It looked like he was going to fight her, after all.

The captain didn't pull the pistol all the way out. He stared at Ted. "I know you won't understand this. You work a lifetime, rise to the top, and still have nothing to show for it. I'm not going out like that. I've got dibs on the entire state of Vermont." He held the radio to his mouth. "Kill them," the captain deadpanned.

The whip-bang of a rifle discharge jarred Ted out of his decision loop. At that moment, he didn't care whose side the captain was on; he'd given the order to kill his niece. If the bullet was meant for him, he'd die trying to wrap his fingers around the man's neck. Ted lunged for the captain as the nearby sailor fell sideways.

She shot him.

He had enough time to appreciate he wasn't the one getting shot, but Van Nuys almost had his pistol out. There was no doubt who it was intended for. He tucked his head and squared his shoulders as he rammed into the navy man's ribs.

"Stop him!" the captain yelled.

Ted was willing to die to accomplish his task, so he wasn't as concerned about the Marine as the captain probably hoped. He had no idea why she shot the sailor, or if she was coming for him next, but blood surged through his veins like Niagara Falls during a thunderstorm. Nothing could stop him from killing the bastard.

The captain wasn't a pushover. He fell with Ted's thrust, but he didn't crumple into a ball. He rolled sideways and forced Ted to roll with him.

"Cancel the order!" Ted shouted, spitting anger all over the other man's face.

Van Nuys didn't flinch. "Marine, kill him!"

They rolled again, with Ted getting on top of the captain's chest. He tried to straddle him, so he could get solid leverage and snare his neck, but Van Nuys pulled up his knees and forced Ted off.

The opening gave the captain another chance to reach for his pistol, but Ted pivoted and thrust himself back into a second tumble. The violent jarring sent the pistol skipping over the pavement and out of reach. Ted tried to land a punch, but they were both off balance.

His vision compressed down to pinpoints as he only saw the enemy's smug face.

"Marine!" the captain yelled again as he fought to get up on one knee.

Meechum wasn't far. She stood a few yards away, M27 rifle in hand. However, she seemed to be waiting for the result of the fight before making a move. If he was to be shot, he was taking the captain with him.

He ripped several buttons off the white navy uniform as he yanked the man back onto the concrete. The movement caused the captain's head to strike the ground, which seemed to temporarily stun him. It provided Ted another chance to fall upon him and grab his neck. A distant voice told him to stop trying to do the same thing over and over, but all he wanted to do was choke the life out of him.

"Kill him!" the captain repeated.

Ted still didn't look at the Marine, figuring he was dead if he relented or lost contact with the captain. They rolled from side to side, trading clumsy punches and elbow jabs, but Ted finally managed to hold the captain in place. They'd both exerted themselves toward exhaustion, though Ted was younger and in better shape. He had the advantage. "I'm going to kill you, you son of a bitch," he wheezed.

Van Nuys struggled, but the ending was set.

"Hey, guys, someone's going to get hurt." Meechum's casual voice made her seem like a mother breaking up a pair of toddlers.

"I'm going to kill him," Ted chuffed.

"I don't think your niece would like that." She held Van Nuys's radio.

Ted froze at the sight of it, which gave the captain an opening. Like before, he kicked and shoved Ted off his chest. While Ted rolled right, he rolled the other way. As the gap increased, Ted concluded the Marine and the captain were working together. In fact, the captain had rolled his way over to his discarded pistol.

Ted froze in a half-standing crouch. With two threats in front of him and no gun, he had few options. His only defense was to raise his hands, which counted for little in total war.

The captain laughed to himself as he caught his breath. He also raised his pistol and pointed it at Ted, though he had to bend over again to pick up his discarded hat. "Nice try, Major. I'm afraid you lose. David is going to reward me greatly for taking out the last in the line of succession for the presidency." He positioned his cap on his head, then aimed the pistol at Ted's midsection.

Ted reflexively covered his face with his arm.

The gunshot blast made his insides recoil.

"Oh shit!" he blurted, thinking he was hit.

A few seconds went by before he chanced a look up. Van Nuys fell sideways onto the tarmac. The pistol skittered out of his hand, though away from Ted. A large exit wound had replaced the salad bar of ribbons over his heart.

The Marine stood over the fallen captain, leaving no doubt who was really in charge. She'd brought down two of the men she'd come with.

Was he next?

Vacaville, CA

Dwight's headache had been dialed up to icepick-through-the-temple pain as he drove across California. The motorcycle engine and the screaming wind worked together to annoy him, as did Poppy's endless complaints. However, the real cause of his suffering had nothing to do with the outside; his body desperately missed the usual flood of alcohol in his veins. He'd been dry for almost twenty-four hours.

Poppy still flew alongside him, flapping her wings into colorful green blurs. She'd been quiet for a few miles, which suggested she was ready to listen rather than yell at him.

"Keep your eyes peeled, Pops. I want to lose this guy as soon as I can." The bird looked down at him, then nodded ahead, like there was something to see. And there was—a large group of bikers had pulled over to the side of the highway, though many walked up a nearby embankment toward an overpass.

Bernard waved him to pull over. For a few seconds, he considered shooting under the bridge and never looking back, but he knew his skills on the bike weren't any better than passable, especially with his headache and other imbalances in his skull. Poppy was already slowing down.

Fine.

After setting the kickstand and walking up the hill, he and Bernard joined other black-clad bikers. He recognized them from the warehouse. Bernard gave him a nudge when they got close. "Looks like they found some survivors."

The notion excited Dwight, as they would almost certainly be normal Americans, like him, but when he got into the mix of things, he quickly came to the conclusion they were not like him. They were tied up and made to stand at the edge of the bridge.

"What did they do?" he blurted out.

A fellow rider heard him and replied, "Found 'em up in the foothills. They'd been inside a cave this whole time. We caught them heading back to San Francisco."

The crowd clapped for a few seconds, making it hard for Dwight to reply, but then everyone began to chant, including the man who'd answered him.

"Free America. Free America. Free America!"

The chant went on for half a minute—long enough that he figured out he needed to join in. It didn't make him happy to say it, but Bernard always seemed to watch him. In fact, the guy seemed to keep an eye on everyone in the black jumpsuits.

A concussive roar ripped through the crowd.

"Shee-it!" he shouted reflexively.

Some of the others jumped too, but most broke into cheering and laughter.

Wisps of smoke blew by, and he got a good look at where the captured cavers had been standing. When he didn't see them, he shuffled through the happy revelers so he could look over the side of the bridge.

The normal Americans, like him, had been shot dead. Their bodies lay broken and bloody on the pavement below. One of his fellow bikers yelled for someone to clean the road of the bodies, which resulted in numerous replies from within the crowd.

"Cleanliness in all things," they murmured.

The ice pick in his brain suddenly slid all the way through to his spine.

"God, Poppy, what country have you brought me to?"

ELEVEN

Montauk, NY

"Kill them," the voice replied from the radio.

The sailor on the boat glanced up at her and Emily with a "my pleasure" look in his eyes. He leaned over to set the radio on a bench, which briefly pulled him out of her line of sight. It gave her a chance to retrieve the gun tucked in at her right hip.

When the man came back up, he fiddled with his rifle, perhaps flicking the safety off, but his eyes doubled in size when he saw her weapon pointed at him. Kyla didn't give him a chance to surrender, or to fire at her and the VP. She steadied her aim, pulled the trigger, and braced for the kickback.

The gunshot sounded like a canon. At first, she believed it was her gun making all the noise, but when a second shot shook her teeth, she realized Emily was also firing a pistol. Kyla reoriented on the injured sailor and fired a second shot.

The man never had a chance. Both women landed at least one shot in his chest, even though they fired four or five shots apiece. Others might have been on target, but he fell out of the boat.

"Holy shit," Kyla wheezed. "You have a second gun, too?"

The VP smiled. "Your uncle insisted on it. Now I know why."

Kyla's ears rang like her head was inside a church bell, but it was exhilarating to have taken part in fighting back against someone bent on killing her.

"That was Van Nuys on the radio," she said flatly.

"The captain?" Emily asked.

She nodded gravely. "We've got to warn my uncle. Hell, I've got to warn Meechum." Kyla worried her friend was already dead. If the captain was working for the other side, the last person he'd want around is the friendly neighborhood Marine.

Unless she's a bad guy, too.

"I'll get on the radio," Emily replied as she trotted into the shallow water in front of the black boat.

Kyla reached down to pick up Emily's discarded rifle as someone shouted "Halt!" from the woods. A new sailor came out of the trees beyond where the boat was parked, his rifle pointed at Emily. She assumed he had a clear view of the injured or dead sailor, who was in the water on the other side. He'd heard the shots, for certain.

The order had been given to kill them, so she continued and picked up the rifle, intending to go down fighting. Time seemed to get stuck in molasses as she brought the black-barreled weapon up to her shoulder. It took forever to click over the safety.

At the same time, the sailor already had his rifle aimed at Emily. She was defenseless in knee-deep water. She didn't even have the time to grab her pistol, which she'd put back in her waistband.

"I give up!" Emily cried out.

Kyla was no more than twenty feet away from the attacker, though he had a few small trees in front of him. She lined up his profile and gently pulled the trigger back. The metallic clang of the AR-15 was distinct from the smaller pistol, but also somehow quieter. She squeezed off as many shots as she could, while the man also took his shot at the vice president.

Emily dove into the water.

With the foliage in the way, it was hard to see if Kyla had struck the man, so she stopped firing for a few seconds while taking some steps forward. She had to crouch down to see him better. When she did, the guy had his rifle pointed at her.

They fired at the same time. She didn't have nearly the experience as the professional warfighter, but she knew there was no going back. She launched into a frenzy of trigger pulling, doing her best to keep the barrel pointed at the target. The staccato fury amped up as she imagined bullets whizzing back and forth from twenty feet away.

At one point, it seemed like a bee stung the side of her neck, but otherwise she kept up the fire until the man slumped to the ground. After a brief pause to ensure he was no longer firing his weapon, she deliberately shot two more times. She'd seen too many movies where the bad guy got that last shot at the good guys. Emily was nearby in the water.

"Emily?" she asked warily.

"I'm good!" The VP came up out of the water, soaked, but she had a better view of the sailor. "He's down!"

When Kyla finally lowered her gun, her pulse quickened, and blood coursed through her brain like a levee break had taken place. She fell to one knee, glad to be alive, but a wet liquid ran across her shoulder, as if she'd been hit with a water balloon.

Or a bullet.

She reached for her neck, meeting warm blood.

"Emily..."

Montauk airport, NY

On his knees and panting at a hundred beats per minute, Ted was at the mercy of the grim-faced Marine woman. She'd fired the gun at the captain, which registered as a victory for him, but she still stood there with the gun pointed his way.

He blinked in surprise as she tossed the radio to him. He bobbled it for a second until he got a grip.

"Call her," Meechum ordered.

Ted glanced down at it, then back to her. "You aren't going to shoot me?"

She slung the rifle over her shoulder. "I'm on your side, Major. Your niece did the right thing running with you to get away from these guys, but we can talk about that later. Right now, call off the hit on her. Please."

He didn't need more encouragement. "Cancel the last order! Do not kill them!"

In terms of radio protocol, he knew it wasn't going to fool anyone on the other side, but if he could sow a little confusion into their game plan, maybe he could get back to the boat and help them.

A woman answered, "We're fine. We killed two sailors who answered the call to kill us. The birthday girl took a nick to the neck, but she's going to be okay."

The air in Ted's chest rushed out as his body stood down from high alert. There were endless questions he wanted to ask, including how they fought off two traitors, but he didn't want to give anything away. He assumed the enemy was listening to this channel, since it was their radio. "I'm so glad to hear. Can you continue to the rendezvous?"

"We'll be there," Emily replied.

His sign-off was short. "Affirmative. Out."

Ted got to his feet and faced the Marine. "I owe you my life."

"Just doing my job. Sorry about scaring you, sir, but I couldn't tip off my allegiance until I knew for certain the captain was with them. When I said I worked for David and it didn't get an immediate reaction, I knew something was off about him. However, when he pulled out his pistol to shoot you, I knew what I had to do."

He was glad to have her help, but she'd taken a big risk. "What if he'd turned and shot you without asking questions? Then I'd never know you were with us."

She shrugged. "I was pretty sure he was a bad guy, sir. My platoon has been watching this man since he miraculously showed up in a lower hold when the event cleared out the JFK. Since then, the carrier's air defenses have gone offline, the lifts stopped working, and computer systems have gone haywire. We got intel this morning concerning enemy activity at NORAD, so I assumed it was their base of operations. The captain seemed to confirm it, as well as his role in those problems."

"And this guy?" Ted pointed to the dead sailor.

"A man like Van Nuys wouldn't travel out in the wild without a personal bodyguard. A tight-knit group of like-minded assholes. His other two buddies tried to kill Kyla and the vice. The captain's last remaining guard was certainly with him."

He rubbed his stubbled chin. "I guess we have to assume everyone back on the JFK is on the other team? How can we get back to friendly forces?"

"My Marines aren't playing for the other team, sir. They'll straighten things out. Right now, let's gather weapons and gear," she replied, gently kicking Van Nuys as if to ensure he was really dead. "I assume you can fly a plane? Your niece said you were a pilot on Air Force Two."

"I can."

"Good. What are your orders, sir?"

He appreciated the deference to his rank. "Call me Ted until we get out of this mess. I'm not even dressed in my uniform; no sense tipping off the enemy who I am or who I work for."

She seemed satisfied. "Once we're in the air, I'll tell you where we have to take the VP next."

He frowned. "I'm guessing I'm not going to like it?"

"Nope."

On the Interstate, Illinois

After being on the bikes for so long, Tabby was happy to be safe inside another stranger's car. The blue Subaru wagon had plenty of room for the three of them, and the two shotguns. When she found tie-downs in one of the compartments, Peter suggested lashing the bikes to the roof rack, in case they needed them again.

A few hours later, they were on the interstate and getting close to St. Louis. The three of them talked about many things during the drive, including how much they missed Donovan, but they didn't dwell on the negative. She thought it was a good idea to let them reminisce for a short time, but whenever the conversation headed for the skids, she turned them back to happier things.

"As long as we lay low, we can do whatever we want when we get back home. Got any big plans?" Their goal was still to head to Bonne Terre, though she had no solid plans for when she got there. The question was her way of probing whether either of the teens had thought it through, either.

Audrey seemed excited at her prospects. "If we're really the last people in America, I figure it wouldn't hurt to collect the best furniture from all the houses in my neighborhood and put them in mine. I'll have the best dining room table. The finest china. The best jewelry." She extended her wrist from the back seat, as if to show her an elegant bracelet.

Peter went next. "I'm going to have every video game system and every title ever made. If I'm going to die alone, at least I'll win at some of those games."

"Hey," Audrey interrupted, "you won't be alone. You can live in the house next to mine. We can visit every day."

Tabby secretly laughed. It was cute how they talked, and she wasn't ready to break it to them they could live in the same house. No one was going to criticize their life choices, not even her. It would be easy to fall into the role of parenting the pair, but she didn't want that burden for herself. They seemed like smart kids; they'd be fine.

But what about me?

The long drive had given her time to think about her situation from multiple angles: the tour guide, the mentor, the older female friend, the defender. However, it never really sank in that she might not have a male companion for...a long time. Vinny from the TV station was the closest she'd seen to an eligible bachelor since the disaster started, and he was probably dead.

"Hey, what's that?" Peter, in the passenger seat, pointed ahead.

She squinted to see far down the highway. They were in corn country, so the roadway was flat and straight with nothing but young corn stalks on either side. A few cars remained in the highway where they'd stopped, which made the motion stand out. "It's a plow."

She slammed on the brakes.

"What are you doing?" Audrey screamed. "We can't stop here! At least drive over there." The girl pointed sideways off the road.

"No. We'll be seen." She wasn't entirely sure, but it seemed logical. She'd had a lot of time to think about how they'd be spotted from drones, and her conclusion was they were harder to spot when coming directly at a camera, or going directly away, exactly like it would be for human perception. Thus, she put the car in park to cut down on their chance of being seen moving.

"Get out!" she added. "Get to the corn."

She opened the door and got out. The menacing sound of an engine caught her attention right away; the machine coming her way was moving fast and loud. The crunch of metal on metal echoed from down the roadway as the plow struck the abandoned cars.

"Should we take something?" Peter inquired, standing at his door.

The machine was too close for her liking. "Just run!"

The three of them went down a small embankment, then into the adjacent corn field. The stalks were about four feet high and provided enough cover to hide them, but they had to go about ten rows back before she lost sight of the highway completely. However, when everyone was safe, she returned a couple of rows because she wanted to see the machine go by.

It approached with the energy of a chugging freight train. She saw the black diesel fumes belch out the dual pipes before she saw the machine itself. When it arrived, it became apparent a second sweeper was in the other pair of lanes, doubling the volume they were able to plow.

"Stay low," she said, checking behind her to make sure the kids weren't doing anything stupid, like standing up.

When it got there, she thought it might have been a converted train engine. It was as big as an eighteen-wheeler, but it was all one machine, like the box trailer was built into the front part. It also had more wheels than a semi, and they were about twice as large, maybe as tall as a man. The dual-faced plow on the front was low and swept-back, like a graceful wing.

The fast-moving contraption slammed into the Subaru and seemed to lift it off the ground as the scooped plow caught it. It happened so fast, Tabby could barely understand what happened, but along with the bone-jarring crunch and scrape, the car flew sideways off the highway.

She watched as the shattered glass of the windshield caught the sun.

It twirled like a trapeze artist doing a dismount.

And it was going to come down right on top of her.

TWELVE

Newark, NJ

Kyla and Emily worked together to get the big boat off the shore. She was glad to be gone too, since there was one body floating in the water and another in the bushes. A strip of the dead man's shirt was wrapped around her neck, putting compression on the small graze she'd gotten during the gunfight. She thanked God she wasn't lying in the weeds. Exchanging gunshots at point-blank range wasn't a sport she wanted to do ever again.

"Did your uncle teach you how to shoot?" Emily asked from behind the wheel.

Kyla made an effort to keep her hands in her pockets or holding one of the boat's grips. Otherwise, Emily would see them shake. "Yes.

Well, not really. I've been practicing with one of the Marines back on the ship."

"Ooh, a Marine? I bet they were all over you—a pretty young lady." Emily flashed a brilliant smile, like she knew something about which she spoke. She piloted them through the narrow inlet at the beach, taking them from the lake into the open sea.

Kyla shook her head. "It's nothing like that, although I guess a few of them were okay-looking." Carthager was the big, bronzed, figure of a man she might normally find attractive. "No, a woman Marine took me under her wing. Showed me how to be a badass. I mentioned her earlier; she came with me on the helicopter."

"In my experience, Marines are cut from a different cloth. I hope she made it. Male or female, we need every one of those Marines fighting for us. I'm glad you got the lessons, too. It takes some of the pressure off me to defend you until Ted gets back."

"We can defend each other," Kyla reasoned.

"Bingo. Your uncle and I made a pretty good team these past few days. Once he and you are together and safe, we can focus on warning the rest of the world what's going on here."

Kyla looked back. The boat was already hundreds of yards into the open channel. The lighthouse came into view, no longer hidden by the tops of nearby trees. She also saw the beach on that area of the shoreline. A man caught her notice—

"Look! Another sailor." Kyla pointed him out to Emily, but she had a hard time looking back while also piloting the boat on the choppy water.

"Crap burglar," Emily responded.

Kyla noticed Emily kept her head low. "Do you think he's shooting at us?" It would be hard to hear a gunshot from so far away. She figured the only way she would know for sure was if one of them fell over dead. Without waiting for the answer, she hunched over too.

"They've been given the green light to kill us. I'm not taking any chances. Heck, so far, I've been bombed, shot at multiple times, and almost had a plane shot out from under me with a missile. I wouldn't put anything past these guys, up to, and including, a nuclear bomb."

"Wow. My uncle was in that mess, too?"

"In it? He's the reason I'm still here talking to you. I don't know what they taught him in flight school, but he sure knows how to survive. I told him I was going to promote him when—" She stopped talking, like she'd said too much, but quietly added, "—when we get back to friendly forces."

"How far is it to Martha's Vineyard?"

"I don't really know. All I'm sure about is it's a big island below the boot of Massachusetts. As long as we stay within sight of the shore, we should see it."

Kyla finally sat up. The man on the shore had become a tiny point. She didn't know the exact range of a rifle, and it was extra difficult to measure distance on the open water, but she figured they were free and clear of that one guy. He was probably running back to his bosses.

Or maybe he was going back inland to find Uncle Ted.

She looked at the radio the sailor had left in the boat. Should she risk giving herself away to warn him?

In the air to Martha's Vineyard

"So...where are we taking the vice president?" Ted asked Meechum, who sat next to him in the cockpit of the small Beechcraft Skipper—a two-seater probably used as a trainer. The bubble-like cockpit gave them each a wonderful view of the Block Island Sound below.

"Minot, North Dakota," she replied.

"What the heck is out there? An airbase, I know. And?"

She shot him a wary look. "I can't say any more than that until I talk to the vice president."

He held his hands above the wheel. "All right. You drive, then. I'm done." It came across as immature, but he was mad as hell she would hold out on him. The Marine had no idea what he and Emily had been through.

The plane's nose dipped, and Meechum grabbed the door handle like it was about to open and fling her out. "Are you nuts?"

Ted still didn't put his hands on the wheel, though the plane was drifting more to the right than he liked. If she didn't come around quick...

"Fine. It's the missile base. We have to go to the damned missile base."

Ted grabbed the wheel for both of their sakes. Once he had it straightened out, he felt bad about the trick. "Sorry. I've been through the wringer and I guess I'm not in the mood for bullshit. It's dangerous as hell up here."

"Life is dangerous these days," she deadpanned, settling back into her seat. "I take it you mean we are in more danger being up here." The woman was strapped in and snug in her seat, but he noticed her fidgeting with her fingers, like she wasn't entirely comfortable in the air.

"When we flew in across the Atlantic, I'm talking about when the attack happened, Air Force Two came under attack from missile boats. We were pretty far out at the time, but there's no telling what range they have, or if they've moved since then. I like to play it safe."

"Is that why we're flying the wrong way?" she asked matter-of-factly.

He was impressed she noticed. Ted flew them almost due west out over the water, even though the destination was to the east. If they were followed, he planned to cancel the flight completely. They'd ditch somewhere on the mainland, if possible, then get to Martha's another way. If no one pursued them as they headed east and north to the coast, he planned to get lost in the ground clutter of the eastern seaboard as he turned back east, then make a final cut to the island of Martha's Vineyard. It would add time to his route, but he figured they were going two or three times faster than the yacht so they'd get there at about the same time. Rather than explain everything to her, he kept it simple. "We're taking the long way."

That seemed to satisfy her. They shared some silence for a while, before she pulled out a handheld radio. "I need to call my people, let them know the captain was in on it."

The plane bobbed on the wind as he took it over the coastline. In seconds, he was over the houses and forests of Connecticut, as he'd planned. "Sure. Better to call them now, before we get to where we're going. You know, in case we're tracked."

She held up the black box. "It's encrypted. We plan for this stuff, you know?"

He nodded. "I know. I'm just giving you grief, Marine."

"Meh. I'm used to it. Before we came here, I basically had twelve asshole brothers in my squad."

They laughed for a moment, before she got on the radio.

A male voice picked up. "This is Crackerjack, go ahead."

"This is Kit Kat. The otter was a snake. I repeat, the otter was a snake. Plan accordingly."

"Affirmative, Kit Kat. Be safe. Out."

Ted looked over. "That's it? I take it the otter was Van Nuys, but aren't you going to take over the ship? Call in reinforcements?" There were a lot of actions he figured the Marines could take, but he soon realized he'd been thinking like it was the time before the attack. "Do you even have reinforcements?"

She stayed silent for a few moments. "I shouldn't tell you this, but you've protected the vice president, and it seems we're sharing state secrets, so I figure there's no reason not to… Other than a depleted platoon of Marines on the

John F. Kennedy, there isn't a certified allied unit anywhere in this hemisphere that I know about. Everyone is suspect now. Anyone who left the country right before the attack. Anyone who put themselves in a position to be outside the country, even months before. Entire units who transferred before the attack. If you think about the scope of the destruction, lots of people had to know it was coming. You can't scare up a nation-killing attack without someone, somewhere, knowing something."

The cockpit fell into silence again, and he had the time to appreciate the lush, green landscape along the coast. He glanced over to Meechum from time to time, wondering if she would ever settle in, but she always seemed uncomfortable. He'd been with Emily for so long that he actually missed having her with him. She would have kept the airplane stocked with humor and snark. He found himself missing her.

Miles later, Meechum came out of her silence. "You know, you didn't need to scare me into telling you. Any relative of Kyla is a friend of mine. I know it doesn't seem like it, but I trust you with my life. I'm up here in this rickety milk crate, you know?"

He saw an opportunity for a follow-up. "So, I don't need to forget how to fly if I ask you what's so important about the North Dakota missile base?"

"Happy to tell you," she answered with her 'get-some' attitude. "We need to protect the entire United States arsenal of nuclear bombs."

Amarillo, TX

In all his years in Vietnam, Brent couldn't remember a juicier target than the one in front of him now. The international airport was a bustling hub of military and civilian transport planes, which were the main targets. The enemy had also amassed a small fleet of Humvees, hundreds of motorcycles with strange attachments added, and an equal number of little metal machines had been lined up in even rows and columns. Using the binoculars from their hiding spot inside a nearby building, he had the perfect observation point overlooking the whole thing, though they weren't quite strong enough to make out what those lines of machines were for. His bigger problem was that there were so few of them, and so many of the enemy.

"I wonder where the rest of our ex-con friends ended up?" he asked, somewhat rhetorically. Other than those who'd gone to Trish's place, he hadn't seen any of the prisoners he'd let go, nor did he see the other guards who'd slipped away from their duty. If all the ex-prisoners came back, he'd have a more useful fighting force of about fifty. Even if they weren't the most disciplined lot, he could have used the numbers.

"Probably in the strip clubs," Cliff replied, twisting his mustache. He couldn't remember the man's real name, but the inmates had assigned him a nickname because he'd worked for the post office as a letter carrier. The man appeared to be in his late twenties, but his mustache made him look a bit like Cliff Clavin from *Cheers*, a show he was surprised the younger ones even knew about.

"Pfft." Kevin slapped Cliff on the shoulder. "All the strippers are in pole-dancer heaven."

Cliff seemed shocked at first, then laughed cautiously. "That's just wrong, man."

"Well, it's true. There won't be any strippers for a long time, unless you want to find a pole and dance on it yourself."

A few of the men laughed, though Trish acted disinterested in the banter.

"Guys," he said, trying to get their minds out of the gutter. "I need options for how to deal with the problem in front of us. This airport is being used by our enemies to invade the hallowed soil of Texas. Are we going to just let that happen, or are we going to do something about it?" Invoking the name of Texas was a calculated risk. Amarillo's penal system brought in bad guys from as far away as Oklahoma City and Roswell, New Mexico. Not everyone would bleed Texas red, white, and blue.

The men mumbled among themselves for a bit as he kept watch. He assumed he was going to have to think up a plan on his own, but postman Cliff spoke up. "Why don't we drive one of the bigger mail trucks into the middle of that place and shoot the hell out of anyone we see?"

"Screw that," someone replied. "I'm not going in there for any reason. I'll stay right here and launch rockets, or take potshots with a rifle, but if we go in there, I don't think we'd ever come back out."

It was a good point. Each plane brought more bad guys into the airport. How many had come in since they visited earlier in the morning?

"Can anyone fly?" Brent asked, knowing it was a long shot. Most petty criminals wouldn't have the cash or time to get a pilot's license.

As expected, no one raised their hand.

"Can anyone drive a big rig?" he pressed.

A few hands went up.

"Does anyone know how to set up a remote-controlled vehicle?" he asked, knowing it was an even longer shot than flying. If they could organize a fleet of big trucks, then program them to all drive into the airfield, they could tear up the planes, or at least severely damage them.

No one raised their hand, at first, but finally Ross raised his. "I never did no remote control, but I had an old Chevy I wanted to disappear, so I put a brick on the gas pedal and tied a rope to the steering wheel. It went right where I wanted, and fast."

"Where did you want it to go?" Brent asked, afraid to know the answer.

"It was the old lady's truck. She took a tone I didn't appreciate. Said I was a no-good bum and wanted me out of the house. The crazy bitch said I didn't respect her, or her house. I went ahead and jimmied her truck and sent it straight into the Red River." Ross burst into laughter.

Brent ignored how he'd essentially proven his wife's point; criminals seldom thought through the crimes pulling them into the prison system. Those that did often used their time to plan how to do it better when they got out. Still, it planted the idea in his head. If he could find a heavy truck, maybe they could send it toward the airport and do a little damage.

"Gentlemen, we have the start of a plan."

THIRTEEN

Martha's Vineyard, MA

"Protect the whole arsenal?" he said with disbelief. "How?"

Meechum chuckled. "I know how it sounds. I'll tell you everything I know, I promise, but please let me do it when the vice president is with us. What I'm going to tell her is classified as top secret, so I want to be sure she gives me approval. I don't want to lose my pension." She finished with heavy sarcasm in her voice, probably because nobody was around to pay her retirement plan anymore.

"I can wait," he said, understanding where she was coming from. He also had a high-level security clearance; he'd been through a new check every year of his life since becoming a senior pilot with the Air Force. They always told him it was to ensure he was qualified and above suspicion for leveraged attacks, such as blackmail. However, he always suspected they also wanted him cleared in case an emergency happened to the president. If the VP suddenly found herself promoted to the head office, she wouldn't get far along if her crew lacked the clearance to talk to her.

"For now," he added with a chuckle.

The flight in was uneventful, for which Ted was grateful, but he didn't see Emily's boat as he came in, nor were she and Kyla waiting for them when they arrived. At first, he paced around the terminal, which was about the size of a high school gymnasium, but after about fifteen minutes, he couldn't take it anymore.

"I've got to do something," he lamented. "Do you want to help me find an airplane big enough to take us all to North Dakota? That way, when Emily and Kyla get here, we can jump on and be gone. They might be hiding from pursuit." He thought they were fairly lucky to avoid any drone activity. The captain most likely called his bosses to report he'd found the most important woman in America. Every resource they had should have been sent right to the lighthouse, and the skies and seas around it. However, it wasn't his place to correct the mistakes of his enemies.

"Sure, this place gives me the creeps, anyway." Meechum pointed to the floor of the terminal, which was layered with gray tiles, but also peppered with the clothes of the fallen. It made him appreciate that he no longer saw the clothing the same way he did back at the terminal building at Andrews Air Force Base. It was still haunting, but it didn't give him the creeps, as Meechum described it. If anything, seeing those clothes made him more determined than ever to strike back at the sickos who'd done this.

Martha's Vineyard Airport was essentially a miniature version of any big city airport. It had two runways, a proper taxiway, several enclosed hangars for storage of planes, as well as the terminal building itself. It also had the true measure of any named airport: car rentals. The larger scale also meant there were larger planes parked on the tarmac. If he could find a twin-engine jet, it would get them where they needed to go a lot faster than the single-engine Beechcraft, or any of the other small airplanes parked nearby. It wasn't that the small craft couldn't get them there, but it would fly slower and require more fuel stops. Since he didn't know what to expect out there, he wanted to cut out as many stops as possible.

He went right toward four modern aircraft parked a hundred yards from the terminal. "Any of those would do." He had his eye on a Cessna CitationJet CJ2, which could be piloted by a single person, such as himself, though the distinctive Avanti P-180 was also attractive.

"Won't we need to find keys?" she asked. "Are they in the pockets of one of those people back in the terminal, do you think? Like you found it in the other airport?" They'd discussed his escape from the lighthouse, as well as how he got a plane working at the Montauk airfield.

Ted shook his head. "Smaller planes have keys, a lot like automobiles, because they get left at small airports around the world. No one is there around the clock to watch them, so the keys make people feel safe. Bigger planes, like these here at Martha's, would normally have full-time security watching them, so they don't require keys. Of course, now that no one is here…"

"We can take what we want," she finished with a smile.

"I just have to pick the best one," he added with dry wit.

He strode around to get a look at his options, but as they walked, he wondered how much she knew about the big picture stuff. Despite spending time with the vice president, a woman who should normally be the center of an intelligence operation unmatched in history, he'd barely heard any news since the attack. "Do the Marines know how the hell they did it?"

"The attack?" she said, tracking his thoughts.

"Yeah."

She shrugged. "They didn't tell us what to expect when we went wheels up from Yorktown. We ended up in the lower part of the boat because Lieutenant Keller wanted his platoon off the main decks, so we could observe. He got caught doing recon on an upper deck when the big zap happened, but his positioning of the rest of us saved our lives. Kyla was saved by being in a lower compartment, too. Whatever it was that did it, the metal of the decking must have blocked it."

"It means it had to be an energy weapon of some sort, right? What else could have penetrated some decks, even if it didn't get through all of them?" He'd had a little time to think through various scenarios, but it was the first time he had confirmation of how the survivors made it through the assault. "And how would you deliver a nationwide, uh, zapper?"

"Beats me. I work with everything from a knife up to a Javelin anti-tank missile, but they never told us anything like this existed."

"It exists," he said matter-of-factly. "At some point, we're going to have to figure out how they did it, then take it out. They've threatened other nations—"

"I know. We operate a secret shortwave radio and have been keeping track of friendlies all over the world. It's a shitstorm, though. Several EU countries have already pushed out every American they could find. The Middle East, too."

"What about Great Britain?" he interjected. Though she'd become little more than a casual acquaintance, he had no ill feelings for his ex-wife. She was stationed in the UK, at least for the time being.

"I think they're fine," she replied.

It dawned on him how big the war had become since Meechum and Kyla arrived. Now he knew a little about the actual attack, he'd been alerted to the necessity of taking Emily out west to a missile base, and he'd been warned about terrorists possibly taking over an aircraft carrier. He even knew how the enemy was communicating. If they could get Emily and Kyla to show up, he'd be well on his way to mounting the first counterattack—a role he relished.

Come on, Kyla, make it back to me.

Highway in Illinois

"Move!" Tabby shouted. She guesstimated where the Subaru was going to land, then lunged away with as much thrust as her legs would give her.

"Yee-ow!" she screamed as the car came down inches from her backside.

The crunch of metal and further shattering of glass rang in her ears as she tumbled through four rows of cornstalks. One of the bikes had been flung sideways, and it cut through the corn about five feet to her left. The bell rang wildly when it smacked the dirt.

She'd fallen almost face-first, giving her a taste of the nasty soil. While she spit it out and wiped it from her cheek, she rolled to her side to see if her friends were all right. "Peter? Audrey?"

They'd been a bit behind her, but she'd given them a brief warning. She assumed they'd been watching the plow go by and were ready for the flying car, but with those two, she never knew. Seconds went by, and she began to fear the worst. Tabby prepared to crawl over to search...

"We're fine," Audrey finally replied from the other side of the car.

"Thank God." Tabby fell back to the ground, content to sit for a moment and make sure she didn't toss her cookies. The roar of the plows faded as they drove on, but new engine sounds followed; other vehicles were on the interstate, including the rumble of semi-trucks—lots of them.

She took a centering breath, then got to a crouch in order to see over the stalks. For a second, she imagined life going back to normal. The highway was filled with box trucks, flatbed trailers stacked with shipping containers, and tanker trucks. They all followed the mega-plows like ducklings behind their mother. A few cars were sprinkled in, furthering the illusion. However, the flow of traffic took up all four lanes and all of them were going north toward Chicago. And worse, lots of the flatbed trucks carried the robot horses.

It wasn't a return to normal; it was a full-on invasion.

Peter and Audrey scooted over to her while she observed the procession.

"Hey, tour guide," Peter laughed, "what's next on our itinerary? I'm bored."

Audrey slapped him across the chest.

"Ow!" he said with mock pain.

Tabby laughed at the crazy situation she found herself in. It had been mere hours since their friend had been gunned down and they were joking again. She wished she could bounce back that fast. All she thought about were the trucks driving by, and the enemy within. Those were real people, not robots. They were the jerks who killed her parents, and everyone else. In her head, they were senseless, drooling, maniacal killers, ever searching for the next innocent they wanted to murder. She would never see them as proper soldiers on the march.

Tabby spoke dramatically. "I'm going to kill them. Every freaking one of them."

"Say what?" Peter asked seriously. "I was kidding, you know. We almost died a second ago. I was making a joke about being bored."

Tabby caught herself, then glanced back to the kids. "Oh, right. I don't mean right now. But someday. Those people driving those trucks, they're going to pay for killing Donovan. For killing our parents. I know we can't do anything at this moment, but I'm going to be on the lookout for how I can."

From tour guide to G.I. Jane? It sounded insane when she thought it through, but nothing so far gave her any hope they could peacefully surrender. Gus and Vinny had said their co-workers tried to surrender and were killed on the spot by real people. No one asked Donovan if he wanted to surrender; the robots didn't seem to care, either. She shook involuntarily at the idea of having no way to protect the two happy-go-lucky teens in her charge.

It took about five minutes, but the parade of tractor-trailers came to an end. A single military armored truck trailed behind. It had eight wheels, a muted gray hull that reminded her of a narrow turtle, and a small turret on top. A pair of men sat in the open hatches on the turret, dressed in black uniforms and black hats. She was close enough to see them laughing as if one of them had told a funny joke.

The face of the enemy.

She crouched lower, afraid men with real eyes would turn and see her in the corn.

"Stay down," she hissed, sure Audrey or Peter would be standing too high.

The wheeled vehicle rolled by without slowing. She had no idea what it was, or what military it came from, but she didn't want to tangle with it. They'd been lucky so far, and she wanted that streak to continue.

"We have to collect our stuff," she said, only after the convoy was a distant hum.

"What do you mean?" Peter asked. "The car is toast."

"Some of it had to survive. Our guns and stuff are in there." She pointed to the ruined Subaru, which was lying on its side. "We'll get what we can and find another car. We'll have to take backroads."

"Won't we get caught with those things on the highway now?" Audrey said with worry.

"Well, we can't walk home. We have to get there before more of these jerks show up. I want to be somewhere familiar, you know?" All at once, getting the kids home seemed like the most important mission in the world.

She'd gotten up to full height when stalks of corn crunched from behind her.

A drone?

More stalks tipped over. Like in the movies, she saw an object running through the rows, heading right for her. She reached around to the gun at the small of her back, but the fear made her clumsy and slow. Having it probably wouldn't matter if a mechanical horse-drone found her.

Of course they would scout alongside the highway.

She crouched down, intent to at least block the drone and maybe give the kids time to escape.

Then a dark shape came out of the greenery.

It went right for her.

FOURTEEN

Martha's Vineyard Island, MA

As Kyla and Emily motored along the shoreline of Rhode Island, the boat traffic increased greatly. Unlike the automobiles on the highways that ran into things, or stopped when the clutch wasn't engaged, boats kept going until they ran out of fuel. Some of them had crashed into land, or headed out into the ocean, but the congestion as they approached Martha's Vineyard suggested it was a fishing and pleasure boat anchoring area; lots of white dots were adrift on the blue waters.

"Do you think anyone's alive out there?" she asked Emily, who sat resolute and mostly silent at the wheel.

"No. Nobody's alive. People have all been cleaned away, just like they said."

Kyla wanted to argue the point, show some hope in front of the leader of the country. Tell her she was wrong, and this was why. But nothing came to mind that would prove her right. Eventually, she drifted to sleep with the rhythm of the waves...

A change in the engine pitch startled her awake.

"Whoa!" she blurted, tipping forward a little.

"It's okay," Emily reassured her. "We're here."

They were in a small bay with dozens of single-mast sailboats anchored behind a rocky sea barrier, so waves wouldn't strike them. A large renegade ferry had sped through the mooring area, creating a path of tipped hulls and debris. The ship had run aground on the beach beyond the boats. Emily pointed to it. "I bet Ted could get that running and use it to take us out into the ocean."

"Wouldn't the missile boats get us?" Kyla asked in return.

"I don't know," Emily remarked. "Maybe they aren't prepared for ships to come through, only airplanes. Who would be looking for a wayward ferry? Maybe it drifted loose, with all the other boats?"

It made sense. "We could drift our way across the ocean! They couldn't destroy every sailboat and dingy loose out there." They'd already seen plenty of boats on the water. Any of those small ones could survive the voyage, though fuel would give out long before they made it to Europe. A larger ship, like the ferry, might have enough fuel to go the distance. It was an idea to keep in her back pocket.

"We'll park alongside this dock. At least we'll know we have one option of escape at our command if we don't find your uncle right away." Emily guided the boat next to an empty wooden pier, and Kyla jumped out and secured the mooring ropes to a pair of cleats.

Together, they walked the pier toward the shore. Emily carried her rifle and the holstered pistol. Kyla only had her pistol tucked into her belt.

Ahead of them, they entered a pleasant street filled with seafood restaurants, boat rental shops, and tourist trinket kiosks. The summertime clothes strewn all over the sidewalks reminded her she was dressed like a Marine. Though she was grateful for Meechum giving her clothes to wear besides her fast-food-styled polo shirt, she wanted to dress more to her taste and comfort. There was no way she could be convinced to pick up any of the clothing belonging to the missing tourists, but there were lots of shops.

"Do you think I have time to run in and change?" she asked, stopping suddenly at an open storefront. When Emily turned around, Kyla motioned to her own attire, as if it would be obvious why she needed new threads.

Emily relaxed, then looked inside the windows. "Be quick. I could use a change of clothes myself. These have been in the ocean. Twice. I feel like I've taken these jeans as far as I can without washing them."

She went inside with Emily. Eighties music played in the background, and the cheery lighting made the place seem normal. But it was nice she didn't need money. It was like winning a radio contest where she could buy anything in the store, as long as she did it within three minutes. Emily ran around and yanked clothes off the racks, then hurried into the changing room, even though there was no one else around. Kyla changed right on the main floor.

When Emily came out and saw Kyla buttoning her new shorts, she laughed. "I guess old habits are going to stick with me for a while. You're younger. Obviously, you've adapted to having no one else around."

Kyla shook her head. "I didn't think about it. I'd change in front of a crowd if it meant we can get going to my uncle that much faster. I can only imagine what he and Meechum are doing right now without us. Probably building a tank or something." She laughed at the image.

"That sounds like him. Hey, what do you think?" Emily half-turned to show her flowery outfit. She'd put on a sleeveless summer dress that ended a little below her knees. The pink and teal flowers went perfectly with the dress's white background, giving it a happy, summery look. "It's less formal than I would like, but this is a beach bum kind of place. There isn't much here for the business-minded woman."

Before Kyla could respond, Emily pointed to her feet. "Plus these. My other boots were soaked, and these were the only things I could find, besides flipflops." She'd found a pair of thick, black combat boots that went up to mid-shin. Emily was a pretty woman, so the look worked for her, but she appeared anything but professional.

"It'll all come together when you pick up your rifle," Kyla joked. "How do I look?" she went on. She spun around, too, but was inexplicably self-conscious about her appearance in front of the important woman. Instead of a feminine dress, she'd pulled a random pair of olive drab cargo shorts off the rack and matched it with a sky-blue T-shirt. It had a lobster outline on the front, with the words *If you pinch me, I'll bite* stenciled above it, and *Martha's Vineyard* below.

"For a five-minute shopping spree, I think we both did pretty good." Emily grabbed her rifle, but she didn't know what to do with the pistol. There was no belt to tuck it in, nor did the dress have pockets. "Oh, wow, I didn't think this through." The VP glanced around the place, then grabbed a fashionable over-the-shoulder beach bag. The pistol dropped right in. "Solved!"

"Good call," Kyla replied. Her cargo shorts had pockets barely big enough for her fingers, so she was forced to put Carthager's pistol back in her waistband.

"Come on, we've wasted enough time," Emily huffed as she headed for the door. Before she went out, she yanked a pair of sunglasses off the spinny-rack near the exit. She held them up for Kyla. "Snag a pair. It helps to have eye protection when we're firing guns."

"Listen to the vice president," Kyla mused. "She's got fashion sense and a mind honed for combat."

They went outside, sunglasses on and rifles over their shoulders, but Emily held her back. "You know, I never wanted any of this. My political career has been based on non-violence and helping people. What we've been forced to do is…"

"It blows chunks," Kyla interjected. "I know. I won't think any different of you. You've got my vote, no matter what."

Emily cracked up. "That's the last thing on my mind. Getting you back to your uncle is what really matters. He's been looking forward to this since I met him. Let's get over to the airport and do this."

They easily found another car and got it started. Emily drove like she knew where to go. Kyla really hoped being reunited with Uncle Ted would end the nightmare, but Meechum had taught her to be suitably cautious. She'd seen it herself in New York City. No matter if they escaped by boat or plane or anything else that moved, the fight was far from over.

Still, when they pulled up to the airport and she caught sight of Uncle Ted with Meechum next to him, she forgot all about her horrible attire.

"Uncle Ted!"

Martha's Vineyard Airport, MA

"Uncle Ted!"

Those were the sweetest words Ted had heard the entire week. His niece ran into his arms and they hugged for a moment, until the barrel of her rifle bonked him in the head. "Whoa! Where'd you get this hardware from?"

Kyla took a step back. "You won't believe it! When that guy said to kill us on the radio, Emily and I both got out our pistols and shot the bastard dead. Then, when another guy came out of the woods, we killed him, too."

Meechum came up next to Ted but looked at Kyla. "So, you learned a few things at the firing range, huh?"

Kyla nodded enthusiastically. "I kept my breathing calm. I aimed with my dominant eye. Then I squeezed the trigger, like you showed me a million times." Without prompting, she lunged for the Marine and gave her a hug, too.

"I'm more worried about your outfit," Meechum said dryly.

Kyla jumped away like she had a week's worth of pent up energy. "Yeah, I look like a tourist.

The uniform was too uncomfortable. Besides, it takes off some of the pressure. When I dress like a Marine, people expect me to do heroic things. At least, that's how I feel."

"Sounds like you did some heroic things anyway," he suggested.

He'd been talking to the two ladies, so he almost missed when Emily came around her borrowed car. Like Kyla, she'd changed since he'd last seen her. Now, she wore a shapely little dress which made her seem the opposite of presidential. A colorful scrunchy bunched her brunette locks into one big ponytail. The oversized combat boots made her seem more like a broody teenager than the leader of the free world. However, cleaned up as she was, he had to admit she was extremely pretty.

Ted wanted to compliment her in some way, but he couldn't think of anything appropriate in the moment. He diverted his eyes from where they wanted to go and instead saluted her. "Ladies and gentlemen, I give you the President of the United States." He remained serious for a couple of seconds, but then had to laugh.

"Yeah, yeah," Emily said, "yuck it up, funny guy. I can have you demoted, you know."

"Is she officially the president?" Meechum asked, glancing over at her like she was seeing her for the first time.

Ted turned her way, to alleviate his discomfort at how Emily was dressed. "Yep. I was at the White House. The president died in the attack. She's the next in line, if we ever get the country running again."

Meechum whistled quietly, like she was impressed. "That changes everything. We figured Tanager was dead, which is why we wanted to get to Ms. Williams, but I guess this makes it official…" She gave Emily a belated but proper salute.

"Please, none of that is necessary. I may be the president on paper, but I'm deferring to Major MacInnis for my security. I never even dreamed about a scenario this dire." She gestured for Meechum to step closer. "When we came in, we saw a big ferry beached up in the port. If we could free her, we might be able to put out to sea."

"No," Meechum interjected. "You can't, ma'am. The reason we were trying to find you is that...well, normally this would be classified..." She glanced at Ted and Kyla.

Emily caught on immediately. "Whatever you can say to me, you can say to them. We're way past classified and top secret, you know?"

Kyla stepped forward and held up a finger. "Wait! Are you saying the president can tell us if there are aliens at Area 51 and all that? If so, I'd really like to know."

He flashed her a look of disapproval, though he gave Emily a sideways glance. It was an excellent question.

Emily appeared torn, and he wondered if Kyla had hit upon a hot topic. She leaned closer to Kyla and waved him and Meechum closer. "I did hear about an above top-secret memo about aliens. Do you want to know what it said?"

He leaned in harder than the girls. "Hell yeah, I do."

She smiled. "So do I!"

Ted rolled his eyes as Emily and the others laughed. "There's no such things as aliens. Not as far as I know," she amended. "Now, Lance Corporal Meechum, please tell us what you know."

"Of course," the Marine replied. "The reason I came looking for you is that you have the codes for the nuclear briefcase. If we can get you to the missile base in Minot, North Dakota, we can deprogram the entire defense system."

Emily absently rubbed the waistline of her dress. "Why would we need to do that?" She paused for a second and lit up. "It's so they can't use it!"

"Right," Meechum replied. "It might already be too late, but we think there's still a chance they haven't figured out what needs to be done. It isn't something commonly known to government agencies. If they had traitors on the inside, it's still unlikely they knew how to re-program the whole system."

"Do you know how to do it?" Kyla asked the Marine.

"No. I was hoping she did."

All eyes went to Emily, even his.

Folsom, CA

As much as Dwight wanted to get on his motorcycle and disappear in the farmlands of the Central Valley, he had no choice but to stick with Bernard and the larger group of motorcyclists. They went east for another hour, traveling through the empty city of Sacramento along the way. The crowded buildings tempted him to make a run for it there, but he admitted he was too scared to risk it. The men around him were willing to kill innocent people by shooting them and then dropping them off bridges. What would they do to him? A guy who shouldn't even be there...

When they reached the next city, the bikers began to peel off in blocks of five or six. He stayed close to Bernard, mainly because he didn't know anyone else. When he saw Bernard turn down a side street along with a small group of his own, Dwight followed. Eventually, they turned down another street lined with single-story storefronts. It reminded him of an old-school mall without a roof.

Bernard pointed to each man, and the bikers drove toward stores where he motioned to them.

When he got to Dwight, he did a doubletake, then pulled next to him so they could both put their feet down. "You aren't part of my team. Did you get lost again?"

Poppy squawked from the gutter of a nearby building.

Yeah, I'll be careful, he thought.

"I've been lost this whole time, Bernie. Can I ride with you until we get where we're going?"

Bernard smiled. "We're there, friend. And sure, why not? It will help me meet my target that much quicker. Then we can go to the designated hotel and relax until the big show tomorrow."

That sounded good to him. If he could get himself alone in a room, maybe he'd get the opportunity to flee he'd been waiting for. Surely, they couldn't watch him every second of the day. The first thing he was going to do was find a—

"Right here!" Bernard gestured toward one of the shops. "This is your place." It was a sporting goods store he'd never heard of. Since he didn't have to move, he shut off his motor. Bernard sped down the street about fifty yards before he stopped, too.

The other men walked around, holding the flamethrower poles that had been secured to the backs of their bikes. He took his off and tried to mimic what the nearest man was doing. He seemed to turn a crank, push a button, then hold the metallic pole a bit like a gun.

Poppy cackled from above the sporting goods store.

"No, I won't shoot my eye out. Where do you get such crazy ideas?" He spoke low, so none of the men would hear him. "I don't know what we're doing, but I'm getting out of this as soon as I can. Keep your eyes sharp. Help me, Poppy."

Before she could answer, one of the men down the line seemed to explode with fire...

"Good night!" he spit out. The man's hose had a jet of fuel shooting from the end, and it turned into a long stream of fire. The splashing flames went through the glass store front, as well as soak the wooden façade on the front.

The next black-clad man in line did the same thing. He aimed his flamethrower at a building, unleashed the spray of liquid by itself for a second, then it ignited and sent flames in an arc to the wooden structure.

"Oh, crap." It was his turn. He had to keep up appearances, so he tried his best to mimic them. He squeezed a trigger, which unleashed the flow, then he searched for a trigger or button for the spark. It took him a few extra seconds, but he found the red button on the side of the handle. Once he pressed that, an intense heat hit his face.

He was suddenly holding a cone of flames shooting directly through the front doors of the store thirty feet away. The pressure was strong enough to send the fire well into the store. When he let off the throttle, the flamethrower kicked off, and he saw his handiwork: fire quickly spread in there.

Bernard also had his flamethrower operating. The whole group sprayed, then lit, then shut off, then moved to an adjacent store.

Dwight figured he had no choice. He sparked it up again and threw the flames all over the front of the store, then, like the others, he aimed for the neighboring buildings. He was out of juice less than a minute later; he was the last one to finish.

He slung the business end into the holster and was finally free to see the damage they'd done. The entire street reminded him of a valley, with walls of fire on the outsides, and him and the bikes on the pavement in the middle.

Poppy screamed at him from up above.

"No, I didn't mean to burn your feathers. Come down from there!" In seconds, they'd laid waste to a quarter of a mile of storefront, and the fire would certainly spread to the untouched buildings close by, and probably the homes and businesses behind them.

Why are they doing this?

FIFTEEN

In the air over Lake Huron

Ted eventually chose the P.180 Avanti as their ride. It was a distinctive twin-engine turboprop aircraft with large wings in the back and two small wings near the nose, making it look like it had whiskers. Other than the looks, he'd selected it for its ability to make the flight from Massachusetts to North Dakota in one hop. Some of the other planes were nicer and could go faster, but the Avanti also had the most fuel, so that won the day.

Once they took off, he'd gone directly north to avoid New York City and the chaos at Newark. He kept as low to the ground as possible on the way out, but once he was two states away, he figured he'd be outside the radar range of any airport in the New York area, so he leveled out at a more comfortable, and less dangerous, cruising altitude.

Emily sat in the co-pilot's chair, though she wasn't familiar with the cockpit. On the way up, he'd shown her what he knew, though he had only seen the avionics in the model one other time. They took turns working the controls to give her more experience; it paid to be prepared.

"You haven't said much since I came back," Emily said from behind her fashionable sunglasses. "Anything you want to talk about?"

At first, he was going to tell her she was way off the mark, but he begrudgingly admitted she was right, to a degree. Finding and saving Kyla was a huge burden off his shoulders, but now he was directly responsible for her safety. To make it all worse, the pragmatic Marine told him he had to take her toward danger, not away.

"I like your beach bag. It looks like you're on spring break." The colorful bag sat behind her seat. She'd showed him it was where she kept her pistol.

"Ted?" she sassed, knowing that wasn't what was bothering him.

He sighed, beaten. "Do you think I could convince Kyla to wear a parachute, so I could toss her out over Canada?" The direct route to North Dakota had them going over Canadian territory. If he threw her out, he'd get her away from the possible danger of going to the missile base, though traveling north of the border was no picnic, either. The intel he'd heard while on Air Force Two suggested most of Canada had been taken out.

"Hell no," Emily said right away. "She's definitely not going to back away from any fight. She didn't flinch when she had to kill those traitors, Ted. I think she wants to impress you, and her Marine drill sergeant."

He chuckled. "Yeah, Meechum is one serious badass. Normally, I'd have some concerns about my daughter hanging out with a Marine, but in this case, I think it has done wonders for her. Boy, I tell you, my sister would have hated to see her carrying guns and…" A bubble of sadness welled up, knowing he'd never see Rebecca again. However, he fought it back down. "And carrying on like a Marine."

Emily reached over and touched his arm.

"How do you always know?" he said, appreciating the human contact.

"A president just senses these things," she said in a dead serious tone, before giggling. "You're a tough guy on the outside, but I've been with you long enough, and through enough crappy situations, to know a little about what makes you tick."

He straightened, not willing to dwell on his own weaknesses. "I think you and Kyla have been talking about me. It's not fair, you know?"

She pulled back, still laughing a little. "I'm sure you think all we did was sit around saying how great you are."

Ted turned on the charm, to be as funny as her. "Did you?"

They shared a moment, and he thought she was going to say yes to prove him right, but she flicked on the radio and set it to the 100.0 frequency for Southern One Hundred.

"Speaking of talking, it seems S-O-H is back to playing music."

The high-flying solar aircraft broadcasting music to America were sixty thousand feet above them. If he wanted to listen to music on the flight, they were the only station left on the air. However, it was owned by Jayden Phillips, the guy who said he was responsible for attacking America. Ted wondered if there were signals or hidden messages in the songs, akin to how allied forces sent information to French resistance fighters in World War II. At that moment, the station played a violent rap song. He couldn't imagine what message could be hidden inside.

"I'd shoot down all those flying transmitters if it would shut off this music."

"What about free speech and all that?" she replied with a laugh. "I'm supposed to protect it."

He had some opinions on the subject, but a blip appeared on his central avionics screen. The TCAS, traffic collision avoidance system, showed another aircraft nearby. The reliable limit of detection was about thirty nautical miles.

"We have company," he said, all trace of humor gone.

He watched intently as the unidentified craft hovered at the extreme edge of his system's range, almost directly behind them. It went on for several minutes, and nothing changed, leading him to wonder if it was a malfunction.

"I'm going to change heading a little to see if he matches." He conducted a gradual turn toward the north and watched as the other plane shadowed his maneuver. When he turned back to his original course, the other guy hung with him. "Uh oh. I think we have a problem."

The P.180 Avanti was built for small, private companies, and tiny airlines away from major hubs. The dual-prop design was great for fuel savings versus a jet, but it sacrificed speed. If the craft behind him was with the enemy, they were almost certainly traveling by jet. The Avanti wouldn't be able to outrun or outfly them. Even a marginally-trained pilot only needed to keep them in range, so other units could pursue.

He looked outside. They were almost at Michigan. Lake Michigan was spread on the horizon ahead. Not nearly close enough to North Dakota to give up.

"You know how I mentioned parachutes?" he said with worry steeped in his voice.

"Yeah," she responded.

"If that's what I think it is, we might all need them."

She leaned toward him. "You know that's impossible, right?"

The door to the outside would never open while they were in flight. There was no way to jump out, even if they had four parachutes ready to go. He nodded. "Just trying to keep morale above room temperature."

The transponder signal on the screen still hadn't moved.

"Well, before we frighten the first-class passengers, let's wait a little while and see what this thing does. Maybe it will assume we're a friendly and let us go."

She took the controls and jinked a bit to the left. They watched as the other plane took a second to re-orient, then it moved to the spot directly behind them again.

"Or," she began in a hushed voice, "maybe this thing knows exactly who we are, and where we're going. It's tagging along because there's no need to grab us until we land at our destination."

"How could anyone possibly know all that?"

Emily looked over her shoulder and whispered, "Are you positive that Van Nuys character didn't know about what the Marines were doing on his ship?"

Ted trusted that Meechum was on his side, but he couldn't vouch for anyone else back on the JFK.

"We'll just have to wing it," he snarked.

Highway in Illinois

The dog flew out of the cornstalks, which forced Tabby to brace her arm against the inevitable attack. She'd recently tangled with those lost dogs back in Chicago, so her reaction time was heightened. However, when the gray dog switched from attack mode to rain-of-kisses mode, she was completely shocked.

"Deogee?"

The excited pup looked up at her with anticipation and a lolling tongue, then it barked once as if she'd gotten the answer correct.

"It is you! Guys, look who found us!"

A black dog came out of the corn, panting hard as if it had been trying to keep up with its friend. Once it saw Deogee getting lovin' from Tabby, its tail spun into high gear and she came up to get some attention, too.

Audrey and Peter crawled over and joined in the reunion, but as soon as Audrey put her hand on the big wolf, she recoiled. "She's been burned."

Tabby had been so wrapped up in the shock, she'd failed to notice patches of fur along one side had been burned down to the skin. It wasn't totally debilitating, since the dog was playful and alert, but it couldn't have been pleasant. She immediately wondered where she'd gotten the burns from. "Where's Sister Rose?" she asked the dog, as if it would answer.

"And who's your friend?" Peter asked, petting the black lab. He settled the pup long enough to get a look at the dog tag hanging below its neck. "This one's named Biscuit."

"Biscuit and Deogee," Tabby declared. "How did you find us?" It was a small miracle to be sure, though she wondered if it was due to the fact there weren't many people left in the area. If the dogs had somehow tracked her and the kids, it was probably because they were the only ones making tracks. She and the teens had come up the same highway earlier on their way to Chicago. The dogs were simply moving slower.

The joyful reunion was a small consolation prize for losing their car. She wondered if the dogs would have gone all the way to Lake Michigan before they realized she'd turned around and gone back toward home. Were they that smart? Could they be useful to them, since they were all on foot?

The three of them spent the next half-hour clearing what they could from the broken car. The shotguns were scratched but otherwise undamaged. That was her main concern. If those plows came back, she wanted to be ready.

Eventually, a vehicle passed on the highway, heading toward St. Louis. It was an average-looking four-door car, a lot like the Subaru in the corn. A few minutes later, a big truck passed on the northbound lane, heading for Chicago.

"It looks like the route is now open again," she said cautiously.

Audrey held Biscuit by the collar. "We should stay away from the interstate. Whoever those people are, they aren't our friends."

Tabby sighed, wondering if there was a right answer for what to do next. They could cut across country and probably find a car soon enough, but she had no map. If they left the interstate, she wasn't sure how to get home.

"I want to get this trip over with," she said. "The plows went north. We're heading south. There are still lots of cars in the ditch alongside the highway. I'm sure we can find a working one and get the heck out of here. It doesn't look like they're driving special cars or anything, now that the road is open. We'll blend in."

Peter laughed. "You don't think they're going to check our IDs?"

She tried to think logically, for all their sakes. Hundreds of millions of her fellow Americans were dead and gone. Other than the convoy, she'd seen no living souls between the big cities. If these new people were taking over, they couldn't be everywhere at the same time. They'd probably only be watching where the interstate met other highways, or over the Mississippi River.

"I vote we get a car and head for St. Louis. We'll drive slowly, in case they have roadblocks or whatever. When we get to the river by the Arch, we'll spy on the bridge to be sure there's no one there, then we'll cross. If we see anything along the way, we can pull over and hide, like we did here. All we have to do is stay vigilant."

Audrey and Peter shared a look before the girl replied, "We trust you."

Peter wrapped his arm around Deogee. "You'll be our guard dog, won't you?" The wolfhound licked his face, making him fall over on his side giggling uproariously. Again, she thought of how easily the teens were able to blot out the loss of their friend.

Deogee soon left Peter, sniffed all over Audrey for a few moments, then she came and threw herself at Tabby. For a few minutes, she rolled and played with the dog too, trying to forget all the problems swirling around outside their patch of cornfield. She didn't make a big deal out of it when another car passed by on the road, but it reinforced the idea she was doing the right thing.

Driving straight home was the smart play.

SIXTEEN

Over Wisconsin

While Emily and Uncle Ted sat up front, Kyla had eight comfortable seats in the back to share with Meechum. The plane was barely big enough for one small restroom, which was a godsend on the long flight, but it had no door between the seats and the cockpit. She chose to sit near the back, if only to give the pair privacy in the cockpit. She had her suspicions about what they were talking about; she'd seen the way her uncle was gaga over Emily's dress.

"Do you think they like each other?" she asked Meechum under her breath. Kyla wasn't a gossip at heart, but this was a special case. She thought back to all those fake boys she mentioned to her partner Ben back on the job.

She'd exaggerated and made stuff up to avoid telling him she wasn't dating anyone. It was all fake, but it passed the time. However, there, on the plane, she was convinced real things were happening.

She shifted positions to better see Meechum.

The short-haired woman sat across the aisle from her. She had her rifle in pieces for the umpteenth time since they'd taken off. She'd seen her do it before, which led to her thinking the woman was super thorough about cleanliness and preparation, but Kyla now believed it was a trained habit designed to keep her endlessly occupied, possibly because she'd said flying wasn't her thing. The Marine didn't even glance over. "It wouldn't be proper for me to get into it. She's my commander-in-chief."

"Oh, come on. You mean you never speculated about who Tanager would end up with?" President Kirby Tanager was famous for entering office as a bachelor, but that didn't last long. He married one of his spokeswomen who was as loud and obnoxious as he was. For the brief time before he settled down with her, the tabloids were on fire with speculation about who would make the perfect first lady.

Meechum stared at her. "Do I look like the type of woman who cares who other women are doing? I have enough trouble finding a man, and I work at a company with nothing but men." When she'd made her point, she resumed working on her rifle.

"I bet you scare the hell out of those guys."

"Marines aren't afraid of anything," she deadpanned. "I just don't go for the big, stupid types. I also don't go for men in my unit. Do you know how much trouble it would cause? Those dumbasses would lay down their lives one after the other to protect me when the bullets came our way."

Kyla detected an undercurrent in her words. "But there is someone, isn't there?" she taunted in a friendly manner.

Meechum's lip almost formed a smile, until she caught herself and turned the tables. "What about you? Did you date that fellow you were with when we found you?"

She recoiled at the thought. "Eww. Hell no. Ben was married with kids, plus he was old enough to be my father. Oh yeah, and this is a disqualifier of epic proportions in my book, he was working for the bad guys." Meechum knew the story of how she'd shot Ben as he tried to get off the boat, so her reason for bringing it up was to deflect from her original question. However, rather than press her on who liked whom, she tried to move the conversation away from the subject.

"How much damage do you think Van Nuys did before you killed him?"

Meechum paused her task and looked up. "If we would have had the authority to detain him at the outset, we would have kept him in that hold at the bottom of the ship. His story was fishy from the start."

"But you couldn't?" Kyla asked.

"No. And with no other crew around, we needed him to get the ship out of port. He did us a favor by doing that much, but his plans were probably threatened when the Marines on the *Iwo* showed up. At that point, it might have been possible for the captain of the *Iwo* to take command of the carrier, but we didn't have any evidence backing up our hunch."

"But now you do," she reasoned.

"Yep. That's why I radioed a message back to my team. They'll work with the other captain and hopefully gain control of the JFK. I only wish I was there to bang some heads with the rest of the boys."

Kyla didn't have to ask if it was because she loved a good fight, or if there was someone she wanted to see again. She began to understand the dynamics of the other woman and came to a new respect for her sense of duty for going with them out west. She was about to ask if she had a sense of the odds of their journey, but the plane lurched and bounced violently before she could speak.

Uncle Ted called over the intercom, "Ladies and gentlemen, we've crossed most of Wisconsin. Next up, Minnesota."

Over Wisconsin/Minnesota

"Airspeed: four hundred miles-per-hour. Altitude: ten thousand feet. All instruments look solid." Emily pointed to the radar screen; it still had the contact at the extreme edge of their TCAS screen. "Except for this guy, we've made great time."

"Whoever they are, they must know the Avanti's capabilities, including what distance they needed to maintain position off, or at the edge of, our avoidance system."

Emily sighed. "We saw them the whole time. I guess they messed up."

Like he'd done with the Cessna 172, he'd turned off the transponder before they took off, so they couldn't be tracked as easily. It meant they wouldn't show up on the enemy's TCAS system, since it collected data from nearby transponders. However, if they weren't tracking by TCAS, it meant they probably had active radar on board. It suggested a military aircraft. "Whatever, or whomever, they are, we aren't going to lose them in flight. I'm afraid if they stay with us until Minot, they may figure out what we're doing."

She chuckled. "Taking the vice president to a nuclear missile base to enter a code in a computer, so real Americans maintain control of the United States ballistic missile arsenal. You really believe it's the first thing they'll think of?"

He stretched his legs and leaned her way. The pilots' chairs were comfortable, but they'd been in the air for almost three hours. The lower half of his body was crying out to shift positions. "When you put it like that, lady, I don't believe they'll come up with it at all. However, the fact remains: they're watching where we go."

"Then we have to go somewhere that throws them off the scent," she said dryly.

Ted had been thinking the same thing, but he'd kept it to himself for as long as he dared. It was too easy to sit in the plane and cross the endless miles of land below, but the cold truth was they were literally on someone's radar at that moment. They had to ditch them before they could make their move toward North Dakota.

"I don't want to turn around. That would make it obvious we didn't have a real destination. From where we are, we could go to Duluth, Rochester, or Minneapolis. All are about the same distance from us."

"Where do you want to go?" she asked.

"Well, considering the size of our strike force, I think it would be easy to get lost in any one of those cities, but if the aircraft behind us is also carrying military personnel from the enemy forces, I think I'd rather be in a large city. It will give us more places to hide."

She huffed. "Why does it sound like we're in for some trouble? Everywhere I fly with you, more trouble!"

"I'm sorry," he said, really meaning it.

She grabbed his arm. "I'm kidding, of course. You know I trust you. This sounds like a really good plan. We'll swoop down, jump out, and make a run for the city."

He reflexively put his hand on hers, but he pulled it off a second later, fearing he'd make things uncomfortable. She held her hand where it was for a few seconds, smiled with a hard-to-read expression behind her eyes, then pulled back. He thought about telling her how nice she looked, or how her hair was attractive in the summer-themed scrunchy, but nothing sounded professional in his head. Failing that, he picked up the intercom microphone and went with what he knew. He pushed the yoke forward to dip the plane toward Minneapolis.

"Ladies and gentlemen, please put your seat backs and tray tables in the upright position. We're about to descend into the Minneapolis-Saint Paul International Airport. Oh, and if you have running shoes available, please have those ready. We'll be doing some light jogging. Thanks for flying with MacInnis Air."

Amarillo, TX

Brent issued his orders and sent his band of merry men out into the greater Amarillo area to retrieve the necessary supplies. They avoided the airport, since that seemed to be the hub of enemy activity, but the rest of the giant city was ripe for the plucking. They'd found throwaway cars and split up; a move he hoped wouldn't come back and bite him in the ass. There wasn't enough time to play it overly safe.

They all rendezvoused on a residential street deep inside miles of suburban housing. He was pleased to see everyone had come back from their first mission with the right vehicles. Nine or ten big trucks were already there.

Kevin, a small black man with the deepest voice Brent had ever heard, knew a guy who managed a car repair shop. He owned a giant wrecker, which was now parked on the street. Carter, the alleged pyro who may or may not have burned down his family's failing pool supply store, said he knew of a trucking company they'd done business with inside the city. A tractor-trailer with that company's name sat behind the wrecker. Brent didn't let Trish go off alone, so they'd gone together and brought back two tankers from a truck stop.

As he climbed out of his rig, he noticed a line of trash trucks down the street. "Who brought those?"

Andre raised his hand. "It must have been trash day in this part of the city when they attacked us. Me and Ross brought in six of them, and we didn't have to look that hard."

Brent rubbed his hands together. "Good job, men. Let's make one more trip to the truck stop I just came from. You aren't going to believe how many of these shiny tankers are there."

"Are they full?" asked Kevin.

"I think so," he replied. He wasn't a trucking expert, but the engine strained to pull the one he'd taken. It had to be close to full, and the numerous hazard signs convinced him it was carrying gasoline.

The rest of the daylight hours went by as Brent and his men improved their collection time. They figured out it was best to pair up—one man would start a civilian car found in the subdivision, then they'd go to the truck stop. They'd leave the little car there, then bring back two trucks. When Brent arrived in another tanker, the whole street looked like an oil refinery.

"This should do it, guys." He was proud of what he'd been able to accomplish in a short time, but the real heavy lifting would begin once it got dark. He looked over the nearest truck, and his guys gathered around.

In the evening, a flatbed truck rolled up the street and parked next to Brent. It was a rental from a Home Depot store, painted in the distinctive orange color of the home improvement chain. Its arrival meant the completion of another of the missions he'd created for his men.

"What did you bring us?" Brent asked the driver.

Cliff waved at him. "Check it out." He pointed to the flatbed.

Brent moved around to get a look at his cargo. The familiar orange buckets were filled to the tops with metal objects, making it look like he'd brought back a king's treasure that was spilling over into the truck's bed. Instead of gold, however, they were large bolts and strips of rebar. There were also twenty or thirty cinderblocks stacked inside.

The driver came around behind Brent. "I filled up the buckets like you said. It was easy to do when there was no one inside to stop me. I just dumped out the boxes of bolts. I, uh, might have driven my truck right in through the front doors to make it easier."

"Smart thinking," Brent replied.

The man went on, "I also got all the emergency roadside kits I could find, as well as two dozen ten-foot lengths of copper wire, though I have no idea what it's all for."

Brent couldn't wait for the sun to go down. He'd had nothing but time over the past few hours to imagine how they were going to assemble all that they'd brought together into a weapon designed for war. It wasn't Vietnam, and those weren't regular soldiers at the airfield, but he was about to teach all of them, friend and foe alike, what it meant to be a pissed-off American warrior.

"I know exactly what it's all for," he said dryly.

SEVENTEEN

Minneapolis, MN

As soon as Ted touched down at the Minneapolis-Saint Paul Airport, the plane behind them disappeared from their system. He had no illusions of losing the enemy craft; the only question was whether the opposing force had radioed to ground units already in Minnesota or not.

They ran through the darkened airport terminals, careful as always to avoid the piles of clothing. There were long lines of passengers at several of the gates, as well as lots of traffic inside the food court. All four had the same idea when they ran by a food kiosk; he grabbed a couple energy drinks and several bags of chips. The others pulled off their favorite junk foods as they ran for the pilot's lounge.

"Through there. Hurry!" he yelled. Ted had been to the airport in the past, but he'd never spent much time there. Most airports had a restricted area where pilots and flight crews were able to relax. Often, airport administration and operations were nearby. "Yes, that's it." He pointed to an exit.

The door was closed, and it had a security panel that required a keycard to operate. He didn't have the required card, but several of the airport employees nearby had what he needed. Ted respectfully pulled the card off one of the maintenance uniforms and got them through.

They went up several flights of stairs before entering the square room with huge wraparound windows displaying the airport and the nighttime skies above the dark city of Minneapolis. Dozens of workstations had chairs with civilian clothes piled on them, each placed in front of radar, weather, and communications terminals.

"It's still working," he said breathlessly. Most of the airport had gone dark with the loss of power, but everything in the air traffic control tower was lit up. He figured generators would have kicked on the second main power went out, but since he didn't know when the switchover happened, he worried everything was going to shut down as he watched. "We have to hurry."

"What are we looking for?" Kyla asked.

Meechum ran to the nearest working terminal. "We want to see if we're being chased, right?"

Ted nodded at her. "Yes, exactly. I wanted to get up here before that other plane had a chance to clear out or land." He jumped in front of one terminal, then slid two or three down the line until he found the one he wanted. "Got ya!"

The others gathered around. He touched a bunch of numbers on the screen. "Uh oh. We weren't being followed by just one plane. Look at them all." He pointed to a half-dozen aircraft coming in from the south, in addition to one that was a lot closer. "They're running with transponders on, so they can ID each other. We had our transponder off, to stay hidden, but they must have caught us on radar along the way."

"Should we have kept it on?" Kyla said reflectively.

"No, we were unauthorized, either way," Emily said.

"So, what does this mean for us?" Kyla pressed.

They all bunched up at the workstation as Ted explained. "This is the one that was following us. You can see how it's the only aircraft close to the airport. It's a..." His voice trailed off.

"What?" Kyla asked, crowding in on his left.

"It's a civilian craft. I was sure it was military based on how it kept pace with us. It's a Bombardier 850. Basically, a big executive aircraft." He had no illusions about the intent of the pursuit. Maybe they couldn't spare a military plane to investigate a little puddle-jumper flying across the Great Lakes. The pilot only needed to stay close. But it was the other aircraft which bothered him, since they were moving a lot faster. "These are military." He pointed to the six dots at the lower part of the screen.

The group watched the moving dots for half a minute before he realized they were mesmerized by the active radar's sweeping motion.

"It looks like they're coming for us," Ted said in a steady tone. "We better get moving." He leaned away, hoping the others would follow. When he looked to the next computer screen, he noticed it was a TV station that had been shot to pieces. His attention was drawn to the scene.

The big number 5 behind the anchor desk had distinct holes in it, as did the wall next to it. The lights were funny, like a few had been turned off, or the station was running on low power. A small counter ran at the bottom, suggesting the shot was live.

"Hey, guys, check this out." Despite the impending threat, they had time before any aircraft got to the ground. He risked a look at the computer system. It was designed to record live television, like a Tivo. He figured the video monitor was useful for air traffic personnel during emergencies.

Maybe I can see the instant of the attack.

He paused the live shot, then reversed it. It went by slowly until he hit the button again. The reverse speed increased until it was going by hours at a time. The studio remained the same as he watched, but suddenly, the number 5 fixed itself in an instant. The rewind went on until two people appeared at the desk.

"Stop!" Meechum ordered.

He cued the tape back and forth until he found the precise moment he wanted. As one, they held their breath until the moment they all knew was coming. The well-dressed man and woman at the news desk spoke about breaking news happening on the West Coast, then they disappeared from existence.

"No effing way," the Marine remarked.

"Show it to me again," Emily requested.

They all got as close to the screen as possible to see it happen. The newscasters were there one second, then gone the next. As they watched it over and over, it seemed less real to him, like someone had edited the tape.

Silence descended on them for half a minute. The instant of the attack was there, recorded for posterity, though it did them little good.

"Can you fast-forward the tape?" Kyla asked. "When you were rewinding, I thought I saw some other people, like when the place gets messed up."

Ted looked at his niece. "Sure."

He went forward again until he found the moment the anchor desk was shot. For a split-second of fast time, a group of young people sat at the desk, followed by the destruction of the set.

"Hey!" he barked. "You were right."

Ted cued up the tape to the exact moment before the strangers appeared. When he had all eyes on the screen, he hit play. A pretty young woman came up to where the female anchor had been during the attack. She wore yoga pants with a white long-sleeve shirt; three long braids rolled off her head as she leaned over. She picked a lapel microphone off the chair, then shoved the woman's clothes onto the floor.

"Hello? Is this thing on?" the woman asked to someone off the screen.

"I hear you!" a girl replied. "Your voice is coming through the speakers outside."

The young lady stared at the screen for a long time but didn't say anything. Ted recognized the look of someone who was in shock.

"Say something," a young man's voice insisted.

"Here we go..." The girl took a seat and motioned for unknown people to join her.

Two teen boys and girl closed ranks with the young woman in the seat, but they didn't sit down. The dark-haired girl held hands with one of the boys; he was big-boned, though not overweight. The girl in the seat was younger than Kyla by a few years, but she seemed composed and didn't hesitate as she spoke.

"My name is Tabitha Breeze. I'm from Bonne Terre, Missouri. I survived the poison gas with three students from Seckman High School." The three others waved nervously. "This is Peter Ellison, Audrey Hampton, and Donovan

Callaway. We're here in the studios of Channel 5. Please help us evacuate."

Poison gas? It was the first he'd heard of such a theory.

They watched the entire exchange, including an older pair of men who joined them. One of them looked old and filthy. The other was younger, with a blue sports cap. At the end, Ms. Breeze apologized for giving guns to the younger teens, though he sensed in her voice she was secretly glad to have weapons. He wondered about the two men and how they'd all found each other.

Everyone drifted off screen as the live shot continued, but he didn't turn it off since the big number 5 was still intact. "Wait, guys. It's going to happen."

He held his breath despite himself. As the seconds ticked by, he was tempted to hit fast-forward again, especially since there were aircraft on the way, but he let it run in real time. Eventually, two or three minutes later, the distinctive crack of a shotgun rattled the camera. Kyla and Emily reacted to the intense situation by pulling back a bit.

"Was that a gunshot?" Kyla asked. "I'm sure it was," she answered herself.

Still, Ted didn't move. The number 5 was still intact. He watched, even as the others hovered behind him. "Wait for it," he said dramatically.

It took another minute, but the rattle of a chain gun made the shotgun seem quiet by comparison. He imagined the young kids getting torn to bits by the war machinery, though there were no clues as to why those youngsters were getting tangled up with such weaponry.

The next part happened so fast he almost missed it. The young man in the blue hat ran behind the anchor desk. A moment later, the backdrop number 5 was eviscerated by bullets.

"Run!" Kyla shouted to the screen. The man's blue hat hovered at the back of the desk, then the guy seemed to duck off screen.

A second later, a large mechanical robot paced by. Ted had seen a similar one before, in front of the White House. It stood as tall as a man's waist and looked like a four-legged animal, if the creature was only made of metal. "Oh, man. They're in some shit."

"They have mechanical horses?" Kyla asked.

"I thought it was more like a robot cat," he replied absently, unable to stop watching.

"Cat, horse, whatever," Emily stated, "those children are in trouble."

As he watched, the machine dropped its head so the chain gun mounted on its back had clearance to spit out untold rounds.

The horse-robot plodded off screen, presumably to follow the man in the blue hat. The video image returned to how it was when he'd first seen it. The big 5 was damaged. The wall was full of holes. No living people were in view of the camera.

"We're not the only ones fighting for our lives," Ted remarked.

East Saint Louis, Illinois

Tabby had made sure everything she did was average. She picked a boring-looking four-door car, gray in color, and used that to drive on the highway toward St. Louis. She did the speed limit and kept an eye out for any signs of walking or flying drones, giant snowplows, or strangers lurking around the shoulders. An hour later, as the sun was going down, she exited the highway in East St. Louis, intending to get one quick look at the bridge over the river. She was convinced it was the only place where they'd find trouble.

They drove around for a short time, searching for the perfect place.

Finally, with Deogee and Biscuit at her feet and the two teens close by, she studied the city from the rooftop of an old warehouse. It provided a perfect overview of downtown St. Louis and the highway bridge a little to the south of it. The city was ruined. Many of the tall buildings near the Arch were either filled with smoke and fire or had recently been burned. Ash rose into the sky beyond, as if the area on fire was much larger than the downtown. Still, her attention went to the interstate bridge to her left. From her vantage point, it was obvious there was activity at the near side of the span, and it wasn't a bunch of people fleeing the inferno. "Look at the bridge, guys."

"I see them. What are they?" Audrey asked.

"They look like giraffes," Tabby replied. "There's two of them, like they're standing guard. One is in the middle of the eastbound lanes. The other is in the westbound."

"You don't think they're protecting us from going into the fire, do you?" Audrey asked, full of doubt.

"No. They aren't the same as the horse models with guns, or the floating ones with speakers. I think those are a type of guard model. Why else would they sit up so high?"

"I don't care what they're for," Peter laughed. "Can we run them over?"

Tabby thought back to a recent visitor to her family's Bonne Terre mine tour. The man had gotten up early to drive his family from across the state. They'd made it almost all the way there, but they'd hit a large deer a few miles before town. When they pulled into the parking lot, Mom and Dad took her outside to see the car. The front end had been mangled, and the glass windshield had a bloody hole on the passenger side. The giraffe model was a lot bigger than any deer, plus it was made of metal.

"No, that wouldn't be wise," she replied.

Peter huffed. "Then what do we do? We have to get over the river."

"I know," she said dryly. There were other bridges, some not far away. They could also find a boat. Perhaps that would surprise the invaders more than running over their sentinels.

Deogee nudged her leg, though she waved her off. "Not now, girl."

"Do either of you know about other bridges to the south? How far do you think we'd have to go before we found another one?" Tabby was embarrassed to ask. She'd been driving for two years, since she turned sixteen. She should probably have a better grasp of the area.

Deogee growled, getting all their attentions.

"What is it?" she asked with a touch of impatience.

She had no idea what to make of the sound, or the dog's odd behavior, but Biscuit behaved like Deogee was threatening her. Ears back, head down, tail between her legs.

"What the?" she asked.

It wasn't Deogee scaring her. The sound of a flying drone carried over the air. It was getting closer. They were standing on the roof, in full view of the city—a mistake which only became painfully obvious as she turned for the door.

"Run!" she whispered.

EIGHTEEN

Minneapolis, MN

Kyla stood there as Uncle Ted flipped off switches and buttons up and down the row of terminals in the control tower. Some of them turned off the radar screens, but he got to one computer which seemed to control the runway lights. "Why are you doing that?" she asked. "Shouldn't we be running?"

Once they'd seen the video of the girl, Tabby-something, and the robots shooting at her and her friends, she had a new respect for the enemy invasion force. They weren't only blips on a screen or traitors on a boat. They'd come to America armed with a superweapon that erased all the people, and they were obviously using robots to clean up whatever was left. She wished she could go back in time and ask Ben if he knew about all this. He had warned her the bad guys knew how to survive.

"If we can delay them getting down here, we'll have a better chance of finding a car and getting the hell out of Minneapolis. I'm shutting off what I can, but yes, we're leaving immediately."

"Just shut it all off?" she asked, looking at a nearby computer.

Uncle Ted nodded seriously. "Yes. Everyone can hit power buttons. Do whatever you can for the next sixty seconds, then we haul ass for safety."

At the appointed moment, they all converged on the exit door. Her uncle seemed satisfied at what they'd done, but not all the way. "I can't shut off the lights on the third landing strip. It's either controlled from a second tower or is on a different generator."

Emily smiled. "You did good. It's almost black out there." The city of Minneapolis was mostly dark, except for five or six fires burning in the night. The power feeding into the city must have failed over the past couple of days.

"Okay, go!" he insisted.

Kyla followed Meechum down the stairs. No matter how much she tried, Kyla wasn't able to get the jump on the Marine, so she had to trail behind rather than lead.

They ran through the empty terminal, which was now almost completely dark, save for a few emergency lights. Even with that bit of illumination, she stepped on clothes left by fallen people—an act which gave her goosebumps no matter how many times it happened.

"Can we set up a decoy? Make them think we're holed up in a room or a cafe?" Meechum spoke in a low voice as they passed more gates.

Uncle Ted cursed at himself. "I should have left the plane running. It might have bought us some time. As it is, I think our only chance is to run where they least expect. We have to get a car and get out of here before they arrive in force."

"How long do we have?" Emily asked.

"If those jets come directly to this city, they were about thirty minutes out when we were up top. Now we're talking about twenty minutes, tops. The chase plane who followed us is a lot closer. They could land at any time."

She looked outside, hoping not to see a plane landing in the darkness.

They all had weapons, so she wasn't as scared as she might have been otherwise. Almost getting her head shot off in Central Park had given her respect for what it meant to get into a gunfight, and she wanted to avoid it if at all possible, but she would fight hard to defend Uncle Ted, and Emily, if she had to. There wasn't a doubt in her mind Meechum would do the same. The sense of camaraderie helped a lot.

Uncle Ted took them through a door that once had a jetway attached to it. Instead of the long walkway, there was a short flight of stairs. "We're going that way." He pointed to the end of the taxiway, which was a wall of blackness, even compared to the rest of the darkened city. "I think it's a river."

They ran alongside the terminal, dodging parked planes, luggage bins, and maintenance vehicles. As they neared the end of the building, she wondered if they were missing the obvious. The little flat-topped vehicles were a lot like the ones she'd seen inside the aircraft carrier. When she passed close to one, she halted.

"Hey, Uncle Ted, why don't we take one of these?"

The rest of them stopped, and the clopping of feet stopped, too. That made it easier for her to hear the approach of a jet.

Minneapolis, MN

"How much fuel does this thing have?" Kyla asked from her spot on the back of the airport dolly tug.

Ted knew it didn't have fuel; it had a battery. "We've got a good charge." The low-profile design allowed for two people to sit in the front, and the other two could spread out in the small cargo bay. It had no roof, and only sat about three feet off the ground, allowing it to go under the wings of aircraft. It wasn't made for long trips. "I have no idea how far that will get us."

The first plane landed while they rode into the woods beyond the landing strip. They got lucky, however, when it came down on the lone runway with power. It was on the far side of the terminal, relative to their escape route. By the time they'd cut through a short stretch of woods and sped onto an urban bike path, they were beyond sight of anyone at the airport.

"This thing runs on electric," he said over his shoulder. "I hope the battery charger was on until the last second." It almost certainly wouldn't have been one of the things on the generators. "Or that the kid driving it thought enough to put it on the charger at all, right, Kyla?"

He beamed a smile back to her; the moon provided enough light to see her teeth. Her mother had told plenty of stories about Kyla's teen antics with electronics. Keeping her off the tech was a constant battle his sister hated to fight, but one he often told her was important. However, no matter how much he bolstered her, she couldn't teach Kyla the importance of keeping things charged all the time. Was she still like that?

"You and Mom talked too much," she deadpanned, before falling silent.

He thought she'd taken it the wrong way; he only wanted to kid around with her to keep everyone from thinking of how they were riding a piece of airport equipment down the middle of an urban bikeway in downtown Minneapolis. A few seconds later, and right before he was going to apologize, she added. "And she only told you the bad stuff about me, I'm sure." Her light laughter unloaded the ton of bricks weighing down his chest.

"My sister told me a lot of things—you know how much she loved to talk—but she never had anything bad to say about you, Kyla. In fact, she could never believe her luck at how well you turned out, considering she was by herself." He didn't dare open the can of worms about her father. It was bad enough her mom was gone.

"Thanks, Unk," she replied.

They rode the bike path in darkness for another hour. It remained paved and sufficiently wide for the small four-wheeled tow truck, but it couldn't do much more than ten or fifteen miles an hour. When the path went below a bridge, he knew it was time to switch modes of transportation. He ran the cart under cover but didn't drive out the other side. "We have to leave this here. If they somehow figure out we took this, they'll have to find it on foot. The bridge will block them from above."

"Smart," Meechum replied.

Emily hopped out and came around to him before he could get out. "Will you let me drive next? You haven't had a break...since last night."

"Neither have you," he said defensively.

She put her hands on her hips in a pose that all women seemed to know. "Are you going to let me or not? I could order you, you know?" Her smile was so big, he saw it despite being inside the dark tunnel.

Ted sighed. "You love playing the presidential card, don't you?"

"Hey, if I can't rule over you, what good is it to be in charge?"

Outside, the distinct whine of jets echoed in the night.

"Sure. You can drive. As long as we get the hell out of this city."

Folsom, CA

After Dwight and his partners burned several blocks of Main Street, a woman on a little scooter came through while blowing a whistle. When she had their attention, she pulled out a small bullhorn, allowing her to be heard over the roar of surrounding fires.

"Your presence is required at the next rally point. Your fire team leaders know the coordinates. Please leave this area immediately."

The other burners secured their flamethrower equipment to their bikes, as did he, but the second he had it on tight enough, he started his bike and sped away from the raging fires. However, he had no intention of going far; what he needed was only two blocks over. Poppy had been looking all over town for him, and she led the way.

"You were wrong, Poppy. The store was an extra block over." He didn't hold it against the little bird. She'd gotten him close.

Poppy yelled back at him, but he didn't think her bad language required a reply. He'd done his mission for Bernard and his people. Now it was his time. The liquor store was unlocked, as was everything else, which made it easy to get inside and go right for his favorite aisle—the biggest bottles with the highest alcohol content.

He picked up a plastic gallon-sized bottle of Tequila, ripped off the paper around the cap, then tried to unscrew it. His hands were trembling as if California was having an 8.0 earthquake, so it became impossible.

"Stop it!" he ordered his hand.

Poppy laughed. She sat on the checkout counter, perhaps wanting to see if he'd leave some money in exchange for taking the bottle.

"Shut up, bird. I know what I'm doing." He threw the bottle on the floor in frustration. It bounced with a sickening sloshing sound, but it didn't pop open as he'd hoped. While it spun around on the floor, he held up both of his hands, palms up, and couldn't believe how much he was shaking.

"This isn't me," he complained. "I just want a bottle and a warm place to sleep."

Bernard and the others were out there, probably looking for him. A remote section of his brain registered that as dangerous, but he'd been without his fix for over twenty-four hours. His body no longer cared about danger or rules. It simply knew what would happen if he didn't have his drink.

He went down the aisle until he found a glass bottle. It was a 750-milliliter of gin. It didn't matter to him what was inside, he'd have drunk cough syrup if it was all he could get. He took the bottle to the front of the store and smashed the neck on the checkout register.

"Open up!" he demanded.

His first strike didn't break it, so he had to do a second one. When the bottle cracked open, it sent gin spraying all over the register and counter.

Poppy complained as usual, but he wasn't listening to her.

He lifted the broken bottle to his lips but happened to look at the front door. Bernard had found him and stood there quietly observing his breakdown. Poppy spoke again, and that time, he listened.

"I see him now," Dwight replied to her. Somewhere in his subconscious, he remembered he could get into trouble for being inside a liquor store. The words wanted to come bubbling out of his fuel-starved brain, but it remained mired deep inside. If there was a price to be paid, he was willing to pony up, as long as he could taste alcohol one more time.

He lifted it close to his lips but hesitated. Bernard still hadn't moved. It was unnatural.

He slammed the bottle on the counter, nearly breaking down into tears. "I know what you're going to say, but I don't care. I didn't come here to burn things, man. I don't think I can do it again."

Bernard stepped closer. "It's your call what you want to do. I can't babysit you around the clock, and there's a whole country of liquor stores ripe for the picking. However, you might want to hold off until you see the big event. Once you know what our true goal is, and how fast we can achieve it, you might think twice about going back to your old habits."

"Something big is happening?" he asked.

The other man nodded.

Poppy flew to the back of the store, but she whispered in his ear as she went by. She asked if he would at least let her out the door before he killed himself. Her blunt assessment of his actions made him reconsider, or at least delay.

"All right, for her sake, I'll check out your big surprise."

Bernard tilted his head like he'd heard him wrong, but then relaxed and waved him out. Dwight set down the bottle of gin, opened the door for Poppy, then walked out to his bike. He rolled it into the middle of the street, intending to hop on and follow Bernard, but the other man stayed back. In one smooth motion, Bernard kicked on his flame thrower, shot a stream of gas into the liquor store, and lit it up.

The resulting explosion knocked him backward off his bike. It hurt nothing but his pride, but the jarring hit knocked some sense into his crippled brain.

Bernard and his people played for keeps.

NINETEEN

Minot, ND

Ted woke up in the front seat of a strange car. The world outside was flat for as far as he could see, and the starry sky met the line of the horizon wherever he looked. The driver had the car at a high rate of speed, but the headlights weren't on, adding a strange element of danger to his spot in the front seat. For a moment, he had no idea where he was or who he was with. He'd been having a weird dream he was traveling with the President of the United States, a female Marine, and, strangest of all, his niece. None of which could be true.

"Hey, sleepyhead," a woman cooed softly. It sounded like Nancy, but he'd had a dream he was divorced from her.

What?

He sat up in the seat, sure his eyes weren't working right. He focused on the road, which was whipping by in the night with barely more than the parking lights of the car he was in. And it was the president. Emily was behind the wheel. Ted looked into the back seat. As expected, Kyla and a Marine woman were back there, each asleep on their side.

He whispered, "I'm awake."

She kept her eyes forward, which seemed to be a necessity. As they sped along, she shifted lanes, and he saw a dark shape as they passed it on the interstate. As the world settled back to reality, he figured out what she was doing. "Keeping our profile down by not using the headlights, huh?"

Emily glanced over for a second. "We're lucky the moon was almost full. We're also lucky there aren't many vehicles on the highway in the middle of North Dakota. I've been able to make good time."

"How long?"

"Seven hours," she replied. "Including one fuel stop."

That surprised him, and he couldn't hide his expression from her.

"Yep, you were so tired, you didn't wake up when I went into the hardware store, got a siphon, and took gas from a second car there in the parking lot. I'd planned to use another car, but you all were zonked, so I tried not to wake you."

He was happy to be at the target city, no matter how they got there.

"Were we followed?" he asked. When they abandoned the airport tug, he'd been on the alert for aerial reconnaissance aircraft, certain they'd track them down and take them out with missiles, guns, or the thing that zapped everyone else, but none of it came to be. They found the fuel-efficient sedan and had apparently avoided detection all night, given they were still alive.

"I haven't heard a thing, and the sky has been quiet. If anything was up there, we'd see it. The skies are so clear up here. It's easy to forget how beautiful it is out in the country when you spend so much time in Washington, D.C."

He figured she was talking about herself.

"Where are we?" he said, getting back into the proper mindset of the mission.

"The signs took us through the town of Minot. It was completely dark, like power was gone. However, you can see the lights up that way." She pointed out the windshield. "The signs for Minot Air Force Base have been coming hot and heavy the last few miles. We're almost there."

The base glowed like a circus tent, lit up to draw patrons from miles around. However, now that he was awake and aware, he had Emily exit at a cross-street and pull to the side of the road without using her brakes. "Let it roll to a stop, then jam on the emergency brake."

He half-turned to the back. "Hey, Kyla. Wake up. Lance Corporal Meechum, wake up."

The Marine woke up with her pistol already in her hand, though it wasn't pointed at anything. He held up his hands anyway and tried to be friendly. "Don't shoot."

"Are we there yet?" Kyla mumbled. A second later, she glanced over at Meechum and her gun. "Wait. Where are we?"

The Marine stowed the weapon in her holster, then sat up straight, yawning. Kyla gave him a bleary-eyed thumbs-up sign as Emily stopped the vehicle.

"All right, guys, we're going to leave the car here, but remember where it is for when we come back. I think we're far enough away not to be noticed, even when the sun comes up. The airport has to be at least two miles away." There wasn't a hill in sight, but Emily found a fallow field with some high grass that shielded them from being spotted.

They all carried their weapons as they walked through the high grass toward the airport. The runway was closest to them, while the rest of the buildings on the base were behind it. If they'd come in from the north, it would have been a lot harder to see what they were dealing with. As it was, he had the perfect angle to see the planes on the three-mile-long runway.

Ted was proud they'd made it to the air base, but it was out of his knowledge as to where to go from there. "Well, we made it, Marine. What do we do next?"

Everyone looked to Meechum.

East St. Louis, IL

Tabby and the two teens ran to the roof's exit door with plenty of time to spare before the airborne drone arrived. However, after making sure Audrey and Peter went through and headed down the stairs, she turned to see Deogee and Biscuit running in circles all over the rooftop.

"Come!" she cried out.

Deogee seemed anxious to go to her, but the other dog wasn't cooperating. She knew the puppy crazies when she saw it. Biscuit had been spun up by all the running, and she thought it was a game. Instead of going into the dark staircase, the dog instead chose to stay on the roof where it was lit by the fires across the river.

The whirring sound of the drone came from somewhere nearby, probably close to the door and top of the staircase. She didn't think it was safe to go out and try to chase the dogs, but she wanted to take another shot at calling them over.

"Deogee, come!" she hissed, afraid being too loud was going to give them all away.

That time, the wolf almost made it to the door, but Deogee looked back at the black dog, still running in circles. Biscuit wasn't going to come over without someone grabbing her collar and dragging, and the wolf wouldn't leave her.

Tabby decided to let the dogs stay on the roof. If the drones found it odd, then so be it. Her primary concern had to be for the kids. She left the door open for the pups but chased after Audrey and Peter. They were somewhere down in the darkness of the old warehouse.

"Guys? Where are you?" she asked, turning on her little wrist light.

"Over here," Peter replied from not far away. "We can't see anything."

Her small flashlight helped her pick a way through the debris on the floor of the abandoned building, but she turned if off when they met up. "I know. Let's stay here until we know what's going on."

"Where are the dogs?" Audrey asked with concern.

She sighed with disappointment. "I couldn't get them to come down from the roof. They're running around in circles."

"Maybe they're scared," Audrey added. "We should go get them."

"No," she said sternly, "we have to stay here. If those things find us, it's all over."

A metallic clang resonated from the far side of the warehouse floor, like someone had taken a big sheet of aluminum and pushed it over. After the noise settled, the distinctive fan-blade sound came from the enclosed airspace above them. She reached over and found the shoulders of the teens and guided them down. "Stay low," she whispered. A second later, the drone turned on a small red laser light that swept back and forth across the room.

Tabby looked up the steps to the dim light coming through the doorway thirty feet above. There were drones on the roof and drones inside. If they were going to escape, it had to be by getting outside the warehouse, or below it.

"Look for a sewer lid," she suggested. They'd used the same method to escape from the buildings in Chicago, so she hoped their luck would hold with a second escape. It bummed her out to leave the dogs, but they still hadn't come down the steps. In fact, as she looked back up, the barking became noticeable.

What are you crazy dogs doing up there?

A second ripping noise came from across the warehouse, and a car-sized hole opened in the wall, as if a section had been torn out. The airborne drone remained in the rafters above them, but two of the horse-drones appeared in the new gap. They had red lights too, and the beams seemed to be part of their search mechanism.

"Come on, crawl this way," she advised. There were no obvious sewer lids by the steps, but she was forced to turn on the flashlight when they got away from the stairway. She used her T-shirt fabric to block most of the beam, leaving only enough to see the floor ahead. It seemed like she was playing it safe, but she'd not even gone ten feet when the red beam appeared on the hand holding the light.

A female computer voice spoke from above. "Warning: This area is off limits by order of the

Illinois State Police. Please confirm name and social security number to improve chance of rescue."

Her stomach turned to iron. "Back," she hissed anxiously at the two teens behind her. They turned around in half a second, but the light split into three beams, one for each of them.

The drone spoke again. Its voice wasn't encouraging. "Warning: Avoidance is not advised. Your safety is our primary concern. Please stand by for security intercept."

The clops of the horse feet echoed from several places inside the dark warehouse. She believed the sounds kept getting closer, but it wasn't until one of them turned on a spotlight that she realized where it was.

"Ow!" she cried out. The source of the light was almost in her face.

"Security inquiry: Please state your name and social security number. This is a non-human restricted zone."

"Non-human?" she replied.

"Correct. Human inhabitants are confined to local headquarters. This area is off limits. The penalty for repeated noncompliance is termination."

"That's harsh," Peter jibed. He had his shotgun at the ready, as if looking for the proper target. However, the horse-machines had guns bigger than anything short of a tank. Vinny and Gus hadn't been able to fight off one horse. Now, there were two. Their shotguns would be useless against them.

More lights came on as the two horse-robots closed the distance. The big canons weren't exposed on top of their framework, but she knew they were there. It was enough to keep her from doing what she really wanted, which was running like hell.

A drone floated about ten feet above the scene, providing a small cone of natural light. "New directive: Please state the nature of your presence here inside this facility. How did you survive the National Reboot?"

"National Reboot?" she asked.

"Affirmative. This area was inside the reboot footprint. Please explain how you avoided detection and termination."

Peter laughed. "Yeah, because we want to help you improve your operation. If you expect us to answer that honestly, you're pretty stupid."

One of the horses pushed up against her arm, seemingly wanting her to go somewhere. The floating machine offered a clue. "Advisory: Please stand against wall for positive identification."

As they walked the short way, mechanical squeaks and shuffles came from the framework of the robot horses. Though they were behind her, she figured out the sounds were caused when the chain guns came out of their backs. When she got up against the wall, the two robots had their guns at the ready.

"We want to talk to our parents!" Audrey shouted in outrage. "You can't do this to us!"

Peter looked at Audrey and caught on. "Yeah, we're just kids. You can't hurt us. It's against Geneva's convention, or whatever it's called. That thing about war. We learned about it in school. Look it up, assholes!"

"Warning. By order of the Governor of Zone 21, you have been found guilty of trespassing, property destruction, security interference, impersonating new citizens, and willfully avoiding the National Reboot. How do you plead?"

Tabby stood up straight, ready to go for her pistol. "If you mean we willfully avoided getting killed, then we're guilty as charged. Who wouldn't—"

The machine cut in, "Sentence will be delivered immediately."

Both horse-drones braced their feet.

She knew what came next…

TWENTY

Minot Air Force Base, ND

"What are all those aircraft?" Emily whispered from close by. The four of them had snuck across a field, so they could scout what they were facing at the base. The dark gave them cover, but he worried about infrared sensors. However, if they were able to drive a car across the lonely state without being spotted, he thought they simply weren't looking for strangers.

"They sure make it easy to see them, don't they?" he replied. "It's like they don't even know a war's going on." The long runway was designed for the heaviest and biggest aircraft in the United States' arsenal. He guessed it was every bit of three miles long. In a wartime scenario, the base would have all its lights off and the valuable aircraft would be spread out or stowed away in hangars. The neat rows of fighter jets suggested it wasn't a fluke they weren't detected. Whoever was running the base apparently had no fear of being attacked.

Meechum slid over to him. "I count fifty jets, twenty of the big transports, and at least seventy-five private jets. There's likely more in the hangars, but the doors are closed."

He privately thought of how much damage he could inflict if he could steal a fully-loaded fighter. It would only take one strafing run along the row of parked planes to destroy a good part of the air fleet. The Imperial Japanese Navy did the same thing to the USA back at Pearl Harbor. It was almost a textbook example of what not to do. He was wary about underestimating a military opponent, no matter how inept they seemed at face value, so he continued his observations.

"And you should know," Meechum continued, "most of those planes aren't ours."

At first, he thought his eyes had played a trick on him, or Meechum was wrong. The Air Force

C-5 Galaxies were right in front of him, obvious to all. However, as he looked behind the first of the four-engine transport jets, there were similar cargo haulers from other nations. A big Antonov Condor sat in the line, as did a Chinese Y-20 Chubby Girl. Twenty of the largest transport aircraft in the world were lined up as one juicy honeypot.

"You're right. Many of the heavies are from other nations. The fighters aren't all ours, either," he added. "I recognize the Russian and Chinese airframes, but there're some on the end I've never seen before." He reflected on what it all meant. Were they there to protect the nuclear arsenal of the United States, or were they there to capture it? If the call had gone out asking other countries to help, any of the planes could have flown over the North Pole and landed in North Dakota within twenty-four hours of the attack. Why they were Russian and Chinese, rather than allies like Great Britain or Germany, he couldn't say.

"What the hell are those?" Kyla pointed to smaller objects moving at the edge of the airstrip, a bit outside the ambiance provided by the powerful spotlights on the tarmac. They were on the near side of the pavement, walking in the tall, reedy grass.

Ted watched for a full minute, content to study the new threat before making a call about what to do. The problem was, he wasn't sure what they were. At first glance, they looked like a couple of people walking in the grass while holding a mailbox high over their heads, post and all.

"They look like giraffes, don't they?" Kyla finally asked.

"Yes!" he said excitedly, but also at a whisper. The giraffes loped through the grass with about a hundred yards between the two. As they kept watching, a third appeared another hundred yards behind. "Whatever they are, they're walking in a loop around the runway."

"Guards?" Emily asked.

"Sentries," Meechum added. "And that's not all. Look over there." She led Ted's eyes to a distant section of the airport, next to one of the giant hangars. There was a large space between the cargo planes and the next row of fighter jets, which allowed him to see the lighted area behind them. Four military tanks sat in a perfect line.

He sighed, still unsure what was going on. Were they the good guys or the bad guys? Ted wasn't up to snuff on every tank in the world, but he figured the Marine ground-pounder would know. "Can you make out who those tanks belong to?"

She squinted as if trying hard to make the ID, but she gave up and glanced over at him. "I want to say they're M1s, but they have some sort of mesh camo on their upper hulls. If they're American, they're configured in a new way."

He chewed on his lip, working out what to do next. They couldn't go forward, that was obvious, but they needed to get inside.

"Meechum, can you tell me which building we need for the computer coding we're going to do?"

She studied the base for a few seconds. "Not from here, but I'm sure once we get in, I'll recognize it." She hesitated before going on. "If we get separated, or I don't make it, the building is labeled as Maintenance and Parts."

Kyla scooted closer to him. "Uncle Ted, do you think this is a good idea? Just the four of us against an army?"

What could he do? The President of the United States needed to disarm the nuclear arsenal. Who else had the ability to do it? He immediately thought of where he might send Kyla so she was out of danger, but unless he was willing to tie her to a chair, she would never allow him to get away with it. Her mom would probably rip his head off if she knew where he'd taken her, but there was no obvious place where she'd be safe. Therefore, logically, he figured the safest place was with him.

"Let's retreat for tonight. We'll study the base operations tomorrow, in the light, to see if patterns emerge. Some of us have to find a way inside." He didn't beat her over the head with the word 'some,' but he'd laid the groundwork for having her wait outside the base while he went in.

I can't afford any losses.

The Stinky Place

Deogee was as happy as she'd been since leaving the Bad Place. She'd found her new friend Biscuit and together, they'd taken off after the scent trail left by the young female human who'd befriended her. Today, they'd been reunited.

"Biscuit! Stop running!" Deogee cried out for her friend as the black dog ran circles around the two-legged Tabby. Biscuit was overly excited, and she wanted her to settle so they could both cash in on the lovins from her new human friend.

She looked across the river to see the hot flames ravaging the tall rocks standing there, but she didn't stare for long. Fire had burned her back at the Bad Place, and she wanted nothing to do with it ever again. However, she kept one ear on the crackling noise coming from across the river to ensure it wasn't getting closer. If it did, she was going to warn her humans.

"This is hilarious!" Biscuit barked at her with relentless running. "I'm making myself sick to my stomach going in circles!"

Deogee loved having Biscuit around, but it was a lot like what she imagined if she had pups. The black lab was always playing, always getting into trouble. "Then stop running!"

Their conversations were never quiet. She knew humans didn't like her loud voice, but she wanted to control Biscuit for them.

Deogee managed to nip at her flank, but she got away.

"Faster! Faster! Faster!" Biscuit insisted as her spiral loop got tighter around Tabby's feet.

All at once, Deogee halted. A new odor was on the air, even more odd than the smelly place below them. Tabby kept using the word warehouse, whatever that meant. A few seconds later, a whirring sound caught her attention.

Must warn her!

Deogee ran by and nudged one of Tabby's two, long paws. "We have to leave!"

Her human waved at her. "Not now, girl." Instead of running for safety, Tabby continued talking with complicated words Deogee didn't understand.

Deogee worked through how to warn her pack. She gathered all her anxiety and fear into a ball and let it out as a long growl.

Biscuit finally stopped when she heard the call to order. The lab got into fight-or-flight mode, dropping her tail, bending her ears, and paying attention. Deogee was pleased. The humans came to attention, too.

Tabby's scent changed immediately. She oozed worry as the unnatural noise came closer. It was the same sound made by that white floating box that showed up when she got burned.

The humans got the message; they ran for the door back into the stinky warehouse. However, before she could follow like she wanted, Biscuit resumed running in circles. This time, it wasn't for fun.

"Come!" the human Tabby cried out. A deep instinct told her to respond to the female pack leader, but she was responsible for her friend Biscuit.

Deogee barked repeatedly, hoping Tabby would understand. "I can't come yet!"

Biscuit ran in more circles, as if she was broken. "It's too much! The smells. The orange across the water. Something's coming!"

"Deogee, come!" Tabby shrieked from inside the doorway.

"I want to," she barked back.

Biscuit's claws tapped on the hard roof as she ran all around with the crazies. Deogee was torn. She'd been given a direct order. Save her friend or follow the alpha? After fruitlessly yelling at the lab, she turned to the door, but Tabby was gone.

They always disappear.

Her focus went back to Biscuit, and for several long minutes, she chased the other dog, knowing it was the only way to stop her. It wasn't as easy as running on grass, and it took much longer than it should have. The smaller dog was able to cut corners sharper than she could, and in the end, she only managed to stop the insane pup because she ran out of gas.

They both panted with relief.

"Are you better?" she asked Biscuit.

"Where did the female go?" the black lab asked, apparently oblivious to the last few minutes. "And what's making those sounds downstairs?"

It was difficult to understand the world of humans. They lived in strange houses with many things that weren't a bowl of food or a warm bed. They also went from place to place in little houses with black wheels. Those were made from material she couldn't chew through, and they carried horrible smells.

Below, at that very moment, one of their strange objects was making the same sound as those ugly machines. Even from so far away, she smelled the scents from all three of the humans. They were in fear for their lives.

"Come on, we have to help them!" she ordered.

Biscuit didn't complain. She followed.

Deogee went down the stairs and jumped into a battle blur to help. The rattle of a noisy black tube destroyed the lower part of the steps, nearly hurting Biscuit. The humans had noisy sticks, too. They caused such intense roars over and over. Still, Deogee bit into an enemy's metal leg. The big, disgusting animal threatened her alpha.

Biscuit offered moral support as she barked behind her. "Kill it! Get it! Tear it in half!"

Deogee wished she could yell for her friend to grab onto the second monster, instead of Biscuit running around being her usual chatterbox self. However, she couldn't let go of the first beast to get the words out. One of her teeth cracked under the weight of holding on, but she wasn't giving up. Not while Tabby was afraid of the two monsters.

She thought she was doing good until a wall collapsed, and a new sound turned on. It was immediately painful, as if Biscuit was barking right in her ear.

A new human machine approached. It had strange, elongated feet that dragged it close to Tabby. It was huge, maybe ten Deogees in height. It was unlike anything she'd ever imagined in her puppy dreams.

The new sound from the odd machine kept ramping up, but she still hung on to the smaller metal animal with her teeth.

Must protect the Tabby.

Deogee hadn't realized the noise could get louder, but soon it became painful. Her eyes vibrated in their sockets and she greatly wanted to put her paws over her ears. Still, she refused to let go and run.

Her human alpha exploded with the smell of fear, like she was about to be left alone at home for the day. Tabby was next to the giant machine, waving her upper paws and yelling at it, "Wait!"

In a flash, the painful sound got in her head, and everything went black, like Deogee had her eyes closed.

Tabby? Where are you?

East St. Louis, IL, three minutes earlier

Tabby and her two friends were up against the wall with two machine guns pointed at them. One of the white floating drones hovered above the two horse-robots, and there was nowhere left to go. It seemed like her time on Earth was reaching an end.

All I need is a blindfold and a cigarette.

The drones were so confident of their supremacy they didn't even ask her and the two teens to drop their weapons. She hung onto her shotgun, tentatively pointing it at one of the horses, figuring maybe she could damage one before it shot her dead.

A flash of darkness caught her eye, and it went toward the horse-drone closest to her. The machine stumbled sideways as if someone had climbed on. A second shape came down the stairs after the first, which seemed to catch the attention of the remaining drone. Tabby did the math and figured out the happy-go-lucky Biscuit had followed the much more serious Deogee, now chomping repeatedly at the first drone.

"Leave them alone!" Tabby shouted as she lunged at the robot. The instant she touched it, her ears nearly burst with all the explosions generated by the chain gun on the back of the horse's framework. The steps where Biscuit had been running were ripped apart by the bullets, though she couldn't see if the dog caught some of the shots, too.

The floating drone acted like the brain for all the others. "Warning: To avoid additional pain, please cease resistance."

"You want us to make our deaths easier on ourselves?" Tabby shouted, sure the programmed voice had no sense of humor, even the dark kind.

"No thanks!" Peter shrieked, before letting loose with his shotgun.

Tabby joined in, knowing there was nothing to lose. She'd been holding her shotgun at the ready, so she separated from the robot and trained the barrel on what should have been the face of the mechanical creature. Her ears had been dulled by the intense concussions of the heavy machine gun, so the shotgun blast sounded tame by comparison.

The shot ricocheted off the heavy shield-like mantlet protecting the head in a thunderous light show of sparks.

She fired again, but her aim was ruined when the horse snapped a leg sideways, pushing her onto the filthy tiled floor. That gave the machine time to reorient on its companion and aim its gun toward Deogee as if it had no care for hitting its partner robot.

"No!" she screamed into the din.

The machine gun barrel on the first robot started spinning, but then it stopped before any bullets came out. Deogee continued to maul the second robot, though Tabby figured her efforts were hopeless if her shotgun couldn't even dent it.

The floating drone came down a few feet, hovering over the madness. "Warning: Breach imminent. Please step away from outer wall."

Tabby jumped toward Audrey and Peter, who were both still up against the wall. Peter held his shotgun without shooting, and Tabby stopped her firing, too. They couldn't shoot while Deogee was tied up with the machines. Biscuit was in there, too. The black lab ran in circles around one of the enemy shapes, barking constantly.

The wall next to them caved in, filling the immediate area with an explosion of dust and debris, followed by giant spotlights. A tracked vehicle came through the breach and haze. It was as big as a tank and seemed to have no trouble getting through the brick wall and rolling onto the warehouse floor.

At first, she huddled with Audrey and Peter, simply to stay clear of the machine and the junk falling from the wall. However, when she regained her presence of mind, she stood in front of the kids, though fighting a tank could only end one way.

When the smoke cleared enough to see movement, and the last few bricks fell from the wall, the white drone floated back into view with a new message. "Please stand by for localized reboot."

"Screw that," she said under her breath.

Deogee hadn't let up a bit on the backside of the robot horse. She kept her grip on wires and hoses that seemed to come out of its rear leg. The dog snarled and shook itself back and forth as if the haunch was a chew-toy.

The second horse stood there looking at the first, its gun trained on Deogee as she moved. Tabby figured it would open fire the moment it was clear of its partner, which made her hesitate to interfere. If she called the dog off and made her come over, the second machine would shoot her. If she let her continue, the best case was she somehow managed to disable the robot and then get shot by the other one.

The tank's wheels squeaked in the treads, like metal on metal, but she didn't look back until a hum started up. She glanced back, aware that the deep resonance of the hum was so low as to barely be heard. It was, however, shaking her teeth with bass.

"What the—" She turned around to process what the tank had become. Unlike every other tank she'd ever seen, this one had no gun on the top. Instead of a turret, the metal superstructure had spread out, a bit like a radar dish. It was curved, about ten feet tall and twenty wide, and it crackled with electrical energy. It pointed toward the two metal horse-bots, which created the illusion the net was going to be used to retrieve them.

Deogee hadn't let go of the backside of the robot, and even though Biscuit wasn't chomping at metal, she barked excitedly next to the wolf, as if telling her what to do. Tabby took a step in the tank's direction, afraid it was going to hurt the pups. "Wait!"

The hum rose to such a level that she had to put her hands over her ears, though it barely helped. She happened to be looking at the wolf-dog as it relentlessly tore at its target. As the hum became unbearable, Deogee disappeared. Biscuit seemed to run behind an invisible curtain as she went away, too.

The robots were still there. They recovered from their assault and both shifted orientations, so they faced her and the kids. One of the tracks on the tank went backward, scraping the floor with a squeal, which changed the facing of the metal mesh of the radar dish. None of that mattered, however, as she figured out the dogs were gone.

"You killed my dog," she said dryly. Then, realizing it had really happened, she lost it. "You killed my dog!" She oriented her gun on the drone, which shifted up to avoid what was coming. Tabby fired but missed. "I'm going to kill whoever is behind that drone!"

The tank's hum began again, as if it needed a short time to build to critical mass.

She fired repeatedly, vaguely aware the mechanical horses had come to attention nearby with chain guns trained on the three of them left in the warehouse. She'd never been more frightened in her life, but she'd never been as sure of the need to fight back.

The flying drone made it behind a metal pillar as Tabby and Peter both unleashed shots at it. The intense gunshots no longer mattered. The painful hum almost drowned out both shotguns, and it made it easier to crank out all the rounds she had left in the magazine.

In the back of her awareness, she knew there was no hope. If the machine guns didn't cut her down, the hum was going to make her disappear like the dogs. An enemy with such incredible weapons couldn't be stopped.

Out of ammo, she held the shotgun out in front of her as a blocker. The barrel was too hot to hold, so she kept her hand on the front stock. Peter was out of ammo, too. He held his shotgun like a baseball bat.

"Come on, you bastards!" she shouted. Her legs wobbled in her stretch pants, but she made herself hold position. Audrey covered her ears.

Peter stepped in front of her. A few moments later, the intense auditory assault rose to such a level, it could have been coming from inside her brain.

Whatever it was that zapped out and got Deogee and Biscuit, it was coming for her next.

Love you forever, Mom and Dad.

TWENTY-ONE

Minot, ND

After getting a first look at their target, Ted insisted they retreat to somewhere safe, so they could talk about what to do next. They got back in the car and drove a few miles down the road to a small abandoned food store. Once inside, they made a layout of the base using canned goods. While eating their favorite foods, they talked about possible entry points that would put them closest to where Meechum thought they'd find the correct building.

After an hour of talk, and with a full belly, Ted's eyelids suddenly weighed fifty pounds each, despite the important business they were conducting below the bright halogen lamps. Emily noticed his condition after one or two head bobs. "Ted, we both could use some sleep. Why don't we get a few hours of shut-eye?"

He waved her off. "I slept in the car. You ladies can hit the hay. I want to stay up to keep watch."

The three women looked at each other in a way he didn't like. Emily turned back to him. "No one gets good sleep in a car. These two got some decent zees in the plane; they'll keep watch for us." She motioned to Kyla and the Marine.

He tried to blow it off again. "I'll drink some coffee. There's a whole store of the stuff."

"Nope," Emily replied. "Are you going to argue, or am I going to have to pull rank? I'm your commander-in-chief. I can order you to rest." Before he could think up a response, she grabbed his arm and dragged him away from the soup-can mockup of the air base. Meechum and Kyla stifled laughter on his way out.

"Come on, tough guy," she said quietly. "I found some throw pillows you can use for your head."

In his mind, he fought the noble battle to list the reasons why he needed to stay awake, but he couldn't come up with good ones. Flying the plane and riding in the world's most uncomfortable car had taken their tolls on him. The stress of getting close, but not too close, to the runway had added to the physical toll. By the time she had him on the floor, pillows as promised, he was ready to listen to her.

"You know, you're pretty handy to have around, and not just because you're the President of the United States..." He hung it out there, implication thick on the air, but he didn't follow it up with the words his heart truly wanted to say. He'd been with her almost every waking minute for the past three days and he'd come to depend on her, but he couldn't come out and say anything more personal. Not in the middle of a military operation.

"Oh?" she said with exaggerated doubt. "I assume you mean because I can fly a plane and drive a boat, right, Major MacInnis?"

Her brown eyes shimmered in the harsh white light of the grocery store, and he was tired beyond belief, but he knew she was yanking his chain. Still, as much as he wanted to pull her down and kiss her, he closed his eyes.

"No, it's because you can drive a train..."

Emily stood there for ten or fifteen seconds as if building to a reply, but he heard her shoes turn on the tiles and take a few steps away. "Good night, Ted. You're pretty handy to have around, too."

His last thought about Emily was more practical.

This really is a comfy pillow.

Folsom, CA

Dwight managed to stay upright on the bike as he followed Bernard to the supply truck. They took turns filling up their flamethrower tanks, then they drove a few more miles to a rocky field where a large troupe of other bikers had bedded down for the night. He pulled out a light sleeping bag that had been in one of his bike's saddlebags.

Bernard took him to the far end of the field, so they were in an area with less people. Poppy laughed the whole way, asking Dwight over and over how anyone could sleep with two motorcycles breaking the silence. He, in turn, shushed her several times. It would cause too many questions if a talkative bird woke people up.

When he finally laid down on the hard ground, he fell right asleep. However, hours later, his slumber was interrupted when Poppy pecked at his exposed head. He retreated down into his bag but left a small opening so he could talk to her.

"No, you stupid cow, I'm not going to get it out now." He didn't want anyone to know he'd taken an extra bottle from the liquor store. It was only flask-size, but he'd snagged it when he followed Bernard out the door. Why Poppy wanted him to get it out was beyond him, though he really wanted to drink it.

The bird cawed loudly, and he craned his neck a bit outside the bag to see if anyone had heard her. Bernard was about ten feet away, behind his parked motorcycle, but he didn't stir, even when Poppy flapped a few feet above his head.

"Why don't I leave?" he asked, repeating her question. "Do you see all these men in black? They aren't here for a Johnny Cash convention!" He clumsily pointed left and right, speaking as quietly as possible. "They're here to destroy everything in the cities."

She laughed at his hypocrisy.

"I don't want to see the big surprise. Why would you say that? All I want right now is a warm blanket and something warmer in my stomach." Suddenly, he realized he did want to bring out the flask, no matter who was close by.

Poppy wouldn't let it go, and he wouldn't agree she was right, so he got into a spiral of arguments with her. At first, it was about the surprise, but the back-and-forth started to include the hidden flask, his shaky hands, and it came back around to a heated argument about how many cats were sleeping in his bed at that moment back in San Francisco. From there, their chatter descended into one of his "crazy scenes."

He knew it was happening while it took place, but he was powerless to stop it. The voice coming out of his mouth seemed detached. He had plenty of room to roll around in his sealed sleeping bag too, as if it helped him make his point. By the time Bernard stopped him from rolling and shook him like a madman, he sensed that he'd been shouting at Poppy at the top of his lungs.

Dwight sprang up like he'd awakened from a nightmare.

"Did anyone see us?" he asked Poppy in a lowered voice.

Despite it being the middle of the night, dozens of men sat up in their sleeping bags. He saw them in the starlight.

"Someone did," Bernard answered dryly.

Amarillo, TX

Brent's plan had to be simple, given the composition of his ad hoc fighting unit. The petty criminals weren't good at strategic planning, but they did know how to drive trucks and tell time. After getting a few hours of sleep, he had everyone ferry the trucks from their suburban oasis to two locations closer to the airport. He chose to park his group of trucks along a four-lane road about two miles from the paved runway. A small rise in the grass fields between there and the airport terminal blocked direct line-of-sight to the destination; he'd scouted the location earlier in the evening.

A second group of three men prepped their trucks a mile away. He'd spread them out so they wouldn't all be caught if the enemy finally scouted the area. He also figured it doubled his chances of hitting the long airport runway. However, those men had rejoined him so they could hear his pep talk.

"Gentlemen, and lady," he said, looking at Trish, "I want to explain what we're trying to accomplish, because once we do this, I think we're going to be on their shit list. If anyone wants to back out, be my guest. I'll give you a head start on your escape from them." He chuckled, confident no one was going to abandon him. They'd all seen the attack firsthand and on the replay tapes back at the prison.

Brent's team gathered in a half-circle around him as he stood on the sidestep of a brand-new tanker truck. "The bastards over there are so confident we're dead, they aren't even out here looking for us. We'll only get one chance to do this right, so that's why I've had you all bring as many trucks as you could get your hands on."

They'd used the early evening hours to prepare the basics on each vehicle. That included attaching the five-gallon buckets of bolts and rebar, rigging up the copper wiring into the cabins, and preparing the heavy cinderblocks for each gas pedal. The last piece of the puzzle was in his hand.

"We've got to be careful with these babies, okay?" The orange road flare was about eight inches long and an inch wide, with a removable cap on one end. "Once we open the spigots, you can't get sloppy with these." He waved it in his hand, making sure everyone saw it.

"Does anyone have any questions?" He hadn't yet given them the final plan, so he expected some confusion, given that it was three in the morning. His intention was to execute his plan at the time of day when the enemy was most tired, but his men were tired, too.

Trish raised her hand. "Are we going back to the same house where we parked the trucks earlier?"

At first, that was the plan, but over the last few hours, he'd begun to worry more and more about being discovered. If there were satellites watching from space, they might be curious about why all those trucks had parked there and then moved. If they went back, they might find themselves in more trouble. Instead, he'd come to a different conclusion.

"After the attack, I want you to drive that way." He pointed west on the four-lane highway. It would go through the town of Amarillo and from there, they would get closer to the prison. He didn't want them going straight there, though, lest they bring the bad guys with them. "Not back to our home, but to the Cadillac Ranch."

The ranch was a local tourist trap where someone had buried ten old Cadillacs in a field, face down, so their back halves stuck out of the soil. The graffiti-laced cars were right off the highway on the far side of the city. Once they linked back up, he would return to the prison using a longer route.

Silent nods all around.

"All right. Let's do this. Check your watches. It's now coming up on three-oh-five." They used the new watches from Walmart to synchronize with the three men at the other job site, so they all launched the attack at the same time. "We start in ten minutes, at three-fifteen precisely."

He watched and waited as the three men drove away, but ten minutes passed in what felt like seconds. "All right, open the valves and start your engines," he said to Trish, Cliff, and Kevin. "It's time to kick the tires and light the fires."

He hopped into the cabin of the tanker truck and started her up. The lights had all been punched out with a hammer, so there was no chance of exposing them to the enemy. He drove it about twenty yards off the highway, facing the airport. It was easy to do since the grassy ground was almost perfectly flat. While the motor idled, he climbed down and opened several valves under the tanker, so fuel spilled into the soil. The two others did the same for their tractor-trailers. Kevin stayed in his cabin, since he drove a dump truck.

After completing their tasks, everyone returned to their cabs.

"This is it," he said to himself, putting it in gear.

Cliff had his truck moving, as did Trish. Kevin was a bit slower getting his trash truck rolling, but soon the four of them slowly drove their big rigs toward the airport.

He picked up the flare, wondering if he was about to blow himself, and everyone else, to Kingdom Come.

If this is how it ends, I pray it goes fast.

Brent removed the cap, touched off the flare to start it, and tossed it onto the floorboard of the passenger seat. By the time it got to the airport, he expected the whole interior of the cab would be up in flames, spiking the chances it would touch off the rest of the tanker when the truck hit a plane or anything else at the target site.

He gave the rig more gas, working through the gears until he was in third and the truck was moving at about fifteen miles-per-hour. It took a bit of effort to move the cinderblock where he needed it, but once it was on the gas pedal, it wasn't going anywhere. He patted the five-gallon bucket of buckshot seat-belted into the passenger seat. The last thing he did was link a carabiner onto the steering wheel. It was linked to the copper wire, which was bound to the far door. It would keep the truck pointed in the right direction.

"Give 'em hell," he said to the big rig.

Brent opened the door and easily jumped off, though his arthritic knees screamed at his insensitivity toward them. As he struggled to his feet, a driverless dump truck rolled by about ten yards to his left. A second tanker went by on his right, spilling fuel by the gallon since its spigot, like his truck's, was wide open. He could barely see the orange glow of the flare in the other cabin.

"Don't stop now!" he yelled to his friends as loud as he dared. He'd planned it so each person would launch four trucks. He figured they could do one per minute, easily, but more than that would increase their risk of getting caught or having something go wrong. He liked to have a wide margin of safety for his people.

Three minutes later, sixteen giant trucks lumbered across the pre-dawn expanse of Amarillo soil toward bright "hit me!" lights on the horizon. As they stood there watching the shapes move away, he likened them to deadly torpedoes dropped in the water, heading for the enemy aircraft carrier.

"Let's hope the others got their trucks launched," Trish remarked.

"I didn't hear a premature explosion, so I guess Carter didn't screw it up," Cliff laughed.

"Yeah, maybe he didn't burn down his dad's place, after all," Kevin agreed.

"You were all innocent, the way I heard it," Trish joked, coming out of her shell a little.

"We're all guilty tonight," Brent cautioned. "Let's get the hell out of here, guys. Cliff, you take Kevin with you. I'll drive with Trish." He wanted to watch the explosion to see if they'd succeeded, but the fire would soon follow the spilled fuel back across the field. It would effectively create an arrow pointing to where the attack had come from. "Move out!"

Once he and Trish were on the road, he looked in his rearview mirror almost constantly for the next five minutes. If the trucks kept pace and stayed on course, they should have crossed the two miles in less than ten minutes. As they sped into the empty city, he began to wonder if all the torpedoes had missed.

Trish watched her side mirror constantly. "Will we even see it?" she wondered aloud.

"I would think—"

The horizon behind them glowed for an instant, like a single burst of lightning had struck. A few seconds later, when it didn't show up again, he was convinced the attack had fizzled. Maybe the flares didn't touch off the big tanks of gasoline, or the buckets of shrapnel didn't fly through the air and blow apart neighboring planes, or the trucks blew up before they reached the target...

Before he could voice his misgivings, a second light made a more substantial impression in his mirror. A plume of fire rose up like a miniature nuclear bomb had gone off. It kept growing bigger in his mirror, causing him to wonder if they were in any danger. Despite the threat of being chased, or getting hit with flying debris from miles away, he had to stop the car.

"What are you doing?" Trish asked with surprise.

"We just hit them back. I'm going to take a minute to enjoy it." He kept the car running but opened his door and stepped outside.

Secondary explosions ripped through the airport, each sending up new plumes of fire that joined the big one towering above the others. The shockwave of each new blast pushed against his face, and he heard and felt the rumble of the deadly explosions. An experience he found strangely comforting.

He gave the airport the finger. "That's what you get when you mess with Texas."

TWENTY-TWO

Minot, ND

Ted woke up to the sound of motorcycles on the road outside. Emily was asleep next to him on one of the throw pillows and she stirred at his movement.

"Someone's here!" he whispered.

The roar of the bikes went on for almost a minute. He ran to the front window of the store, rifle in hand, and found Meechum and Kyla already looking outside. He had to shield his eyes from the sunshine, rising low in the southeast. The last few bikes went by on the rural, two-lane road. The flat terrain let him see there were at least a hundred bikers riding on heavily-modified machines. They carried a strange tank behind the driver's seats. They looked a little like giant vacuum cleaners.

He tapped Meechum on the shoulder. "Were these the first ones to go out?"

"Yes," she replied. "There hasn't been a single vehicle all night."

He looked to the left, toward the air base, and noticed a smaller group of riders approaching. They slowed as they got close, giving him pause. "These guys are stopping."

Emily had come up behind him. "What's happening?"

There were seven guys in two rows behind the leader. They were dressed in black uniforms, though he saw no flags or other designation as to what nation they worked for. The leader waved to his followers, and Ted was sure they were coming into the food store parking lot.

"No," he whispered, clutching the rifle.

As they reached the turnoff to the store, the leader gave his bike a little gas and turned into a lot across the street. A fast-food burger joint sat diagonally to the food store on the other side of the two-lane roadway.

"Phew," Kyla exhaled.

"We have to assume they'll come in here. We've got to hide," he insisted.

"We can fight," Kyla said with determination in her voice.

It warmed his heart to hear her say it, but the time wasn't right. If they killed someone so close to the base, it wouldn't be hard to find who did it. Plus, there were at least a hundred motorcyclists available to hunt them down. The smart play was to hide.

Ted tried to be diplomatic. "And we will, Kyla, but right now, we have to lay low. Our mission is to get into the air base, not protect some little mom and pop shop."

Meechum looked outside while hiding behind a shelf full of two-liter Mountain Dew bottles. She tapped on one to get his attention. "They're off their bikes. What are they doing with that equipment?"

The men had parked their bikes in a semi-circle around the burger shack, leaving about fifty feet between the bikes and the structure—enough room they'd have to shout if they wanted to talk to someone inside. For a few seconds, Ted thought they were the police and had come to collect a criminal, but then one of the men used his vacuum cleaner hose to spray a clear liquid on the colorful red siding. The others kicked on their sprays an instant later, and then the streams all erupted in flames, which followed the spray until it engulfed the building.

"Oh, hell no!" Emily growled. "We're not going out like that."

Ted couldn't breathe for a few seconds. He could almost feel the heat of those weapons from across the street. Fear reached up from the tiled floor and paralyzed him for a short time. Dying by fire was practically the worst fate he could imagine.

The president touched his arm, which pulled him immediately out of his paralysis. "Ted, what do you want to do?"

He gave her a curt thank-you nod. "We stay here, for now, but I don't think we can afford to let those guys get close. Those flamethrowers have insane range. We'd be on fire before we knew they were here." He had a sudden nightmare about other bikers parked behind the country store. Even at that moment, they could be dialing up their hardware to splash liquid fire through the back door.

"Meechum, you check the back. Make sure we have a path to run if things get too crazy. The car is back there if we need it." Though every parking lot had abandoned vehicles, he'd wanted to keep his car closer to the structure. His worry had paid off.

It only took the fire starters a few minutes to ensure the entire fast food joint was engulfed in flames. They even walked around to the side and torched the drive-through ordering station. When they were done, they holstered their weapons and gave each other high-fives.

"Here we go," he said. "If they come over here, we'll have to—" He cut himself short when the leader started his bike, revved his motor, and did a wheelie across the highway. He put the front wheel down when he came onto the lot for the store.

"Shit," he said with forced calm. "This is happening." He looked at Kyla. "Go get Meechum. Bring your rifle and any spare ammo."

He had a minute alone with Emily. They watched in silence as the rest of the men got on their rides and crossed the street. He kept on the lookout for more bikes up and down the highway, but there didn't seem to be any others close by. That was great, but they still had to deal with the seven right in front of them.

"Can we do this?" Emily asked quietly.

Ted met her eyes. "We have to."

Meechum's heavy boots clopped on the tile floor as she ran back to her spot behind the soda. "What's the plan?" she asked.

Ted gave Emily a serious glance, then looked to the Marine and his arriving niece. It wasn't much of a defensive unit, but they had the element of surprise on their side. The men in the lot hopped off their bikes and still high-fived each other like they'd won the Superbowl, but there wasn't much time to organize his friends.

"We're in a line," he said matter-of-factly. "When they get ready out there, only shoot at the bastards closest to your end. When they get their flamethrowers ready, we'll try to drop them all at once." It would be tough, since there were four of them and seven of the enemy. He'd thought about shooting them as they came into the lot, but he worried the chaos would give one of them a chance to dive behind a parked car or ride away. If he waited until they were primed for the attack, they would be vulnerable.

"Spread out a little." He motioned for the women to give about five feet between each other. What he didn't say was that if one of the guys shot a spray of flames, it couldn't get them all at once. If he'd had more time to prepare, he might have sent someone onto the roof, or the side of the building, to give multiple angles of attack. Unfortunately, he didn't have a second to spare. He had to summarize years of marksmanship into a few canned phrases, mostly for Kyla's benefit, he assumed. "Aim for the big part of their body, not their heads. Breathe steady. Squeeze—"

Kyla interrupted. "I've been trained by the best, Unk. I'll do you proud."

He was a proud uncle, no doubt about it. Her mom would be yelling bloody murder at him for putting her daughter in such a dangerous spot once again, but he figured even she'd be proud of how Kyla was able to defend herself.

"On three," Ted said quietly. He aimed his rifle center of mass on the guy giving the orders, right in the middle of the seven men.

"One..."

The black-clad figures slowly moved into their positions, creating a semi-circle in front of the store. Their leader waved back and forth to spread them out from each other, the same as Ted had done to his force.

"Two..."

Once he seemed happy with the deployment, the head guy lifted his flamethrower wand.

"Three!"

East St. Louis, IL

Tabby faced the unusual tank with her spine straight and without flinching. The hum created by the machine made her eyeballs shake in their sockets, and her stomach wanted to return its contents, but she wasn't giving anyone the satisfaction of seeing her show fear. To make the point, she stood in front of Audrey and Peter.

"Come on! Just try it!" she screamed, knowing it was insane.

The teens had been holding hands, but each also put a palm on her shoulders. She heard them saying "I love you," to each other, adding to the sense it was all about to end.

At least we'll go out together.

The tank's energy seemed to peak, and she believed it was about to zap her, but it abruptly shut off. The heightened tension and unsettling vibrations left her legs wobbly. The three of them had to hold each other up.

That was when the men in black jumpsuits ran in.

"Who are you?" Tabby yelled, still fighting the effects of the machine. "We demand to see someone in charge! Why did you kill my dogs?"

The strange men didn't reply. They searched them for weapons then dragged the three of them into a Humvee parked outside the warehouse. Hours went by as they were transferred to different modes of transportation, including a plane, but they finally ended up in what seemed like a prison van.

"Are we there yet?" Peter laughed from within the small cabin of the vehicle. It seemed like they were in the enclosed back of a pickup truck, but it was small, and quiet, and with barely enough room for the three of them, so she couldn't say for sure. A small window on the back door let in a little morning light, but it was frosted, preventing them from seeing where they were.

The ambush in the warehouse had scared them all, but the brush with death affected them in different ways. For Tabby, after the tank-like machine didn't vaporize her and the kids, the emotional unpacking only made her glad the kids were still alive. She hadn't even tried to fight back against the men. Once captured, she maintained reserved vigilance, sure there would be a chance to escape.

"No, we're not," Tabby said for the tenth time. "You're worse than a child," she sniped, not feeling the least bit like a tour guide or protector at that moment. She turned to Audrey, wondering if she would defend her boyfriend. The young teen had become quiet and withdrawn, saying almost nothing the entire night. There wasn't even a flash of her normal spunky attitude present. It was like she'd given up.

Peter, however, was the exact opposite. He couldn't stop laughing at the fact they'd been captured, chucked into a plane, and flown to an unknown location. When the men in black outfits threw them in the truck after the plane landed, he acted like it was the final insult. He puked out curse words for several minutes, but there was no evidence anyone heard him. From there, he settled for annoying Tabby with his are-we-there-yet routine.

They were on the road for at least half an hour when the vehicle leaned a little to one side, slowed, then turned off. The new pitch made the three of them slide to the right side. "We're there!" Peter yelled.

The machine turned back on, and the vibration suggested the driver was trying to reverse. After the attempt failed, the machine went forward a bit, then back, as if rocking out of an icy patch of road, though it didn't feel cold outside.

The effort went on for a few minutes before the truck stopped moving. The silence was disconcerting to Tabby, since there was no way to know what was out there. They could be at the bottom of a ravine, or along the edge at the top. It was a little like being in the pitch-black waters of the Bonne Terre Mine. If you didn't have a point of reference, there was no way to know where you were or even if you were right-side up.

Finally, a voice spoke from a small speaker on the ceiling. "You need to get out and push." He did not sound happy.

Peter wasn't pleased, either. "Push it yourself!" He looked at Tabby with a bemused expression. "Can you believe these guys? It's just like before. Like we're going to help them kill us!"

She wondered about that. They could have easily killed them with the tank's electro-beam, or whatever force killed Deogee and Biscuit, but it didn't fire at them. When the soldiers in black came in, they could have killed her and the kids without breaking a sweat. The only logical answer was they'd been captured for a reason.

The speaker voice returned. "I'm opening the back door. Get out, but do not run. If you do...well, you don't want to know what we'd do to you." The voice sounded overly dramatic, like they were hoping to scare them into compliance.

"Let's get this over with," Tabby declared.

The door clicked and swung open, letting in bright rays of sunshine. She fought against it until her eyes adjusted. When she climbed out, the scenery was breathtaking, despite putting her foot in six inches of mud. "We're heading for the mountains," she said dryly.

Peter helped Audrey out of the vehicle and carried her across the mud to the paved road next to it. Tabby followed, if only to get out of the slop, too.

"Donny wouldn't have liked this," Peter said in a reflective tone. "He wouldn't have wanted to get his fancy shoes muddy."

She and Audrey chuckled, knowing it was true.

"I wish they wouldn't have taken my police belt," Peter continued, speaking in a more upbeat fashion. "My pants keep falling down."

That got them all laughing again.

The new position gave them all a chance to see what they'd been traveling in. The truck wasn't like anything she'd seen on the roads before. It looked like a little milk truck. It had the cargo space in the back but didn't have a driver's compartment. It had been sealed off, without windows, like it wasn't necessary. There was a grid of solar panels spread out on the top, giving her the final clue about what it was.

"Your solar-powered truck doesn't have the horsepower to get out of the mud, does it?" Tabby spoke to the speaker inside the back, assuming there was a microphone there, too. It was the only explanation that made any sense. The computer or remote-controller of the vehicle had veered too close to the edge of the shoulder. Now, it was mired in mud and didn't have the necessary torque to get unstuck.

She realized what a golden opportunity had been handed to her. Before she listened to the reply, she pulled the two teens about twenty feet behind the machine. "We can get out of here." Tabby pointed to a line of trees not more than fifty feet from the edge of the road. The snow-capped mountains were still tens of miles away, she guessed, but there were plenty of trees and hills. They could easily get away from the silly little truck.

"No," Audrey shot back.

"What? She has a pretty good idea. Let's run." Peter bounced back and forth, as if warming up.

"No," the girl repeated.

Tabby looked between Audrey and the van. The little milk wagon had no guns. It didn't even appear to have a camera on it. They had a chance to run, despite not knowing where they were.

"We've got this," Tabby said in her most confident voice. "We have to escape."

Audrey took a few quick steps back toward the truck, shaking her head quickly. "I can't. I won't. I thought it was all over when we came up out of the flooded mine. Then I thought it was all over when we went to my house. Then... Well, you get the point. I need an injection, too, or I'm going to pass out. You two go on. I'm done."

Tabby shared a concerned look with Peter, but she already knew what he would do. For her part, she wasn't going to run away without the two kids she was determined to protect. If they wouldn't leave, neither would she.

"You chose wisely," the truck voice said as they neared the speaker. The man took pains to emphasize the word wisely.

"My friend needs medical attention," she said sternly, hoping that would get some response.

The speaker didn't respond.

"Hello?" Tabby exclaimed, anger rising.

No response.

She glanced at Audrey, afraid she was in real trouble but not sure what to do for her. In the end, she figured the faster she did as asked, the faster she could get the girl some aid. "Just tell us when to push," she said dejectedly.

"Now would be good," the man replied.

As the three of them got into the wet mud alongside the wayward milk truck, a sleek-looking aircraft came in low from over a nearby hill. Its propeller whined as it flew directly overhead, not higher than a hundred feet. Tabby got a good look at the two missiles hanging from the long, thin wings.

I guess we did choose the right path. This time.

She pushed until the driverless vehicle came out of the mud, but she never stopped looking for the next chance for all of them to escape. Wherever the truck was taking them, it wouldn't be good. They didn't even care about a sick passenger...

TWENTY-THREE

Minot, ND

"Three!"

As soon as Uncle Ted said it, she squeezed the trigger. The M4 carbine jumped in her arms as the crack-bang concussion forced her back. The glass window shattered at the same time, and she closed her eyes momentarily to avoid the tiny shards as they came down.

The others had fired their first shots, but the broken glass interrupted their planned attack for a precious couple of seconds. Uncle Ted got his second shot off at about the same time as Meechum.

Kyla brought her rifle sights back up and found that her original target had fallen to the ground, so she went for the next guy in the line, as instructed. With the glass out of the way, she squeezed the trigger three or four times before she had to adjust her aim.

That man fell aside, too.

A couple of the enemy fell to the ground on purpose, and one of them managed to kick on his flamethrower. A jet of flammable gas launched toward the store.

"Shoot him!" Uncle Ted yelled.

She tried to get a shot off, but her heart pumped the blood directly behind her eyes. It made her hyper-aware of how the thick mist seemed to be headed directly toward her. If he clicked the detonate button...

Kyla dove sideways, toward the others, firing wildly as she dodged the spray.

Ohmygod!

A wall of fire erupted where she'd been standing, sounding like a roaring freight train had come in through the window. At almost the same instant, an explosion happened in the parking lot, which blew out all the remaining glass along the whole front of the store. As she landed on the dirty floor, she was doused with the contents of hundreds of bottles of warm soda.

The fire shot across the ceiling for one brief moment, then seemed to retreat like the tide. Kyla fought to find some air to breathe as she slid on the floor with the others. Her lack of success sent a surge of panic throughout her body, but the air soon came back.

"Holy...shit," Uncle Ted said hoarsely between heavy breaths. "Meechum hit the fuel tank for the flamer. That was a nice shot."

The Marine sucked in air like everyone else. "We all did good."

Her uncle looked over to her. "You okay? He was aiming for you, I think."

She laughed at being alive. "Yeah, he picked the wrong girl, for sure." It took some effort since the floor was slippery with sugary beverages, but when she made it upright, the fire outside had almost spent itself, since there wasn't much to burn. The motorcycles were knocked over on the gravel lot. A few of them closest to the blast had been ripped apart, but their tanks didn't explode. The one that had been destroyed still had a few flames clinging to the ruptured metal.

The sudden violence had startled her, but it didn't make her frightened as it might have done in the past. Her time on the *John F. Kennedy* had hardened her to it, as did the fight out of New York City. She cut directly to what mattered. "Hey, do you think someone else saw what happened?"

Emily brushed broken glass off her summer dress and out of her hair. "If they weren't watching us a mile off their runway, I doubt they had eyes on this out-of-the-way place ten miles away. However, we should go out there and move the debris when it cools enough. Anyone driving by will be curious why seven dead men are lying in the gravel."

They found a few fire extinguishers and got to work putting out the lingering fires on the lot and around the bottles of soda. Working together, they used a tow rope to drag most of the bikes behind the store. Of the seven, two were unrecognizable. A further two were heavily burned and damaged by the blast. However, there were three still good enough to drive.

When Kyla saw Uncle Ted and Meechum each drive a bike and park them next to the store, she saw how they could get into the base.

"Hey, guys. I have an idea."

Minot Air Force Base, ND

Ted was not thrilled with Kyla's idea. It involved high risks, though it also offered high rewards. If they could get inside without using their guns, and without risking their lives in another firefight, it was worth trying. However, he'd been planning to leave Kyla behind, to keep her away from the base altogether. She kept making it harder to ditch her.

"Emily, can't we take a little more time to think about this?" he asked.

"No, the clock has been ticking since the nuclear suitcase was stolen. I want to get inside as soon as we can do it safely. This idea might be the best we ever think up. As you said last night, the air base hardly appears to be aware there's a war going on. We'll be inside before they know what's up."

He sighed, not sure if he had a better answer. Unless they dug a tunnel, there wasn't a realistic way of sneaking in. Time was a factor, too. Kyla's way was the fastest, for sure. Still, he pulled her aside while Kyla and Meechum got ready. "Do we have to take her?"

Emily knew who he meant. "She said she's a programmer, Ted. She could be useful. There's no way to know what's inside. I'm only here for the biometrics. The Marine is here for security. You're the pretty face to get us inside." Her smile was cagey.

Ted rolled his eyes. "How did I ever get stuck with three women? Y'all are crazy, you know that, right?" He poked fun at her to hide his misgivings about having Kyla be a part of the attack. It was going to better their odds, for sure, but it didn't make it right.

"It'll be fine," she said seriously while brushing something off the chest of his borrowed black uniform. She'd smudged her face with soot and pinned up her hair in a style he'd never seen before. It was part of her disguise, she'd told him. "It's a good plan: we dress like them, ride their motorcycles, then slip into the base."

The worst part had been tearing the uniforms off the dead men. They needed to dress like the bikers if they wanted the ruse to work, but he was uncomfortable wearing anything with bullet holes in it. If the others had similar misgivings, they didn't share them. Everyone got on the bikes wearing the black pants and heavy long-sleeve shirts of the invaders.

"I'll miss your beach clothes," Ted said to Emily in a friendly voice. "Especially that big bag. It would have been a nice place to store all our ammo."

"You might see it again," she said mysteriously.

Since the dead men didn't ride with rifles or packs, Ted made the call to hide theirs in the trunk of the getaway car parked behind the store. They'd keep their pistols, and some of them carried more than one. However, the long guns might give them away when they went into the base. It was another of his calculated risks.

Another gamble was identification. They could have all lifted ID badges off the dead men, but it would do the women no good, since none of the dead were female. However, Ted took one from a man who somewhat resembled him, figuring it would give him a chance if someone asked for it.

"I'm Klaus Mitter, from..." He assumed it would have city and state, like every ID badge he'd ever had, but it didn't. "It says I'm from Black Site Mike 10."

"That sounds mysterious," Kyla said dramatically.

"What do you make of it?" Emily asked, more seriously.

He had no idea, but he guessed anyway. "I think they're trying to hide where they're really from. If this said Bob Smith, Albion, Indiana, we'd know how to track him down."

"Well, Klaus, let's go." Emily laughed.

They ran into one last problem before they pulled out of the parking lot. Emily was famous for her ability to operate machinery, but she reluctantly admitted she couldn't drive a motorcycle. He smiled, happy in his own way he'd found another weakness in the woman, but it meant they had to ride in pairs.

Emily rode behind him. Kyla had to ride behind Meechum, since his niece couldn't drive one either. The original owners didn't have helmets, so they traveled without them.

He almost enjoyed the highway speeds as they cruised across the flat plains of the North Dakota highway, but he had to restore his game face as they approached the front gate of the base. A pair of black-clad soldiers stood in front of the heavy mesh gate, rifles at the ready. The first one held up his hand, signaling they needed to stop.

Emily spoke in his ear. "This is nothing like last night. They look like they're waiting for us."

He allowed himself a peek over to the runway on his left. The fighter jets were all gone, as were most of the giant transport planes. It was hard to hear anything with the engine sounds of the bikes, but he looked up on a hunch; sure enough, two jets were high above, perhaps looping the air base as an air patrol.

Ted got close, but he didn't turn off the engine, hoping they would wave him through. However, they motioned for him to shut it off. Emily squeezed him as if they were going to be discovered.

The weird giraffe-things remained along the edges of the runway, but there seemed to be more of them. A couple held position near the front gate, giving him a good look at their construction. Their bodies were about the size of a subcompact car, though it was rounded on bottom and flatter on top. Their long metal legs emerged from joints near each corner, giving the bodies the appearance of animals. The lone neck tube set in the front furthered the illusion of a giraffe. The thin metallic heads were on swivels, and he took a guess they were watching him with mechanical eyes.

The guard came up to him and spoke broken English with an accent he couldn't identify. "You just left. Why back so soon?" Maybe eastern European, or one of the nations in the Middle East.

Ted had his story teed up and ready to go. "We had a malfunction. One of the tanks ruptured and blew up right as we were ripping a new one inside an Arby's restaurant. Almost lost my whole crew." He motioned to the women behind him, hoping they wouldn't get too much scrutiny. If the bad guys didn't use women for their fire duties, they'd have to get out in a hurry.

The man said, "You look like hell. You are injured?"

He didn't take it personally. Their faces were blackened by the initial blast in the store. Kyla even found some strands of her hair had been burned. His niece also wore a strip of black cloth around her neck from her injury. It was an easy sell to appear like they'd suffered a fiery malfunction. Ted nodded grimly and took a chance by glaring at the man square in the eyes. "I lost three men. How do you think I feel?"

Tension ran along the razor's edge as he held the man's gaze, but the guard relented before he did. "Sorry," the guy replied. "We're under strict lockdown. The American leftovers destroyed our forward air base in Amarillo, and command is worried this one might get the hit, too. But you've suffered enough. I'll let you through."

Ted found a suitable reply steeped with regret, but filled with bravery, as he imagined how these men were feeling. "Thanks. When we get back out there, we're going to pay those rebels back ten-fold."

Good job, rebels, whomever you are.

"We're the rebels," the guard said emphatically before speaking more cordially. "Good luck on finding the Americans, though. I heard there's not more than twenty on this side of the Mississippi. Not much to worry about, right?" The guard stepped back and made like he was going to the guard shack to open the gate, but he stopped at the door. "Hey, wait!"

Ted's stomach did a freefall. He had a vision of how that other attack far away had made his life unexpectedly more difficult. He'd saluted the people who may now get him killed. "Yeah?"

The guard reached into his shack and pulled out a clipboard. "I need write in my log. Just tell me your name."

He almost melted with relief. "Klaus Mitter."

"Got it." The man waved to his buddy to open the gate. "Go on through. Hope your day gets better."

Oh, it will.

They were in.

Folsom, CA

"Welcome to the Folsom Lake!" a man in a white jumpsuit shouted into his microphone. "Find your seats and we'll get started momentarily." The eighteen-wheeler flatbed carried a bank of speakers that might have been stolen from a rock concert.

Thousands of bikers had parked along the abandoned four-lane highway, which ran along the edge of the huge lake. Most of them walked up a nearby grass-covered hill, which provided views of the lake and hydroelectric dam to the north and the city of Folsom to the south. None of the people around him knew what to expect, but most thought it would be a flyby over the water of some of the captured military equipment, so most faced that way.

"You feeling better after last night?" Bernard asked him once they'd made it to the hilltop and found a place to sit.

Dwight wasn't certain what took place the night before. He recognized he'd had one of his "episodes," but his lack of ability to remember anything he'd said disturbed him to the bone. His only hope was to pretend. "I feel much better, thanks. My nightmares have been getting worse, I think. Ever since I was in that shipping container." The deflection was a tactic he'd learned on the streets. When the police came over to ask questions, whether he was guilty or not, he acted like the voices were inside his head.

"You came over in one of them boxes? No wonder you've got issues." Bernard laughed, and Dwight found himself liking the guy, despite his role in burning everything.

Poppy soared above the crowd, the stiff breeze letting her sail without flapping her wings. She tried to inject herself into the conversation, but he was glad she was out of earshot. He didn't need to hear her to know she was going to mess things up for him.

The announcer coughed to get everyone's attention, then carried on. "We're getting started. First, I'd like to thank David for the opportunity of a lifetime. I've seen such wonderful things happening the last few days. It's been more powerful than all that I've seen in my life up until this point. I hope you all feel the same."

The crowd cheered. When Bernard clapped, Dwight mimicked him.

"So, it will only be a few more moments. I've just got word from on high."

Dwight looked up, not sure what to make of the man's statement. If planes were coming, maybe the show would begin with a parachute jump. There were no aircraft in the sky, but he did see Poppy still enjoying herself in the mid-morning sunshine.

A new voice spoke on the loudspeakers. It was the one he'd heard two days earlier, in the San Francisco warehouse. "Greetings, fellow humans. I'm speaking to you remotely from my headquarters in my NORAD bunker. Our operations are going completely to plan, and for that, I thank you. Eliminating the people of this land was step one of our mission to reclaim the world. Step two is what you men and women are doing out there on the roads with your flame kits. But even from so far away, I can provide a little extra help for your efforts. For I am David, and I see everything you need."

Dwight almost chuffed out loud at how full of shit the man sounded, but he remembered he was supposed to be undercover. The crowd was applauding, as was he, when he noticed a thin black shape drop out of the clouds. From his position and distance, it appeared to be about the size of a telephone pole. It hurtled down for several seconds—long enough for many of the others to notice.

"What's that?" he asked whoever would listen.

The black shape fell on the flat decking on top of the Folsom Dam and disappeared. He had enough time to wonder if he'd imagined the object before the bottom half of the tall concrete dam bowed outward like a filling balloon. An instant later, fire and debris shot out of the bulge, followed by a white jet of water and a violent rumble under his feet.

The crowd fell into silence, which was a feat in itself.

They all watched the concrete monument crumble from both sides as the water pushed through. The remains of the roadway on the top quickly fell into the torrent, and the gap grew almost as wide as the dam itself. Once the breach started, it peeled away additional layers of stone, further widening the hole.

People started clapping, but he couldn't. He was too shocked.

The flood washed through the narrow river channel below the dam with frothy waves that fought like rabid dogs to get out of the lowlands and up to the neighborhoods of Folsom.

The crowd seemed to catch its breath and people applauded and whistled approval. The churn rushed through the flat valley along the path of the once-peaceful river, continuing its spread as more water gushed out of the lake. As more of the town was consumed, more of the crowd rose in support.

"It's got part of the prison," Bernard said like he was a reporter. "And it's heading for downtown."

Dwight realized none of their fire-starting adventures the night before could hold the flicker of a candle to the destruction wrought by the broken dam. Already houses, cars, and small buildings were being bowled over and washed away. The cleansing of America was happening in real time, and he was there to see its efficiency.

Poppy interrupted his introspection when she yelled a question down to him.

"Yes, I saw the dam break!" he replied with anger. Everyone was whooping and screaming in near-ecstasy at what David had done in front of their eyes, so no one heard him talk to his pet. He was glad for that. It wouldn't do him any good if they saw how upset he was.

"I'm done with this!"

TWENTY-FOUR

Minot Air Force Base, ND

"I was here once on business," Emily said in his ear as they rode through the sprawling base. "Air Force Two had to make a stop before we went to Japan. I got out of the plane for a short while, but I didn't make it to any secret computer labs."

Ted laughed. "Leave seek-n-find to Meechum. You just stay alive so you can unlock the terminal."

To the casual observer, it looked a lot like any small town in America. It had a movie theater, shopping centers, and fast food locations. Since this part of North Dakota was flat, and there were almost no trees for ten miles in any direction, the base seemed even larger. The long central street cut through it all, pointing west, toward the building where Meechum had shown on the soup-can mockup as housing all the computer gear.

He half-turned, happy as could be that they were still alive and free after being stopped at the gate. "You better be right, you know. I don't think anyone would appreciate if we stopped and asked for directions to their super-secret bunker."

The vibration of Emily's laugher traveled along her arms as she still held tight around his midsection.

They'd gone about a mile before they pulled into the parking lot for a nondescript two-story building made of stone blocks. It was about fifty yards square, with tired-looking windows. Compared to the rest of the newer housing and buildings, the place seemed to be from a previous generation. The sign out front said Maintenance and Parts, as Meechum promised.

Emily only let up on her hold when he had the bike off and the kickstand down. He hopped off first and held out a hand, though she didn't need any assistance kicking her leg over.

"Thanks," she said, using him for two seconds of balance.

Meechum strode by. "Ma'am, it's right through here."

He and Kyla followed the other two ladies through the swinging glass doors at the front of the building. There were lots of other cars in the parking area, so he figured there would be people inside. And when they stepped into the foyer, he got confirmation. People scurried about on the other side of the next set of glass doors. However, before they went through, they had to get by the guard.

A tired-looking older woman sat at a wood-grained folding table. She wore the same black on black uniform, but her jumpsuit top was draped on the back of her chair, leaving her in a gray T-shirt. She barely looked up when they came inside. "I'll need your guns."

Ted kept walking. "We don't have any."

She sat up straight. "Hold up, friends. I'll need to wand you." The handheld security wand had been sitting on her lap.

He had to make a split-second decision.

"Sorry, thought you meant long guns," he said nonchalantly, "We do have some pistols, but we're in a hurry." There was no point in pretending they didn't have pistols on them if she was going to wand them anyway. He tried to be a team player.

"Thanks," she said, still holding the wand. "The base commander put us on full alert. I have to wand every person who comes through the doors."

All of them emptied their pockets and holsters. Kyla and Meechum both put their M9s on the table. Emily set down her P229. He tabled his pair of Sigs, plus the little Ruger LCP. He'd intended to sneak it through until she mentioned the wand.

As promised, she lazily checked each one as they stepped through the second row of doors. She seemed to notice the bullet hole in his chest, but only shrugged like even that didn't faze her.

"How do we get them back?" he asked from a bit beyond the threshold. "You didn't give us a receipt."

The woman tapped her head. "I'll know."

He went on, pretending he was used to such treatment. However, when they all got inside the main hallway of the building, they met another surprise. Almost everyone wore different uniforms. Instead of the all-black edition, the new people had black uniforms with red sleeves.

"Where now?" Emily asked the Marine.

The interior had the appearance of being a large call center contained within an old elementary school. Thirty or forty people sat at desks scattered throughout a large room at the end of the entryway. Rows of exposed halogen tube lighting hung above the workers, giving it a cheap telemarketer appearance instead of a military one. Meechum gave the people inside a once-over, then pointed to the left, to a hallway going a different direction. "We could probably use any terminal in the building, but the mainframe room should have the fewest people. The stairs we want are that way, and around the corner."

The four of them walked the bustling hallway, trying to move fast and avoid interacting with any of the enemy wearing the wrong uniforms. It wasn't hard to do, as many of the young workers had their heads down, looking at cell phones or big tablets.

"This is the IT group, isn't it?" he asked, knowing the answer.

"Yep," Meechum said quietly.

Kyla took a double step to get closer to him. "Why does it say maintenance on the front?"

He laughed. "It's an old trick from the Cold War days. If a spy snooped around and tried to map the place out, they'd be confused as to what was really inside the buildings. The US Air Force continued the tradition by mixing up the signage. Everyone on base knows what's in here, however."

"Glad I'm not a spy," Kyla added. "I barely knew how to get to the computer lab while on the aircraft carrier. I'd never be able to draw it on a map."

"You're kind of a spy now," Meechum said, slapping her on the back.

A few seconds later, Ted thought he recognized a face as he walked by the door of a computer room. The man inside the crowded lab was similar to someone from Air Force Two, though it happened so fast, he couldn't be certain. He didn't immediately tell the women, though he knew he had to warn them.

They walked to the end of the busy hallway and Meechum guided them to a right fork. At the last possible moment, Ted looked back toward the mystery man. He came out of the room, obviously sharing his curiosity, but Ted jerked his head back before the bad guy locked on.

Ted ensured no one in the hallway was close, then he spoke to the ladies' backs. "Guys, hold up. We've got a problem. I think I was recognized..."

"Really?" Meechum gasped.

He nodded but looked at Emily. "Remember my asshole friend Ramirez? You sent me and him into DC. He's here. I'm ninety-nine percent sure I saw him." The Hispanic man was a bit on the heavy side for a career officer and was hard to mistake for anyone else.

"Well, let's keep going," Emily replied as she tried to pull his wrist.

"I can't," he said with real regret. "He knows me, but he doesn't know you guys. He couldn't have seen you walk by his door. Ram only looked up when I was in the frame. You've got to keep going."

"I'll stay with you," Kyla acknowledged.

"No, your mission is to protect the president, and she needs you to knock out that nuclear code problem. You have to go with her." He'd come to terms with their roles. Meechum would get them there, Emily would provide the code, and Kyla would be there in case on-the-fly programming was required. His role was taking care of surprises.

He was anxious to push them away. If Ram came around the corner, they'd all be implicated. "Please hurry!"

Emily looked like she was going to speak, but she ended up grabbing Kyla by the sleeve and dragging her away. The president smiled at him, then followed Meechum into a stairwell door.

Ted got up against the wall and crept back to the corner. If the guy never showed up, he'd go down the steps after his team. However, if his old friend Ramirez came around the bend, he wanted to be ready for the reunion.

As he stood there, Ted thought back to his failed mission with ER. They'd confirmed that President Tanager was dead, but Ted was duped out of the nuclear briefcase. He'd more or less forgotten about ER until he saw him a minute ago, but it all made sense in retrospect: the man who captured the nuclear briefcase would probably also be the one to bring it to Minot for reassignment.

Even from around the corner, he heard the heavy footsteps of someone jogging to catch up. Ted hoped he could surprise the other guy.

I'm supposed to be dead.

NORAD Black Site Sierra 7, CO

It had been easier than Tabby thought to get the small milk truck out of the mud, and once it was back on pavement, she, Peter, and Audrey reluctantly climbed back inside. She had no sense where they'd been going, due to the opaque windows, but she figured it was somewhere in the mountains. However, when the automated transport opened the doors again, she was in an underground cave or mine.

Two women in black jumpsuits with silver sleeves stood at the ready as they came out of the truck. "Welcome to NORAD," one of them said to her.

"Your people killed my dogs," she said dryly, repeating the charge she'd leveled at the men who'd put her in the truck, before remembering there was much more to it. "And all of our freaking parents!"

The practiced smiles faltered on both women. The closest one had brunette hair that was gathered in a rudimentary bun on the back of her head. She wore silver earrings, which seemed to match the silver sleeves of her jumpsuit. The other one was a blonde with her hair cut short, like she'd been in the Army.

The blonde replied, "We're sorry about all that. You're luckier than most. You've been invited here by David himself."

Peter chuckled like he'd heard the joke before.

"Who's David?" Tabby asked. "Is he in charge? My friend needs medical attention for her diabetes."

"Of course he's in charge," the woman went on, "though he doesn't like Americans, generally. You three are the first ones he's brought here. They usually get rebooted."

After the long drive, Tabby was in no mood for pleasantries. "Is that what we're calling it now? I watched one of your robots cut apart two men back in St. Louis. It was a little more than a reboot. It was murder!"

The woman seemed ready to defend herself, but she noticed someone outside of Tabby's field of view. When she turned to see what had her captor's attention, a woman in a white jumpsuit walked alongside the milk wagon until she joined the conversation. "Hello, Tabitha Breeze. I'm Charity, one of David's handmaidens. I'm the one who will get you settled." She fluffed her luxurious, long red hair, then extended her hand.

Tabby made no effort to return the handshake, but she did give the woman a thorough inspection. Where the other women were clad in heavy overalls for their jumpsuits, like they were working at a racetrack pitstop, Charity looked like someone out of a rerun show Dad used to watch called *Buck Rogers*. Her tight-fitting spandex one-piece had a half-opened zipper down the front, with long sleeves, and a hint of a belt around her waist, but was otherwise devoid of decorations. Tabby didn't let the oddness distract her. "How the hell do you know my name?"

Charity kept her hand out.

Tabby crossed her arms.

Charity didn't shift an inch. "You know, it's polite to reciprocate when someone offers the hand of friendship. We're not going to leave this room until you shake my hand like a civilized person."

She became uncomfortable as the seconds ran into half a minute. Charity's hand was still out, and Tabby's arms remained crossed. It satisfied her to see the look of horror on the other two women's faces. Whatever she was doing to drive them into such fear, Tabby wanted to keep it up.

When a full minute went by, Charity shifted in her little space-boots. "This doesn't have to get ugly, but you aren't going to win, dear Tabitha. We can either stand here all day and get nowhere, or I can show you where to go to meet David, our leader."

"There's nothing you can do to make me shake your hand."

A look passed over the woman's face, briefly, but her smile returned in a flash. She figured her dad would be encouraging her to keep going, now that she had a chance to stick it to the people who killed her family.

Charity spoke in an unnatural, emotionless monotone. "If you don't shake my hand vigorously by the time I count to ten, I'll put your two friends back in the delivery van and drive it into a lake. David would hate to lose an expensive piece of equipment, but sometimes, the end justifies the *means*."

She counted down, starting at ten.

Tabby waited a few seconds out of anger, but she was beaten. She'd overlooked the easiest and most obvious method of coercion. Before it was too late, she clasped hands with the she-devil in front of her.

Charity shook it vigorously and acted as if the last couple of minutes didn't happen. "So glad to meet you, Tabby. And so happy you brought your friends Audrey and Peter. We will, of course, tend to Audrey's condition."

"Thanks," she forced herself to say.

Peter's eyes darted across the pretty woman's outfit, but he held out his hand like a dead fish. "I guess you want us to shake like trained dogs, too?"

Charity practically scoffed at him. "I think one test was enough, don't you?" She turned to Tabby. "And this is about you, really, so I'm glad I get to help you."

She sighed deeply. "Who the heck is David? How do you even know who I am?" She had no ID on her. When she went to work in the mine, she kept her personal belongings in a locker in the main office. Her phone might have given clues, but she didn't have that, either.

Charity motioned for her to move. "Walk with me."

The three of them fell into a line. Charity and Tabby in front. Audrey and Peter in the middle. The two other women in the back.

Charity spoke. "I cannot say why David brought you here. He only instructed me to get you through decontamination before you have an audience with him."

"Decontamination?" Tabby asked. "Are we in danger?"

"Of course not. I'm talking to you, aren't I? It's merely a precaution. Besides, David does not like things to be messy or out of order."

"The whole world is out of order right now," Tabby said under her breath.

"That's right," Charity went on cheerfully. "It's our job to bring the order back. David has said the same thing many times. Perhaps I understand a little better why he chose you for this honor. You think like us."

"All right. This is too weird. What the hell do you want me to do, exactly?"

Charity pointed to a heavy metal door with the word decontamination emblazoned across the middle. She hit a button next to it, which made the door swing out on a stout hinge, much like a bank vault. The inside was dark, leaving no clue as to what was in there.

"Tabitha, you will be first. I'm afraid the system only accepts one person at a time." Charity motioned for her to go inside, but her eyes became predatorial. They seemed to convey the idea she was not to be disobeyed or someone was going to get hurt. The silver-sleeved women maintained their presence in the back.

She glanced at Peter and Audrey. They'd gone so far together in such a short time. She still remembered that first hour with them on the tour, where Peter had been flirting with Tabby the whole way. It wasn't to hit on her, though she wondered what he would have done if she'd been interested. Instead, the boy was trying to make Audrey jealous. It failed miserably at the time, but their shared terror had kept them together every minute since. Now it felt like good-bye.

Tabby turned to Charity. "You'll send them through after me, right?"

The woman bowed her head. "Of course."

Tabby didn't believe it for a second, but she was at her mercy.

"I'll see you guys in a few," she said with all the cheer she could muster.

The couple waved while still holding hands.

God, please let me see them again.

TWENTY-FIVE

Minot Air Force Base, ND

"Is he coming? Did you see him?" Emily was uncharacteristically frazzled as she asked her and Meechum about her uncle. Uncle Ted stayed upstairs to deal with some guy, which was a bummer, but she understood. He was a warrior, and that was what warriors did. Emily came across as a warrior, despite her diminutive stature, so her concern seemed like more than professional courtesy.

"He'll be here as soon as he can," Meechum assured her.

The three women walked briskly down the hallway, past more technicians who seemed enthralled by their tablets and phones. Kyla tried to get a look at one of them and saw the face of a man talking. When a woman walked by holding her phone at a low angle, she saw the same man's face. The white-haired guy seemed to be giving a speech. The curious side of her wanted to ask one of the strangers who was on their screens, but she discounted it as a very bad idea.

"It's that one, at the end of the hall." Meechum motioned thirty feet ahead. The wooden door faced them and was closed.

As they passed the doors in the rest of the hall, Kyla figured out that this floor was dedicated to computer labs for security of the air base. The screens in one room faced toward them, and she saw what was on the giant terminal: aerial images. Most of them were open, with people going in and out, but the one Meechum called out had no activity.

"Does it need a key?" Emily asked, reading her thoughts.

"Don't know." Meechum whispered. "It wasn't in my briefing."

They got to the end of the hallway and Emily did an abrupt turnaround. "Where is he?"

Meechum went to the door while Kyla pulled gently at Emily's elbow. "My uncle knows what he's doing. If he stopped, it was for a good reason. I'm sure he'd want you to complete your, uh, mission." She didn't think of herself as being on a military mission, but it came out of her mouth sounding that way. Mom would either be so pissed she was doing this or proud of her for avenging her country. She went with the latter.

Emily glanced at her. The woman's brown eyes were balanced between crying and desperate resolution. It confirmed her suspicion that maybe Uncle Ted meant more to her than just another pretty-boy pilot. It grossed her out to think of him that way, but she was proud of him for catching the eye of someone as important as the VP. "Thanks. I feel responsible for him, you know? I pulled him off Air Force Two and made him do special missions for me. I hate being separated."

Oh, yeah. She likes him.

Kyla kept her excitement in check. "Ma'am, Meechum has the door open. We need to get inside and log you in." She tugged at her arm to get her to move. The techs weren't too big on security, based on how they walked around with their noses stuck to their tablets, but someone might recognize the vice president, despite her efforts at disguise.

"You're right," Emily said with a heavy sigh.

They got inside without anyone shouting at them, but Kyla checked the hall once more as she shut the door. Uncle Ted was nowhere in sight. It would have been great if she could cheer up the VP before they got into the system. She had no idea how long it would take.

The inside was a lot like the other rooms on the level, but it was extremely cool. It was about twenty-by-twenty, or about the size of an average school classroom. In the middle, four or five computer desks supported giant desktop cases and even bigger monitors on top. The outer part of the room was lined with computer cabinets, servers blinking and humming inside. An industrial air-conditioning unit sat on the floor near the back, keeping everything cool. A long tabletop hung from another wall. A hundred tablets were lined up in a row, each with charging cables attached. Though she was there for the computer terminal, she trotted to the tablets and picked one up.

"This is what everyone has out there." The lock screen showed the white-haired man's face. She walked it over to the two women.

"That's David," Emily reported. "His real name is Jayden Phillips. Your uncle and I saw him when we were in an apartment the other night." Nosy Kyla immediately wondered if anything had happened that night. It was the type of gossip she used to fake interest in when talking to Ben. He always wanted to hear about who she was dating, so she'd made up a lot of stories. If they ever got a minute where their lives weren't in danger, she was going to plumb Emily for the truth, but it wasn't yet the right time.

"Why are all the people watching videos of him?" she asked.

Meechum seemed agitated. "We're here, guys. This terminal is locked, just like we talked about. Kyla, you need to get your ass in the chair and do your thing. Madame President, be ready to input what you need."

Kyla nodded, singularly focused on the moment. "Let's get this over with."

I have so many questions saved up.

Minot Air Force Base, ND

There wasn't much time to plan what he was going to do if Ramirez came for him. His pistols had been taken at the door, and none of the workers seemed to have any he could borrow. If he got into a tussle, he wanted it to be out of view as much as possible. When the girls disappeared into the stairwell, he continued walking down the hall, purposely avoiding the stairs.

If it's him, he's going to shout my name.

He repeated the thought to make it stick. The last thing he wanted—

"Major MacInnis!" the man shouted.

Ted didn't flinch. He kept walking as if deaf to the name. The rest of the workers in the hallway flinched and stopped, however, which inadvertently made him the one guy who stood out.

"Shit," he said under his breath.

"It's me, ER," the other guy laughed.

Ted increased his pace and angled for an open door, which happened to be an empty room. There were twenty folding chairs set up facing a screen on a tripod, but none of it was in use. He thought about shutting the door, but it would be the end of his battle. He'd be cornered and would never get out. Instead, he took his chances the portly jerk would want him alone, so he took a seat in the last row.

When ER came in, he knew it was him by his heavy breathing. Ted's initial impression of the man was that he was better suited to serve hot dogs at the ball game than be down on the field. The last few days hadn't changed his mind. Neither had the man's change of uniform. As he walked casually around the far side of the chairs, he seemed to show off his black jumpsuit. "It is you," he said admiringly. "I didn't realize you'd joined the winning team, Major."

"Is the president really dead?" Ted asked, trying to cut right to the heart of his intelligence-gathering responsibilities. They'd gone to the White House, but ER had been the one who claimed he'd found the president's clothes. As he sat there, he spun the presidential challenge coin in his pocket, underscoring the only hard data he'd gotten from that mission.

Ramirez laughed and raised his hands, which were partially wrapped with skin-colored bandages. "I got what I needed from the White House, including that nice little fall on the glass. But my mission wasn't to find the president; it was to get his precious suitcase."

Ted nodded. "Which you then brought back here, didn't you? Why would you betray your country so badly?"

The edge of ER's mouth curled up. "Officers like you must live in some world where you see everything in such black and white terms. The rest of us live in the real world. A world where someone can offer you the entire state of Vermont for your service."

"That's funny. I knew a ship captain who was convinced he'd be rewarded with a giant swath of Vermont. Are you sure you've got your contract signed correctly? Might want to have a lawyer give it a once-over. Just sayin'."

The smug look on Ramirez's face disappeared. "What are you doing here?"

He wanted to delay as long as possible. "Thanks for saving me from the plane crash. I at least owe you for that."

Ramirez bowed a little. "I might have killed you if I thought there was even a tiny chance you and I would cross paths again. I figured if the drones didn't get you, the packs of wild dogs would. Plus, I've got to admit, I never thought you'd crawl out of the burning truck."

Ted stood up. "Yeah, well, I guess the Air Force makes us tougher than you Army pukes." He'd said it matter-of-factly, instead of with bile and venom. His blasé attitude worked as intended.

"You have no idea what you're dealing with." He patted his chest, showing off his uniform again. "This army is unstoppable. We took down the entire United States government in seconds. We're cleaning up the rest of your military around the world in mere days. Everything that was once yours is now ours. How does that make you feel, tough guy?"

He took a few steps toward the heavier man, waiting for his chance. "I heard some rebels kicked you in the nuts in Amarillo. It sounds like there's a whole Army division still in play. How does that make *you* feel? Tough guy."

"Rebels didn't do squat. The Reboot Legion must never be compared to the scum we're eradicating."

The man at the gate had also taken offense to his apparent misuse of the word rebel. "Is that what you call yourselves?" Ted asked.

"Rebels, yes," ER said in an agreeable tone. "Reboot Legion. Reb L," he added, shortening it. "Get it now?"

"I call you terrorists," Ted said matter-of-factly.

"We'll see who's the terrorist." Ramirez pulled a small revolver from his pocket. "Remember this? It belonged to the vice president. You gave it to some asshole at Andrews. That asshole shot two valuable members of my team."

Ted reflexively held up his hands, but he was far from surrendering. "That asshole was my friend Frank. I hope he sent your guys to hell. They swept us at the door. How'd they let you keep yours?"

"I'm a national hero. They look the other way for guys like me." The pistol was trained on him for a few seconds before Ramirez dipped it a little. "Wait, you said 'us.' Who else is here? Where are they?"

Aw shit. He'd accidentally said more than he'd needed to. It was a rookie mistake. Emily was going to chew him a new one for it. If he ever saw her again.

"Up yours," Ted replied.

Ramirez snapped his fingers. "You lost the briefcase, right? Maybe you thought you could lock us out using a manual terminal. Such an act could be executed by a skilled programmer, or a high-ranking member of the US government, but you'd have to come here to the air defense mainframe. And that means..." The gun pointed at his face. "Let's go downstairs."

Amarillo, TX

Brent and Trish were the first to arrive at the Cadillac Ranch. He'd driven in a confusing series of turns and backtracks, on the off chance someone tried to follow them. Driving with no headlights was a challenge, but he became accustomed to it as his eyes adjusted. The eastern sky was at nautical twilight as he pulled onto the short dirt road leading to the half-buried cars.

The younger woman had been quiet for most of the ride, but she shifted toward him once they were parked. "Brent, thank you again for coming to my rescue back at my house. I have to admit I never saw any of these guys as upstanding human beings, but you've changed them. They're putting their lives on the line for a cause greater than themselves. It really was amazing tonight."

Brent was taken aback by her dive into the personal. "Well, as long as we're admitting things to each other ..." He took a deep breath. "I've always thought of you as a daughter. Mara and I never got to have any. I reckon you're as close as I'll ever get. That's why I went out to save you from Curtis and his thugs."

She unclicked her seatbelt and leaned over to give him a hug. The personal contact and the smell of her hair almost made him tear up. He'd missed Mara for the past few years, but never as much as he did while in that embrace.

Trish pulled back and looked outside. "Do you think the rest of them made it?"

"I'm sure they did. We saw them leaving." It was true he saw Cliff and Kevin drive off, but not the other three men. They'd all taken different routes through the city.

Dwight didn't know what to say for the next few minutes, so he sat at attention, sure another car would be along shortly. After about five minutes, he saw one. "Thank God. They're here."

The headlights on the lone car came up the abandoned highway but went by the turnoff for the Cadillac Ranch, so Brent flicked his headlights on and off. "They must have missed the turn."

A few seconds later, the car turned around.

"Come on, let's greet them," he said while hopping out. Almost after the fact, he opened the back door and brought his shotgun with him. If the bad guys were out there, he wanted to be able to fight back, no matter what else he was doing.

The headlights were blinding as the vehicle slowly came up the dirt road. They'd switched so many cars over the course of the night's activities, he had no way to know who was driving based solely on the make of vehicle. He had to wait until it pulled alongside him before he got a look in there.

It was a man he didn't recognize...

TWENTY-SIX

Minot Air Force Base, ND

"Can you hack in?" Emily asked over Kyla's shoulder.

She'd gotten through the first password gate with no problem, and now she had access to the mainframe. It surprised her that she understood the operating system. "Yes. Actually, this is a lot like the code I worked on with the Navy. It's probably from the same defense contractor."

The VP tapped her on the shoulder. "Good work. Keep it up. I want it to be ready for when your uncle comes back. Then we're going to get the heck out of here before we get caught."

She typed maniacally at the keyboard, using her polished programming skills to work her way through the file system until she came to a folder with some promise.

Presidential Emergency Satchel

She was hit with a password gate as soon as she tried to gain access to it.

"This is where we get down and dirty," Kyla said quietly to the two women with her. "Though I never thought I'd find myself anywhere near nuclear codes like this."

Emily laughed. "Yeah, well, that makes two of us. I'm supposed to be at a grand-a-plate fundraiser in Ohio today. At least, it's what my schedule said before the world went into the crapper."

"Sounds like fun," Kyla said while breaking into the system.

The vice president didn't sound happy. "It gets old. Trust me. The first dozen are fun. Meet new people. Get press taking your photos. Be the most important woman in the room. But it gets tiring always being on your A-game. You get pictures taken every second of the event, even when food falls out of your mouth."

Prior to the disaster, that life would have terrified Kyla. She liked being by herself, or with one or two others. She avoided crowds whenever she could. However, even a fancy dinner party sounded better than her new existence on the run.

"Yeah, that does sound—"

The door flung open, causing her to stop talking and see who it was.

"Uncle Ted!" she cried out as he was pushed inside. A pissed-off Hispanic guy came through holding a revolver. She jumped out of her chair as her uncle shuffled over to Emily.

"Nobody touch nothing," the newcomer insisted.

Emily caught Uncle Ted and held him close. He stayed there for a moment, then seemed to think better of it. They separated and put about a foot between them.

"Is that my gun?" Emily inquired, not showing any fear.

The man nodded.

"Emily, you remember Lieutenant Eduardo Ramirez?"

"From the plane," she replied with awe.

"I'm glad we could all get together like this. The last time I saw you two, you were both supposed to be dead. Especially you." ER pointed the gun at Emily.

"What do you want?" Kyla volunteered, hoping to take some of the heat off Uncle Ted and the VP.

"What do I want? I want what everyone wants: an upper government official with the authority to transfer command of the nuclear arsenal over to its new owners."

"I want a puppy," Uncle Ted deadpanned.

Ramirez wasn't amused. He swiveled the gun between the three of them.

Three?

She looked around for Meechum, but the Marine wasn't anywhere obvious. Before she gave her away, Kyla turned back to the front of the room. "We don't have anyone like that here."

"You would be the guests of honor under any other circumstances. There are teams of programmers working on changing over the authority of the briefcase without having the correct people present. They would all be glad to meet you. They'd be especially glad to have you help them out by unlocking the system for us."

Emily shifted on her feet. "We aren't going to help you do anything."

"Oh, you don't think so? What if I did this—" Ramirez aimed the gun at Ted's face, which prompted Kyla and Emily to both shout, "No!"

"Well, that's interesting. The both of you don't want me to kill this man?" Ramirez chuckled in an unpleasant manner. "I'd like to do this without hurting a soul, but the only one I really need alive is..." He bobbed the gun between them. "None of you."

His aim settled on Emily. "I need your eyes for the biometric scanner, but I don't need the rest of you."

"Wait a second, ER," Ted pleaded, "let's talk about this."

"Oh, that's so sweet. You two are into some weird boss-underling relationship, aren't you? I wish I had someone to report this to."

Ted put up his hands and took a step closer. "Just tell us what you want. We'll do whatever we can, so no one gets hurt."

Ramirez grinned. "Your little programmer needs to open the interface. I see she's most of the way there." He craned his neck to look at the computer screen. "Then your VP is going to enter her biometric information. From there, we'll transfer full command to the briefcase."

"Where is it?" Kyla asked, not seeing anything briefcase-like in the room.

"Safe at NORAD, with David, of course. He's already working on controlling the arsenal while in the central defense facility, but having access to the briefcase will allow him to move around our new country with it. Once he has control over all the missiles, we can defend ourselves from any and all threats out there. It's one of the important steps in the invasion timetable."

Ted stalled for time. "Why do you need nukes when you have the most powerful weapon in human history?"

"Unlike your people, we conserve our resources. Not every problem is a nail, and not every solution is a hammer. Sometimes, you need nukes. Other times, you need…our superweapon." He smiled broadly.

"You just want to be the hero again," Ted said dryly, taking another small step toward the man with the gun. A second shape moved in the shadows behind one of the server towers. It had to be Meechum sneaking along the wall. Kyla began to understand what they were doing. Unarmed, while in the face of a gun, she didn't think they had much of a chance.

"I'll do it," she rattled off with immediacy. "Just don't hurt anyone."

Uncle Ted spun around. "No, Kyla, you can't!"

The scene served as a distraction for Ramirez. ER didn't see Meechum right away when she came out from behind the six-foot server rack.

But, eventually, he did.

Minot Air Force Base, ND

Everything happened in what seemed like a single second. Meechum charged from behind the bank of computer towers, Kyla got ER's attention by saying she was going to help him, and he was caught in the middle. He had to protect his two friends, so he lunged for the traitor as he turned his pistol toward the Marine.

He'd heard the wheelie gun fire once before, back in Air Force Two, so he was prepared for the loud bang. Still, being close to the deadly weapon made his insides go to jelly.

Meechum fell to the thin layer of carpet like a sack of flour. Ramirez was in the process of aiming and taking his second shot as Ted plowed into him from the side. The other man was fifty pounds heavier, so the impact hurt him as much as it did ER.

The gunshot went wide of its target, given that ER's arm was the first thing he hit. Ted hoped to get him to drop the piece, but he held on even as they careened onto the floor in front of Meechum.

Ted glanced back to Kyla to see her stepping closer. "No! Get Emily to deactivate it!"

His niece hesitated, though he didn't see what she did next. Ramirez pulled him into a headlock. The gun dangled precariously in the man's bandaged hand, but he refused to drop it. However, he couldn't get it pointed at Ted's body without loosening his grip around him.

Ted struggled to maintain his position without getting squeezed any harder. He kept his right shoulder high against the other guy's body, so the lock wasn't total. When he sensed the slightest release, he shoved some more of his shoulder into the weak point.

The next couple of seconds, or minutes, were a blurry haze as he fought to stay conscious. Meechum was nearby the whole time, but she didn't move as best he could tell. The two other women were at the computer terminal; he could barely see Emily's brown hair from where he was. Despite wearing all black, she'd left the summer scrunchy in.

"They aren't going to do it, you know," ER taunted. "We've had teams working on this for three days. She's not going to get in."

Ted had talked to Rebecca many times about Kyla's decision to go into programming. At first, it seemed like a great career path to a steady income and a nice job, but when she started working for the Navy, he had his doubts about her judgement. He figured there were more bucks to be made in the private sector. However, when she landed the job working on nuclear containment on the biggest and most expensive ship in the fleet, he conceded she must have a pretty good head on her shoulder. Now, he was certain of it.

"While you're busy killing me, she's going to shock the hell out of you, asshole." Ted wasn't ready to give up, and he was keeping his head barely above water, but the big guy didn't seem close to giving in. However, as he continued to struggle, the other man breathed heavily. He saw his chance coming up.

Ramirez tried to aim the gun toward Kyla, but a desk was in the way. Ted certainly wasn't going to let him move to get a better line of sight. The bigger man squeezed his arm around Ted's neck and grunted, obviously anxious to kill him so he could get to the terminal.

Ted squirmed as he fought against the pressure, though his vision blurred from lack of blood. It wasn't anything like he pictured as a heroic saving of the women, or the nation, but real-life combat was never like the movies.

Just have to keep him here.

"Dammit, why won't you die?" Ramirez asked. "I should have shot you back on the runway."

A shiny object hit Ramirez on the head with a sickening clunk. The pistol went off at the same time, and the man's grip on Ted immediately loosened. ER rolled to one side, sweeping him underneath for a second before he fell out of the other man's clutches. He tried to tumble away to get free, until he realized Ramirez's gun-arm was free, too.

The pistol was pointed at his face.

NORAD Black Site Sierra 7, CO

Tabby was sure Mom and Dad would disapprove of her actions of the last fifteen minutes. The decontamination procedure was an embarrassing exercise all the way through.

She'd been instructed by a hidden voice that she needed to strip away all her clothes in order to enter the hazardous materials shower. She was willing to strip down to her underwear, but that was as far as she'd go.

Minutes later, after standing alone in the freezing metal room, Charity's voice came over the speaker and reminded her she was the first in line. The other two could easily be tossed back out the front door, come what may.

After that, beaten again, she ran through the shower as instructed. The automatic drier actually felt pretty good, and it was a relief to be clean, but when she came through another door and found her replacement clothes sitting on a chair, she almost didn't put them on. It was the same skimpy jumpsuit as Charity had been wearing, only hers was shiny blue rather than white.

Tabby looked around the chamber for alternatives, but there was absolutely nothing besides the metal seat. "I have to wear this?" she asked the voice controlling her journey.

"David wishes you to adhere to the same dress code as the rest of his Reboot Legion. Your original clothing has been disposed of. You will not be offered an alternative. Blue is a great honor."

"Hardly," she said, unsure if she would be more embarrassed inside the unitard or standing in the nude outside it. In the end, she swallowed her pride and put it on. When she fidgeted and stretched it all it would go, she looked at herself in the shiny metal of the door.

I look ridiculous.

She hurriedly unspooled her three braids. It broke her heart to do it, since Mom had been the one to arrange them, save for one repair job done by Audrey, and it was the last thing she owned of her. However, she was certain her mother would approve of why she'd done it. Tabby arranged her long hair, so it fell over her chest, giving her a tiny bit of extra cover. She kept her front zipper sealed all the way up to her neck.

When she came through the last door, a man in a golden jumpsuit stood waiting for her. "I'm David. Welcome."

"Why am I here?" she replied, unimpressed.

He got closer, noting Tabby's twitchy step in the opposite direction. "I saw you on television, of course."

Tabby had been curious if anyone had gotten her message while she'd been inside the St. Louis television station. It seemed like a long shot at the time, since she learned everyone in the viewing area was dead, but if this guy saw it...

"So, you saw me asking for help. Obviously, my message went to the wrong person. You killed them all, didn't you?"

He stood there looking sad, which was transparently fake. "I hate killing, Tabitha Breeze from Bonne Terre, Missouri, but the world is a cruel place. When I saw you on television, I was struck by how the necessary evil of the reboot had left at least one piece of the old America I couldn't bear to extinguish. I found your passion to find your parents riveting. I, of course, knew you'd never reach them, but that's what made it so tragic, and beautiful. It was an impossible task, just as it was for David to slay his Goliath."

"You're quoting the Bible? After all you've done?" Mom and Dad had made her go to church, which she accepted more as a time to hang out with them than a spiritual exercise. However, she would never in a billion lifetimes believe this man knew a single lesson from the Good Book if he was truly the one responsible for killing everyone.

"All I've done?" he chuckled. "I've saved you from a terrible fate. I would think you'd see that. You called out to me and now I've rescued you."

Her tummy balled up, not wanting to believe the horrible man.

He went on before she could reply. "I caught up with your broadcast hours after you left St. Louis. I was crushed when you disappeared from our intelligence assets, but I knew it was you when we had trouble in Chicago. I—"

"Your drones killed our friend!" she blurted out.

David acted like he didn't hear her. "I sent my fleet of airborne units to sweep the area, but you escaped again, on bikes no less." He clapped his hands in excitement. "But I knew where you would go. All I had to do was keep tabs on the cleared highways until an unregistered vehicle showed up. You went right to that nice warehouse and made it easy, though I almost didn't catch the drones before they did their automated thing and rebooted you." He laughed, like threatening the three of them with the giant tank had been a harmless prank.

"You should have killed me, like you did my two dogs. I don't know why you chose to bring me here, but I'll never cooperate."

He laughed grimly. "We both know that isn't true, after your meeting with Charity. You'll do exactly as I say, when I say it, or things will get ugly for members of your party. And, besides, if you're talking about the two dogs in that same warehouse, I can tell you with authority they aren't dead."

A breath caught in her throat. "Say what?"

TWENTY-SEVEN

Minot Air Force Base, ND

It took Ted nearly thirty seconds to catch his breath. He remained on the floor, next to the still body of Ramirez, while the two girls talked in hushed tones over by the terminal. He heard Kyla say she cracked in, and a short time later, Emily reported success in taking the nuclear briefcase offline. He was content that his role as human punching bag made it all possible.

Meechum crawled up next to him. "Major? You gonna make it?"

Her uniform top had blood splattered all over her left shoulder, and he realized she'd been shot. She saw how his eyes were drawn to the wound and waved him off. "I'm fine. It went right through. I was still able to use my good arm to crack the skull of this asshole." She pointed to ER's bloody head, where a large divot had been created above his ear.

"I bet," he replied, further impressed by her instincts.

Kyla appeared at his side. "We did it, Uncle Ted! We're safe." Then, exactly as he had done with Meechum, she looked at him as if he was broken. "Ohmygod! Are you okay?"

He sat up with her help, feeling better as the oxygen got to his brain. His muscles were sore from holding off Ramirez's arms, but the big man never got the solid hold necessary to choke him out. "What the heck happened?" he asked.

Emily appeared on his other side, crouched next to him. "You and Lance Corporal Meechum held him off long enough for us to finish this. You kept him occupied, and she used a spare hard drive to bash in his head." She gestured to the body next to him.

Ted regained his sense of leadership. "We have to get out of here. The alarm—"

At some point in his dance with Ramirez, he'd fired his revolver. That action had been heard by others and it triggered an alarm inside the building. However, it was silent out in the hallway, as best he could tell. The only ringing came from his ear drums.

"I turned it off," Kyla bragged. "With this." She held up a tablet. "I hacked into the password database and got us the credentials of some guy who had the most access. But we do have to leave before they notice I took control for a few seconds."

Ted's vision blurred when he got up on his feet, but he held onto the corner of a computer terminal while it cleared. He ordered his body to recover so he'd be able to lead them back to the motorcycles. His promise to his sister was in jeopardy if he couldn't get Kyla away from danger as fast as possible.

"Let's get out of here," he said, picking up the Ruger. With it in his hands, he tipped his head toward Emily. "Mind if I use your gun again?"

"Be my guest." She smiled.

On a hunch, he checked ER's pockets for extra ammo. He found one extra speed loader for the revolver, supporting his reasoning that not only would Ramirez sneak in the pistol, he'd also make sure he had more than the five rounds it came with.

Emily opened the door while he picked pockets, and soon they were back in the hallway. He and the others followed her, but they were immediately accosted by a seemingly-terrified young woman.

"Do you know what's going on? They said there's a shooter in the building. What do we do?"

Ted almost chuckled. The IT people in the complex apparently hadn't even considered they were going into a warzone. They also didn't realize how easy it was to sneak in under their noses and score a military victory for the American people. He couldn't express any of his private thoughts, so he kept his voice robotic. "We were told to go to the main entrance and be prepared for evacuation. Why don't you tell everyone you see to do the same? We'll be safe once we're outside."

"Yeah," the girl in the black and red jumpsuit replied. "That's what we need to do. Thanks!"

"No problem."

They walked up the steps to the main floor before Emily spoke up. "Won't it cause a mass panic for the doors?"

He looked behind him before getting all the way up. As expected, technicians ran out of the rooms all along the hallway. They ran in every direction, which further highlighted how ill-prepared they were, but most of them headed for him on the stairs.

"Keep going!" he huffed.

The main floor was comparatively quiet, but the screams and cursing from the people below caught the attention of those walking the main floor. Ted kept his eyes firmly on the front door, where the bikes were right outside.

"Meechum, get our weapons," he advised quietly. The older woman was no longer at the gun-check table. It looked like any weapons she'd collected had been tossed in a big green plastic container and left for whoever happened by.

Emily and Meechum went through the first set of doors and went right for the table. He was going to follow, but Kyla stopped him. She had the tablet in her arms, swiping and tapping at keys. "Uncle Ted, they haven't locked me out of the main NORAD system yet. Those teams downstairs have been trying everything to break into the missile control systems. In doing so, they've weakened all the firewalls and counter-intrusion code for the rest of the defense network. They may not even realize how exposed they've made themselves. I can see it right here." She pointed to the screen.

"It doesn't matter. We've got to go."

"Wait!" she replied, not moving. "If I can get in there, I might be able to steal control of the entire nuclear arsenal from them. I could certainly lock them out. This coding is about a decade out of date. It's stuff I cleaned up a lot when I modified the nuclear containment programs on the carrier. They have all sorts of entry points I can use."

He turned to the hallway on the main floor. The people from down below had made their way up and had their eyes on the front doors. They wouldn't be able to stand there much longer.

"What are you saying?" he pressed.

She looked at him with a serious expression. "I need to go back down to the mainframe terminal. I only need a couple of minutes to get this done."

The people got closer. The confusion might give them an easy excuse for returning inside but going back to the scene of the crime was never a good idea. If anyone in authority found ER's body, they might already be looking for them.

I made a promise.

"We can't, Kyla. I'm sorry. We did what we came to do; let's go while we're ahead." He pushed open the inner door. Emily handed over all three of his pistols as he pushed through the outer doors.

"But—" Kyla replied, before trailing off.

Two robots had arrived outside, stopping not far from the bikes. They stood at attention as if guarding the computer building. As if watching for him, or the President of the United States.

Emily faced the robots as she stood with Meechum at the edge of the parking lot.

"We're screwed," he deadpanned.

NORAD Black Site Sierra 7, CO

"I saw the dogs disappear. They're gone." Tabby shifted uncomfortably in the blue outfit. She kept her arms crossed over her chest as a defense mechanism. This David guy was older than her, maybe in his 30s or 40s, and not the worst looking man in the world. However, his eyes were emotionless—what Mom once said were dead eyes. A trait she warned about when dating boys Tabby didn't know. Seeing it in the flesh made her instinctively want to avoid him.

David brightened. "So, you do want to talk to me?" He motioned for her to walk alongside him. He positioned himself to go into a larger room next door.

"I just want to know why I'm here. Where are my friends? Why—"

He shushed her. "We'll get to all that in a minute. I'll explain why you're here, I promise. But first, I want to show you my toys."

Tabby almost guffawed at how ridiculous the man sounded. She had no more interest in seeing his toys than she had in having her wisdom teeth pulled a second time. However, always mindful of the leverage he held over her, she walked next to him, keeping as much distance as possible.

"Thank you," he chimed. "I built this underground facility inside the original NORAD footprint because I needed a base central to the mainland of North America—" He seemed surprised, then talked to himself in monotone. "I need to rebrand the whole continent. The name America must be stricken from everything, including the landmasses."

David looked up at her. "But never mind all that. Once my agency had this base, I knew it would be an excellent place to start over. It's hardened against missiles. It's got water and a food supply. Those Air Force people really thought this through."

"And?" She was terminally impatient with him. It was the only way she knew to fight back.

"And...here we are at day three of the invasion. We've had total success on all fronts.

I'm already planning for phase two, which will happen once we have some of the new territories cleaned up. I've announced my intentions to the world, I've motivated my foot soldiers, and now it's time to unveil all the wonderful new products we've been holding back for when this became our reality."

They walked through a large chamber with metal walls. A row of pedestals ran along the back—about ten had been spread along the forty-foot-long wall. While the rest of the room looked like a military bunker, the well-lit lineup seemed like it could have come from a museum. David skipped the first one, which was a small box-like machine about the size of a toaster.

The second display case contained a paddle-shaped piece of equipment decked out in white. He pointed inside. "This is a device we've been working on for years. It's designed to scan the human body in real time, parse out the cancer cells based on the unique speed of their subatomic particles and use a tiny burst of energy to erase them."

She cackled. "You can cure cancer, but you can't get your silly little trucks to avoid the mud?

You're joking, right?" The surreal nature of where she was, how she was dressed, and who she was talking to caught up with her.

"I'm not joking, I—"

Tabby hated how she'd lost her cool. "Can this thing also cure diabetes? My friend, um, Audrey is here with me. She could really use a hand."

David looked upset. "If you'll let me finish, I want to show you what else we have. All your friends could benefit from these." He stepped a few pedestals down the row and held out his hand to an object that looked like a ray gun. The silvery metal pistol had a cup at the end, facing away from the handle.

"A gun?" she said with thick sarcasm.

"This is a photon reconnaissance device. It's a practical application we've incorporated into some of our aerial drone programs. Basically, it uses invisible photons of energy to splash light over a room and around corners. The photons bounce on things around the corner, then come back to the source and create a picture."

"Like a bat," she said, seeing the potential.

"Yes, if a bat could see around multiple corners," he replied happily. "All these things manipulate energy down to the quantum level, where things get really weird. Some of these are, in fact, weapons, but my best work is this one on the end."

Tabby followed him, not wanting to admit he was far more advanced than she'd given him credit for. Despite her lame attempts to belittle him and show disinterest, if he had the cure for cancer sitting in some random room in a bunker, he had more power than anyone in history. She was bothered by the fact she suddenly didn't want to decapitate the man who had destroyed the United States. If this was all his work, he needed to be captured and then forced to make things right, as much as was possible. The only thing that would impress her more was—

"If you're trying to impress me, it's failing," she fibbed.

David strode up to the box without rising to her prodding. "You saw one of these in the East St. Louis warehouse. I only have a few in each zone, so consider yourself one of the lucky ones."

A small model of the tank machine that had almost zapped her sat upon the pedestal.

"It's not full scale, of course, but I put it here because it represents the milestone before we finally went big time with our knowledge. I call them butterflies, because the projector array looks like it has wings."

She didn't need to see it; Tabby and her friends had gotten a close look at a real one. "Why are you showing this to me? I'd rather learn about the one that's going to cure my friend. This is just a bug zapper on steroids. It killed two sweet dogs who traveled a long way to find us."

He chuckled softly. "I told you, the dogs aren't dead. This machine requires a lot of maintenance and upkeep, as do all my toys. I would never use it to kill when it would be a lot cheaper to use a lead bullet."

She been running at high alert since she'd come out of the decontamination system, but her heart rose in her chest as she thought up the question. "Does it mean you can bring the dogs back?"

He shrugged. "This mobile design is the smaller version of the one under your feet. This entire NORAD facility was designed like my little butterfly. When its wings unfurled, it wiped away the most dangerous people on the planet: the Americans. You're standing on my greatest museum piece, a triumph of science that will launch man into the next thousand years."

"But can you bring my dogs back?" she said impatiently. The answer to that question had implications she wasn't yet ready to voice. If he thought she was too smart for her own good, or caught on to what he was doing, he might get rid of her.

David strode to another of the steel doors and waited for her to catch up. She reluctantly followed, angry that he was being obtuse about his intentions.

"Tabitha Breeze, old American, I brought you here for a reason. I showed you these marvels of technology as a peace offering. They'll all be part of your life going forward. These and many more, including what's through this doorway."

She shook her head while holding her hands on her hips. It was her mean-girl pose showing how she wasn't pleased at the turn of events. Why wouldn't he simply answer the question?

The door opened slowly.

She expected the superweapon to be revealed. He'd said it was in the NORAD base. She figured there'd be rows of the giraffes, dogs, or hovering drones. Anything that a maniacal leader would install as a way to impress the prisoners. But when the door swung open, she was faced with a far more serious problem having to do with her alone.

"You've got to be kidding me," she lamented.

Inside the hangar-like enclosure, a formation of people stood in rows and columns, like they were part of a military parade. There were about a hundred of them, she figured, with her quick glance. However, they weren't soldiers. They were all women dressed in the same blue suits as her.

David stepped up to the entry and spoke loudly. "First, we took out America. Next, we take out the world. We're going to need young women like you to repopulate God's newest paradise." David put his arm around her shoulders, which poured cold water all the way down her backside.

"Crackers," she murmured.

Folsom, CA

"What an amazing day," Bernard said with reverence. "David really is going to take care of us, like he said."

Dwight had been in a state of panic since the dam fell apart. He'd never been one for superstition or religion, but being in that crowd made him feel like the only saint inside a convention in Hell itself. The cheering for the destruction of the city of Folsom was unnatural to his ears, and he wasn't even a patriotic person anymore. It wasn't right to do, and it wasn't right to watch it. He hated cheering with the others.

He glanced up; Poppy sat on top of his head. She sometimes came down when she really needed his attention, but he didn't want to deal with her at the moment.

"No, I'm not going to do that," he replied. "Stop talking."

Bernard looked over his shoulder. "What?"

Dwight smiled, sure one of these days he would be caught talking to the bird. "Nothing."

Bernard was the last one to fill up his tank of flamethrower fuel. The rest of his seven-man team had already topped off from the mid-sized fuel truck that had come to meet them at a new point in the city. The floodwaters hadn't taken the whole town away, but it had cut a huge swath out of the middle. Bernard said their job was to chip away at what was left.

"What should we burn next?" Bernard asked his team. "Should we get rid of what's left of the prison?"

His team whooped with enthusiasm.

Poppy continued to cry out to him. She knew how he felt about the destruction he'd been witness to, and she wanted to help. He remained still, however, as the bird repeatedly flapped her wings to rise, then bonk his head when she dropped back down.

"You doing okay?" Bernard asked. "You look like you saw a ghost."

The town was full of ghosts. All those little splotches of clothing were ghosts. The water barreling down the valley was now filled with tens of thousands of shoes, shirts, and pants. None of the men around him cared a fig for the dead. What would they say if they knew he was part of this?

"I, uh..." he said as he thought of what to say.

Poppy dug her claws into his scalp. "Ow! Stop it!"

She continued to give him advice, but none of it was good.

Bernard had a confused look on his face. He was seconds from being done gassing up, then it would be back to the road and back to more burning. He was never happy with the idea, but Poppy's complaining, along with his imagining of ghosts, made him think of how he could get out of working with them for a second longer.

I only want a warm bench and a smooth bottle.

Dwight heard himself think and knew in his heart that those weren't the only things he wanted. No matter how many times he'd let himself down in the past, he always tried to be one of the good guys. He'd managed to steer clear of the hard drugs that had brought down countless friends. He'd stayed away from the prostitutes. He rarely got taken to jail, and the times he did were usually for sleeping where he didn't see the keep out signs. Poppy was complaining because she knew...

This isn't me.

He rolled his motorcycle away from the fuel station but didn't hop on or start it up. When he'd gone about fifty feet, Bernard seemed to notice him. "Hey! Wait up! We're almost ready." The leader of their crew talked to the fuel-truck guy standing next to him.

Dwight swatted at Poppy, catching her on the wing. That made her get off his head and fly wildly away from him. She still cawed at him with advice he was reluctant to hear.

"You think it will work?" he asked, terrified of her answer.

The bird told him it would be cleanliness in all things, as they liked to say.

"If you say so," he replied.

He didn't like having the dark thought, but Poppy was right. The work Bernard and his team were doing wasn't for him. They were the bad guys. They were evil. And it was up to him to make things better.

Dwight pulled out his flamethrower tube and hit the electrical ignition. When it came to life, he didn't look up or aim. He simply crunched the handle and sent a jet of liquid onto the men tending their bikes nearby. Bernard screamed for him to stop—a distinctive voice he heard above the others.

"Sorry, Bernard. You aren't a good guy."

The pleas were heartbreaking, but he flicked the switch to touch off his flame. The men went up with wet screams. Every square inch of the nearest twenty yards rose into a plume of hot gas and fire.

Poppy flapped away as fast as she could, but she also yelled down that he'd done the right thing for once.

He didn't stick around to see the grisly end. At some point, the fuel truck blew up, which meant someone was going to come looking for what went wrong. There were thousands of bad guys in the city, if the dam-breaking party was any indication. Hundreds could have chased him if they'd known where he was, but he'd chosen a road that took him out of the city and toward the mountains in the east.

However, the second he felt like he'd put enough distance between him and the city of Folsom, he pulled in front of a liquor store and raided the place. Before, Poppy had been all over him to kill the bad men, but now she warned him against having too much liquor.

"You silly girl! There's no such thing as too much liquor!"

In thirty minutes, he'd drunk himself into his own version of a flammable fuel truck. It took the edge off, then continued its rub until all his senses were numb. He heard the complaints from his bird, but he thought he deserved a little drinky-poo since he'd done the right thing, so he ignored her.

Before his blood alcohol level reached uncharted territory, he saw a man dressed like Bernard come into the liquor store. Then, several other Bernards came in behind him.

"Hey, Bernard! I'm glad you made it. Won't you join the celebration? It's all free for the taking. Look at this place!"

The Bernard look-a-like said Dwight must have forgotten about the tracking device on his motorcycle. The men converged around him, kicking and punching, shouting about payback, but then a white bird arrived at the front door.

The white shape hovered mysteriously, like a ghost, but its voice was human and male. "Stop! Do not kill him. Bring him to NORAD, my rebels. I want to know how the Americans got a spy this deep into my precious legion."

What a wild dream!

Poppy flew rings around a white bird, screaming at it, advising Dwight to run from it, but he was too far gone to even stand, much less run.

"It will be done, David," the Bernard-clone replied.

The last thing he vividly remembered was someone's fist hitting his face.

"Hey, man," he pleaded as blood pumped out of his broken nose. "He said you couldn't kill me."

"But he didn't say we couldn't hurt you," the man in black replied.

Dwight laughed and talked with a heavy slur. "Bernard, I kind of liked you when we were friends, but Poppy said I needed to kill you to keep up with the 'cleanliness in all things' motto you like. Plus, you turned out to be a real asshole."

Poppy scolded him.

"No, I'm not trying to get you in trouble, Pops," he pleaded with her. "Honest."

The bird flew down, green and red wings flapping, and landed on his head. She begged him to stop talking before he got himself killed.

Sometimes, he did the opposite of whatever she said. "Free America, people!" he shouted in glee.

The next punch chased her back into the air.

He didn't remember anything after that.

TWENTY-EIGHT

Minot Air Force Base, ND

Kyla had the ability to hack the NORAD defense system, but she knew better than to push Uncle Ted to let her do it. Over the years, Mom had tried repeatedly to get her brother to do things her way, but he always had the patience to wait her out. Kyla always thought Mom was the stubborn one, since she saw her every day, but Uncle Ted took it up a few notches whenever he was around. "Oh, shit," she said breathlessly when she saw the trouble outside.

Uncle Ted had gone out to the parking lot to be with Emily and Meechum. They'd made it to the bikes but were being "sniffed" by two animal-styled robots. The tall giraffe-like shapes stood over them, heads swiveling around on the upright stalks. Emily and Meechum didn't shrink with fear, but they did act standoffish and wary. As much as she wanted to go back inside and knock out the bad guy's access to the American computers, she owed it to her friends to stick around.

Several of the technicians came into the doorway, and she let herself be pushed to the side. Instead of running with them, she punched up some code on the data tablet. Her eyes absorbed the coding as she tried to modify the screen to let her have access to whoever controlled those things. They couldn't be truly autonomous, or they'd harass friend and foe alike. Someone had to be feeding it the basics, such as who was the enemy.

She walked gingerly down the front steps and stood at the edge of the parking lot. Dozens of people ran by, most heading for the civilian cars and trucks parked on the lot. They seemed untroubled by the robots...

Kyla sped up until she was a lane over from the trio at the motorcycles. They continued to hold position away from the bikes, as if waiting for the robots to discover them. "Uncle Ted!

Look at everyone else! Just hop on the bikes!" She waved her hands to the rest of the people on the parking lot.

He looked at the giraffes, then at the people, then back to her. He stuck his thumb up. Moments after that, he'd gathered the other two ladies and motioned them to saddle up.

She calmly walked over to the bikes, then climbed behind Meechum like the robots were invisible. Emily did the same on Uncle Ted's motorcycle. In seconds, they were on the move, though Kyla kept the tablet out as she held on with one arm.

"Can you drive?" she asked the Marine. "What about your arm?"

Meechum turned back a little. "I'll let it hurt when we're somewhere safe."

Kyla couldn't even offer to drive for her; she didn't know anything about motorcycles. That was a deficiency she had to fix right away, if they made it to that 'somewhere safe.'

"Let me know if I can help," Kyla offered.

"You keep watch, dudette."

Her uncle led them through the base until they got close to the front gate. She figured he was going to try to go out the same way he came in, but he veered down an alternate street shortly before reaching the exit. When clear, he leaned over to her and Meechum. "The base is locked down. They've got it blocked off."

"Where to?" Meechum replied.

Kyla peered at her tablet, hoping she was competent enough to pull off what she needed. Then she spoke to her uncle. "Go over the grass by the runway. I'll call off the drones guarding the perimeter."

"You can do that?" he asked with surprise.

She nodded. "With this account, I have access to the whole system, but we have to hurry. I'm not sure if they'll shut down my link, or if the link has a range."

Uncle Ted drove them around the big complex for a short time until he seemed to have his route planned out. All at once, he goosed the motor and headed onto the pavement of the taxiway. Meechum followed close behind; Kyla looked around her shoulder to see their speed go from twenty to seventy in a few seconds. They passed under the wing of a mammoth gray cargo plane. Then, in seconds, they crossed onto the airstrip.

Meechum groaned as she worked the throttle. She'd made good on her promise to feel the pain later, but it was obviously difficult. Kyla prayed it didn't get any worse, otherwise they'd have to come up with a way to cram four people onto one bike.

Uncle Ted had to slow down when he reached the grass, but not by much. Kyla tried to tap keys on the tablet to get a better idea of the number of drones around, but her cursor became stuck.

"Oh, hell," she exclaimed. "Someone knows I'm in."

Ahead, the line of giraffes patrolling the edge of the property was much easier to see than it had been in the dark. Large, metal dogs also appeared. The tall grass hid their numbers, but they were out there. White flying drones hovered every hundred yards or so.

Kyla's interface didn't show their position on a map, so she had to use trial and error. She tapped the screen and selected a random giraffe to make it deactivate. When done, she searched for a stopped drone, but it wasn't obvious to her. She tapped a few more and saw a nearby giraffe immediately stop.

"There! Go by that one!" Uncle Ted had to look back to see where she pointed, but he soon caught on to the fact a drone was behaving in an odd manner.

They had about a hundred yards to go to the property boundary, and she used the time to tap more of the drones. She tried to find the pattern in where they were on her screen compared to where they were on the security detail. Seconds later, after shutting down three in a row, she finally established the numerical order. Once she had that, she was able to shut down the three different types of drones close to her target. She went out from there as fast as she could click.

Kyla had eight or nine deactivated before one of them turned back on.

"Shit! Someone definitely knows what I'm doing! They're tracking this tablet. They're tracking these bikes. We're lit up!"

"We can't stop now," Uncle Ted declared.

The two original drones were powered down, and that was where they were headed. But other drones were coming back online almost as fast as she could tap them off. A live person was fighting back. It was hard for Kyla read the screen while bouncing on the bike, but she noticed an option to reset the modes of the drones. With seconds to go, she could either try to tap faster or tap smarter.

Here goes nothing!

Amarillo, TX

Brent and Trish had gotten the drop on the stranger in the car. They pulled him out and parked his vehicle behind the Cadillac sculpture to help hide it. They realized immediately they'd found one of the enemy soldiers, mostly since the guy told them over and over that he was done fighting for David.

They'd waited until all members of the team were back before they tried to interrogate him.

"So," Brent began, "tell us again how you came to be here. Are you a deserter?"

"It's all over, man. They're all burned alive. The Americans came back and kicked our ass up one leg and down the other. We were told this was a colonization process, not a war. I don't want any part of the that."

The guy wore black overalls with brown sleeves and traveled with nothing more than the clothes he wore. Brent figured he wasn't a frontline soldier, and he had no weapons, so maybe he could get some intel out of him.

"You said the Americans came and attacked. Who are you fighting for?"

"David," he said abruptly.

Brent looked over to Trish and the others before turning back to the man. "Who's David? Is that a person or a nation?" He figured it might have been a weird acronym or something.

"David is leading us to the promised land. He's our generation's Moses, I guess you could say. But he said everything was taken care of by the reboot. We weren't supposed to have to fight. As I said, I'm not big on war, especially the death part."

"Where does David come from? What nation?" If he could figure out who they were up against, he might be able to craft a proper mode of counterattack. If he could get numbers of men, tables of organization and equipment, and mission objectives, it would greatly help their cause of fighting back.

"He comes from the old America, but he fights for us all—the poor, the dispossessed, those without a homeland. We're his rebels." He stuttered. "Was. I'm not anymore."

"Without a homeland," Brent echoed. There couldn't be many of those. Everyone came from somewhere. He took the man at his word. "So, David came from the United States. Was he by chance at the Amarillo Airport? Did he die in the fire?" If they'd managed to kill the leader in their bold attack, he was going to buy each of his men a new car with the millions of dollars in gifts he'd be given by the returning government.

"No, David stays in a place called Cheyenne Mountain. In a bunker. He told us in one of his speeches."

"NORAD?" he asked with surprise. If the bad guys had managed to hole up in NORAD, it would be nearly impossible to get them out. It was built to withstand nuclear blasts.

"Yes, I've heard them say that before." The guy looked around, scared he was going to be in trouble. "Look, it's all I know. I came over here because I wanted to be one of the homesteaders with a new wife, but look at me now." He pointed to his uniform. "I'm only a common soldier."

"Where did you come from?" Brent asked.

"I'm from Oregon, but I was living in the Philippines. That's where I met David."

"How did you get to the airport?"

"I flew, of course. I had a choice to come over on a boat, but those were full. They added me at the last minute. I guess it explains why I couldn't be a homesteader."

"And what's your mission here? If you aren't a homesteader, as you keep saying."

"I drive heavy equipment. When my assigned burn zone was done, it was going to be my job to level out all the rubble. Guys like me prepare it for the next wave of rebuilders, and the final wave of colonists."

Carter ran his hand over his bald head. "Damn. You people are cold as shit. That's my home you're talking about paving over."

The prisoner must have seen a bad look in Carter's eyes and held up his hands defensively. "I'm done with all that, I swear. I'm an American, too."

"An American?" Brent asked sadly. The others bristled at the man's obvious attempt to curry favor, but he let it slide for the moment. He went through a few more questions, but it descended into a rote formality. The enemy soldier was happy to give up what he knew in exchange for the promise of safety. They learned a bit more about the layout of the Amarillo airport, the number of aircraft probably knocked out, and the overall mission in the area.

The sun shone brightly on the field by the time they finished grilling the guy. They'd asked about the David character, his base in NORAD, and what they might expect if they went to meet him. The guy didn't know much about the top level of their invasion effort, but he was pleasant and forthcoming about spilling what he knew. However, as time dragged on, and Brent ran out of questions, he was forced to admit he had a dirty job to do. They couldn't risk the guy wouldn't change his mind and go warn his old friends.

Brent recalled the discussion with Trish about how one side had to want victory more than the other, and he was about to go all-in for his seven-person rebellion. He took the man behind the brightly-painted Cadillacs, promising that's where he'd be let go.

Dammit straight to hell. I'd forgotten how much war sucks.

Minot Air Base, ND

Ted aimed the motorcycle between the two giraffe-drones that were powered down. Since the machines were no longer moving, they were effectively two goalposts to aim for as he sped across the grassy field.

"We're going through!" he shouted over the sound of the motors, knowing Meechum probably wouldn't hear him on the other bike. He glanced over at his niece. She hung on while tapping the tablet wedged between her and the driver. Whatever she was doing, it was giving them a chance.

A robot horse appeared nearby, with its chain gun apparatus sticking up from its back, but it appeared frozen, like the giraffes. Elsewhere, the sounds of machine guns chattered.

"Stay low!" he yelled to Emily.

The motorcycle rumbled through the defensive cordon, which was also close to the dead end of a paved road heading west. He guided the bike out of the grass, onto the concrete, and hit the throttle.

Meechum wasn't far behind.

Looking back, several of the horse-drones were unleashing streams of machine gun fire, but it appeared as if a few of them were fighting against a larger group still closing in. Ted glanced over to Kyla, who was smiling impishly.

He pointed behind them, then pointed at her. "You did that?" he mouthed.

She gave him a thumbs-up.

There was no time for celebration, however. They were riding two motorcycles across the flattest state in the union. The air base fell behind them, but knee-high grasslands and endless wheat fields surrounded the other three directions. Any competent Air Force pilot would zero in on them in about ten seconds. The jets previously parked on the airstrip had to be somewhere up there.

Ted accelerated. He took at close look at the Victory Hammer 8-ball bike he was on, noting how the speedometer went all the way up to 200 miles per hour. He intended to test every bit of that, but when he hit 120, he could barely withstand the wind blasting his chest, and his eyes were nearly sealed shut by the onrush of air. He glanced over to Meechum and found her lagging behind.

Damn.

He came back down to match her speed, which was a little over 100 on the speedometer. Emily gripped him tighter. "Where are we going?" she asked.

"West!" he shouted.

The entire base was probably gearing up to look for them. He was convinced of that. Their ultimate goal was to the south, in Colorado, but he planned on going into Montana before making the turn in the proper direction. If they could put some miles between them and the pursuit before they really got started, it would give them a better chance of escape. However, much to his surprise, the land dipped ahead of him.

They cruised into a low valley filled with clumps of trees, and a large, meandering body of water. It looked more like a swamp than a river, with gravel roads going off into the woods to the north and south.

He chose to keep going west, over a berm running from one side of the marsh to the other—a span about a half-mile. If they could get to the other side, he planned to detour into the woods. They might be able to lose them that way.

"Oh, crap," he said to Emily as he slowed.

At the very end of the berm, the road ended at a gap where a bridge had been removed. The slow-moving river flowed to the south through the fifty-foot opening.

Ted and Meechum were forced to stop their bikes. Behind them, beyond the length of the berm and a few trees, he once again imagined a pursuit force hunting them down. Minot Air Base was only five miles back there.

"I could use suggestions," he stated dryly.

Emily hopped off and ran to the edge. The reeds and water were only a few feet below the level of the road, and she seemed to walk back and forth, studying the water.

Kyla came over with her tablet in hand. "Uncle Ted! I almost blew it. I tried turning the drones off, but someone came in behind me and restored them in seconds. I figured out there's a maintenance mode. The robots take five minutes to run through the cycle, which can't be interrupted."

"You figured that out while on the motorcycle?" he asked with both surprise and pride.

"Yeah. The tablet is super intuitive. It's the complete opposite of the coding inside the defense systems, which are old and crusty."

"Like me," he laughed.

"Yeah, like you," she said with a wry smile. "I also disabled the beacons on these bikes, but I can't say how long that will last. These guys are really fighting back."

"So they can't track us at this moment?" he asked.

"Correct."

He smiled. "Awesome work, young lady!"

Emily waved him over. "I was hoping we could push the bikes across the river, but it isn't shallow enough."

Ted studied the area. Knowing nothing about North Dakota, it was hard to draw conclusions from the small slice of the valley he could see, but he figured they'd have a lot better chance of survival if they stuck around the river and got into the trees. However, enemy forces were looking for a pair of motorcycles. If he ditched them, his team could blend into the landscape.

The motorbikes were very nice, so throwing them away was difficult, but safety was his priority, not getting cool stuff. If they did manage to avoid detection, there were a million other vehicles they could borrow. He told himself not to get attached to any equipment.

"We're going on foot," he said.

"What? Why?" Kyla asked, still happy from her programming victories.

"We have to get into cover. This place might have the only trees we find in this whole state. It will give us a chance..."

"We should ditch the bikes if they're being tracked," Meechum suggested.

"Push them in," he advised, pointing to the end of the road.

Each bike had two saddlebags. One was crammed with what looked like cleaning gear for the flamer, and the other contained a sleeping bag and some of the previous riders' personal effects. That was a major score, since they had no other supplies. He'd left his prized backpack and rifles in the stolen car at the grocery store, figuring they'd be back through there. After pulling out everything useful, they watched in silence as the metal hogs disappeared into the murky stream.

"Kyla, you have to ditch the tablet, too." He nodded to the black device in her hand.

Kyla was crestfallen. "We can see all the enemy movements with this. We can tap into their systems. With time, I might even be able to access their mainframe."

Ted understood her reluctance. "But you said it yourself: they can track it. We have to ditch every piece of tech that belongs to these rebooter assholes—I'm not calling them rebels."

"Yeah, you're right. I thought this was over. I thought we were home free."

"We are. We know what we have to do to beat them. We'll find a way to communicate with the outside, share what we know about the remaining defense infrastructure, and hopefully they'll send an ICBM from a submarine right through the front doors of David's NORAD base. If they can't, we'll walk in and take it out ourselves. We'll be home free after doing all that, and after a short swim." He pointed across the river.

All three women groaned, though Emily was the loudest. It surprised him to such an extent that he had to turn to face her.

She chuckled in a good-natured way. "I bet you could get us into a lake even if we were in Death Valley. You should know, Major, that the President of the United States is tired of getting soaked."

It wasn't his first choice, either, but abandoning the bikes and crossing the river was the unexpected thing to do. The men and women operating the pursuit back at Minot would spend their time looking for two impossible-to-miss motorcycles driving the open highways. They wouldn't waste time searching reed ponds and streamside forests without good cause.

He rose to her challenge. "Look at the bright side. You'll need another set of clothes. I don't know about you guys, but I'd like to wear anything besides the uniform of the enemy."

"Amen," Meechum replied. "If I'm killed, I don't want to be seen in this thing."

Ted brightened. "Hey, that's the nice thing about this war. They're here to kill us no matter what we're wearing, so we might as well be comfortable." If Emily happened to find another nice dress, instead of the unflattering black jumpsuit, he wouldn't complain.

Eyes on the prize, Ted.

"Come on, I'll lead," he said, to prod Emily. "Keep your pistols above the water, if you can. The sleeping bags, too."

"Last person across has to sleep in the weeds," Emily taunted, seemingly unable to give Ted the last word. "The winners get the comfy bags!"

It was the middle of the day, but he intended to hunker down in the woods until tomorrow. Meechum was injured, Kyla had a neck wound, and the pair of them had been on watch all night. They needed to rest. The group had won a major victory, but as a fighting force, they were all at the breaking point. Still, Ted never himself pushed harder than to get across the river first.

He already planned to give his sleeping bag to the president. If anyone asked, he'd say it was because she was his commander-in-chief.

But he knew the truth.

TWENTY-NINE

The Odd Place

Deogee woke up and sniffed for the expected smell of kibble. Melissa always gave her a big bowl before she went out jogging in her bright yellow, and tasty, running shoes. Today, however, there was no kibble smell.

I had a puppy dream.

The wolf in her immediately went into a guarded posture. Not only were the expected scents not there, but she didn't recognize where she was, either. However, her memory came back a little. She thought Melissa was gone. Her outer pieces of fur had been left somewhere...in leafy bushes. There were no leafy bushes anywhere in sight. She was inside an unfamiliar house.

She barked. "Where am I?"

"Where are we?" Biscuit replied from close by, as if reminding her she wasn't alone.

Deogee nosed the other dog appreciatively, and her memory came rushing back. Melissa was indeed gone. So was her other friend, the human who dressed funny and was called Sister Rose. The fire had gotten her at the Bad Place.

It looked like they were still inside the giant house where the newest of her human friends had brought her. The alpha, Tabby, had been yelling and screaming. There were also much louder noises she could not identify. And Deogee had been chewing on one of the metal monsters.

"Where are my humans?" she asked Biscuit.

"I saw them," the black lab replied. "They were right over there. An annoying sound came next. Then, they weren't over there."

Her friend's simplistic retelling matched her own experience. The humans had been there a moment before, but a sudden pain had caused her to shut her eyes. Everything went black for less than a bark. When her vision came back, the humans and the metal machines had disappeared.

"Does anything smell familiar?" she asked.

Biscuit nosed at some trash on the floor, but managed to say no.

"Follow me. I know where we can see everything." She ran for the stairs to the roof and started up.

"I'd love to play, but the stairs are broken," Biscuit replied, climbing the first few steps. "Well, they were broken, honest. I had to jump when I came down them."

Nothing felt right to Deogee. The air didn't smell right, either. The world around her had changed in the handful of barks since she'd been with the humans. Was it the air? The light? Did Biscuit notice it, too?

Deogee came out on the roof but didn't recognize where she was. The feeling of waking up from a puppy dream overcame her, but she wasn't waking up.

"Whoa!" Biscuit barked.

It had been nighttime when she arrived there with the humans, but now it was day. She knew the connection between the time of light and the time of dark, but the daytime sky was all wrong. It was no longer the usual shade of blue, as she'd heard Melissa describe it many times. To Deogee's eyes, the color was closer to those yellow shoes.

The sky is sick.

The rest of the world wasn't much better. The stones standing up on the other side of the river were still there, as was the tall, silver arch, but many of those rocks were broken. Some had fallen over. Smoke rose from some of them, like the fire had been trapped inside.

Closer to her, an incredible number of the small houses on wheels were strewn over the ground below her. In fact, looking around, she found some of those houses had been tossed on top of the building. She went over to sniff one of them but turned away when the smell of death came out of it. The human was still stuffed inside the house, but he'd been squished.

Deogee barked incessantly, trying call out to her missing pack. Trying call out to anyone within the sound of her voice. Someone had to know what was happening. "Biscuit, where are we?"

The lab ran in circles, misinterpreting her excited manner of speaking. "Who cares? Let's play!"

Upper Souris Wildlife Refuge, ND

Ted stood watch over the three ladies, content they'd done the right thing by ditching the motorcycles and hiking into the wildlife preserve. They'd heard drones overhead a few times, but they seemed to go to the west, where his team was last seen riding. Once darkness fell, he knew they'd managed to give the enemy the slip.

Until tomorrow, he thought.

He'd taken a big risk flying Kyla and Emily across the country, and he'd made some mistakes along the way, but he'd been proven right. The trip saved lives. They'd fought back. They gave the rest of the American population a small victory, even if no one knew about it yet. Passing on the opportunity to take over the entire NORAD system remotely had been the right call to save Kyla. As it was, they'd only made it out with seconds to spare. If they'd gone back inside the "maintenance" building, they'd be sitting in an enemy detention center right now. Or they'd be dead.

Ted looked over at Emily. She was supposed to be asleep on the sleeping bag he'd given to her, but, at that moment, she was sitting up with legs crossed. The bag was fully spread on the ground, making it a large, square blanket. All was quiet in the marsh, so he crept back to talk to her.

"Can't sleep?" he asked.

Even in the middle of the night, he noticed the ring she'd been manipulating with her fingers. The big diamond seemed to gleam in the moonlight. She glanced up at him. "I've been holding onto this ring since I last saw Roger back in my apartment. Once, it meant the universe to me, but not for a long time. For several years, I mostly kept it in my nightstand."

He got immediately uncomfortable. "I'll leave you to it…"

"No, wait," she pleaded quietly. Kyla and Meechum were asleep about twenty feet away. Close enough for protection, but far enough away to give the prez a little privacy. "You misunderstand. I'm holding the last piece of my old life. The life I had before I was President Emily Williams..."

Ted saw an opening. "So, you're calling yourself the president. Does that mean you accept your promotion, finally?" They'd been haggling over whether she was legally the president almost since they'd first met. She tolerated being called the top dog, but she always kept something back, like it wasn't real. Her admission seemed like a huge concession.

"The NORAD system asked for my biometric data. I saw the words 'President of the United States' by my name. I figure that sealed the deal. I can't refuse it any longer." She sighed deeply. "And, if I'm making life-altering changes these days, I might as well take this a step further."

She tossed the ring over her shoulder into the tall grass.

"Wow," he replied. "I don't know what to say, Madame President."

Meechum stirred across their camp site, standing and stretching as he and Emily remained by her sleeping bag. A few seconds later, the Marine called out, "I'm on watch."

Ted was happy to hand it over, though he was never going to stop his amazement at the pain threshold of the warrior woman. A bullet had sliced through her shoulder a few hours ago. She should be out cold, not out on patrol.

Emily tapped the empty half of her sleeping bag. "I saved you a bit, so you don't have to sleep in the weeds."

He crouched next to the bag, not sure if it was proper to sit down with his boss, but when he looked at her in the nighttime glow of the moon, he was flooded with emotions. She'd lost a husband. He'd lost a sister. The nation had lost everyone else. But there, in that quiet patch of forest, the two of them were just people. Living people.

He plopped down next to her, accepting it was just a sleeping arrangement, not an engagement proposal. However, before he let himself get too comfortable, he realized her earlier statement had an obvious flaw.

"Emily, you said the computer system listed you as the President of the United States. Are you positive that's what it said?"

She leaned back on her elbows. "Of course. I told you, it was at that moment I finally accepted the title. Why?"

His stomach hardened as his mind rolled over to anti-conspiracy mode.

One side of his brain said, "Don't ruin the moment, Teddy, old boy."

The other side thought, "How did the hacked NORAD system know she was the president? She was supposed to be dead, along with everyone else. Van Nuys knew she was alive, but he died before he could report it to anyone else. Did someone intercept the captain's radio chatter with the two sailors who almost killed Kyla and Emily? And even if someone did, how could they have known she would end up at an air base at the ass-end of an empty America?"

Emily waited, but he'd taken enough time it became a concern to her. She reached over and touched him on the arm. "What is it?"

He sighed heavily, almost as she had done a moment before. "I have a theory about what's happening at NORAD. Remind me to tell you about it in the morning."

She seemed impressed. "What? You aren't going to hash through all the bad things facing us tomorrow? Haven't you been chewing on a million different problems in the time you've been keeping watch over us?"

He chuckled softly. "I guess you've taught me how to let go a little bit, at least when people need to get some sleep. Everything points to Cheyenne Mountain, Colorado, and NORAD. Tomorrow, we'll make our way to Montana. You said your parents have property there, right?"

"Yep."

"We'll stay as far away from there as humanly possible. That's your only hint about what I've been thinking."

"Sounds interesting," she replied matter-of-factly. Emily patted the sleeping bag again, clearly urging him to lay back and make himself comfortable. He did as she requested, mindful of how difficult it was to shut down his brain. Sure, he'd told her he wasn't going to talk it all to death, but the fact was his officer's mind didn't have an off switch.

He was shocked when she put a hand on his chest and rolled to face him.

"Ted, thank you for making this all possible. I owe you my life several times over, and I'm grateful at all the expert decisions you've made to get us here, but there is one piece of intel you seem to have an enduring blind-spot about."

"No, I don't—"

She interrupted him with a kiss.

The intimacy took him by total surprise, but before he could fully appreciate what had taken place, a girlish giggle interrupted them from close by.

"I knew it!" Kyla crowed.

To Be Continued in *Minus America*, Book 4

If you like this book, please leave a review—even though it is book 3. The series has gotten awesome reviews, and I can always use more, as each one builds my brand a little stronger.

Thank you for being a reader.

I have a short author note to follow.

This book is a work of fiction.

All of the characters, organizations, and events portrayed in this novel are either products of the author's imagination or are used fictitiously. Sometimes both.

Rebel Cause (and what happens within / characters / situations / worlds)

are Copyright (c) 2019 by E.E. Isherwood

All rights reserved. No part of this publication may be reproduced, stored in a retrieval system, or transmitted in any form or by any means, electronic, mechanical, recording or otherwise, without the prior written permission of E.E. Isherwood

Paperback Version 1.1 [3.17.23]

Cover Illustration by 'Covers by Christian'

Editing by Mia at LKJ Books

AUTHOR NOTES

Written December 12, 2019

Thank you for reading,

My computer desk has two monitors. One is for my writing, the other is for the plot outline, web browser for research, and my email. As I type this note in one window, I have the outline for book 4, *Two Wolves and a Sheep*, up and running in the other. As soon as I have the plot solidified, I'll start banging on my keyboard to crank out the next volume of this series. I love these characters as much as any I've written, so I can't wait to crack into the story and see where they take me.

I hope you'll continue with the adventure, too.

We now have a heroine, Tabby, at the heart of the terrorist's operation. When I started writing book three, I had no idea she was going to end up there. In fact, I changed the whole outline when I realized she'd gotten herself into trouble inside that old warehouse. Now that she's captured, it gives us a look into the enemy's operation. Their plan should start to become clear as she pokes around inside their base... At the same time, help is coming for her from multiple directions, even if she doesn't know it.

If you've seen the cover, you know it'll be epic.

The year is racing toward its own grand conclusion. Only two weeks and a few days until 2020. It will be my fifth year of writing as a full-time author. In fact, looking at the calendar, I'm a couple days away from my four-year publishing anniversary. It was almost four years to the day I hit publish on my first book. Since then, I've written about a million and a half words… If you've read the first three books of this series, you've made it through about 230,000 of them.

At this point, I usually ask readers to leave reviews for my book (they've been incredible), but this time I would like to request a different favor. Would you consider sharing my books with your friends and family? Mention me at your book club? Leave a request at the library or bookstore to carry my novels? Anything you can do to show off my post-apocalyptic thrillers to one more reader would go a long way to ensuring I'm doing this for another four years.

Finally, we're a few short days away from Christmas break for my kids. I'm looking forward to having them around for two weeks, even if I don't get quite as much work done. Aside from visiting with family, we're planning to go bowling, see the new *Jumanji* movie, and my son is preparing to go to Philmont Scout Ranch (New Mexico) with the Boy Scouts soon. I'm one of his troop's leaders going with him, so we'll be fitness training over the break. Wish us luck!

Again, thank you for reading this series. I'm honored you've stuck with it for three books. I plan to make the next stories even better.

EE

BACK MATTER

EE Isherwood's Back Catalog at a Glance

Neighborhood Watch Series – Frank retires to a quiet street in sunny Florida, but when the EMP strikes, his retirement is over. Now he must help his neighborhood survive the coming collapse of...everything. (7+ books)

Minus America Series – What would happen if everyone in the US vanished in a flash? Every trucker. Every housewife. Every police officer. Piles of clothes are all that remain. How would you survive in the empty land? And who would come to take it? Five books in this series.

End Days Series (co-written with Craig Martelle) – A post-apocalyptic adventure about a father and son on opposite ends of a continent ravaged by a failed EMP-like science experiment. Six books in this series.

Sirens of the Zombie Apocalypse Series – A teen boy must keep his great-grandma alive to find the cure to the zombie plague, but what if the only people immune are those over 100? They are always the first to die when the world breaks... Seven, soon to be eight books in this series.

Impact Series – A post-apocalyptic thriller about an asteroid of untold wealth slamming across the heartland of America. A Kentucky father must cross the devastation to find his daughter while others rush to exploit the space rock. Six books in this series. (Currently unpublished, relaunch soon)

Website

My updated website now has links to my back catalog on Amazon, so you can see all of them on one easy-to-read page. I've also got links to maps of my books, Kickstarter projects, a Patreon page, and you can sign up to my monthly newsletter.

Please visit www.eeisherwood.com for everything happening in my universe.

QUIET REFLECTIONS

Printed in Great Britain
by Amazon

59522492R10255